344 Days Underground

Novel
Based On True Events

VALERIY GRITSIV

344 Days Underground
A Novel Based On True Events

Copyright © 2017 by Valeriy Gritsiv

Cover design by Lidiya B. Gritsiv

ISBN: 978-0-692-85158-6

Grateful to my wife, Lidiya; daughter, Elina; son-in-law, Grant; and my uncles, Danil and Marat Goldberg, for their support.

"So men must understand and feel that, from the day of their birth to their death, they are always in insolvable indebtedness to those who lived before them."

Leo Tolstoy, *My Religion*, 1904

Introduction

Valeriy Gristiv

FOR MANY YEARS after World War II, my granny Etcia Goldberg often remarked, "I was sure the world would be amazed to learn how we survived the war."

It took my granny a long time to tell me her story. When she finally told me, we were living in the western part of Ukraine during the Cold War era. Nobody spoke about the Holocaust during World War II because nobody wanted to remember.

My granny's story was one of those things nobody wanted to remember. And the story itself was unbelievable.

My granny survived the Holocaust by living in a dark, cold cave called Popowa Yama (Priest's Grotto) with thirty-seven other Jews for 344 days. You see—unbelievable.

My granny's village of Korolówka, like many villages in that region, always had a complicated history. Just before this story begins, everyone in Korolówka was a Polish citizen. The Jewish and non-Jewish communities lived separately but peacefully together. The village was occupied by Russia between 1939 and 1941. Everyone then became a citizen of the Ukrainian Republic of the USSR. Neighbors referred to themselves as either Ukrainian, Jewish, or Polish. This continued as the Nazis marched in and occupied the region from 1941 to 1944, the time when Jews were exterminated and my granny and her neighbors went underground.

The Priest's Grotto story was detailed in a book called *We Fight to Survive*, written in 1975 by survivor Esther Stermer. This book was donated to libraries and Jewish organizations.

In 1989, the Berlin Wall was torn down. This resulted in closer relations between the former Soviet Union republics and the United States. It also contributed to the rediscovery and more mainstream media coverage of Priest's Grotto.

The demise of the wall allowed people to travel in areas previously off-limits to international visitors. In 1993, Chris Nicola, a speleologist from New York, traveled to western Ukraine to explore a gypsum cave near the village of Strilkivtcy.

Chris's exploration of the cave puzzled him. He found evidence of prolonged human habitation such as utensils and tools. These items haunted him. Who had lived in this cave? Why, when, and for how long had they lived there? What happened to the people who once called the cave home?

Chris's perseverance over nearly a decade led him to find the answers to these questions and to uncover the story of the thirty-eight Jews who lived underground for 344 days during World War II.

Chris's work came to fruition when *National Geographic Adventure* covered the story. "Off the Face of the Earth" was featured in the June/July 2004 issue of the magazine.

In 2007, Chris Nicola and Peter Lane Taylor published a book entitled *The Secret of Priest's Grotto: A Holocaust Survival Story*. In April 2013, Magnolia Studios released a documentary called *No Place on Earth*, detailing many Priest's Grotto survivors' memories.

This book will take you on the personal journey of my granny Etcia Goldberg, one of the survivors of Priest's Grotto. The book is not intended to present her as perfect. In fact, some readers may not agree with a lot of her choices. This book was written to tell her story, with flaws and authenticity. She was a decisive woman. Her life journey was remarkable. She loved life despite the atrocities she endured. She made life possible for many and will always be remembered for her humor, wit, and will to survive.

I am proud to share her story with you.

Prologue

ONCE, KOROLÓWKA WAS our land. We farmed the *chernozem*. This rich, black soil nourished potatoes and beets that were envied all over Galicia, the ancient kingdom straddling Austro-Hungary, Poland, and Ukraine, where our ancestors have lived since the Middle Ages.

Galicia is still our land. But for nearly a year, we lived inside it.

The cave where I hid with my children and thirty-four other Jews lies deep under a sea of golden wheat fields, just a few miles from our village where we were suddenly no longer allowed. If seen practically, the cave was a palace. Though the air was laced with bat feces we had seventy-seven miles of free space to roam and to breathe. There was a deep freshwater lake, a gift from God. Our cave was so far below the surface that, if we wanted to, we could scream.

We contained our pain as much as possible, only screaming when we suffered nightmares. Otherwise, we followed the examples of the animals with whom we shared the cave. Like the bats, we spoke only when we needed to, in language so strange our families could barely understand. We slept as much as we could, hibernating to keep the hunger at bay. Like the fox, we hunted close to home with the moon. We conserved our energy so that if we needed to, we could run fast.

The earth has its own storyline. If we had continued to walk in the sunlight, we might never have sensed this. That story is too old for us human beings to comprehend. And so sometimes, when we tried to make sense of our own lives down there, confusion set in. All our worst, most secret beliefs about ourselves became magnified. We read our own appearances by touch, like blind people. Sometimes, we had trouble believing that we were alive.

Anger was always there. It is ancient too. When it rises, you have no choice but to feel it. It can clean you out, that anger. It can keep you alive. The trick was learning to let it go before it soured inside us, before we couldn't spit it out anymore.

There were people in our pack who never left the dark earth—our palace became their prison. Those of us who left always prayed hard to make it back to our families.

During those 344 days, that cave was our home.

My name is Etcia Goldberg. I am the mother of three children. I was the only woman allowed to leave the cave and scavenge for food with the men.

It's a privilege to risk one's life to provide for a family. I kept my bearings by remembering my youngest child Marek's scrawny ribs, putting one foot in front of the other, darting between blue shadows of trees. The eleven men and I who went out of the cave learned to read all the dangers. The longer we were down there, the less familiar the village became. We struggled with ways to describe the changes we saw, to share tales of the scarred place we could visit only as ghosts. We took every precaution to be invisible, but the dogs could still smell us. They followed us. On their heels were the men with the guns.

Walking outside was not easy. Our stomachs seized, our calves cramped, and our knees turned to water. We could never trust that we were alone. The land outside had been poisoned by blood.

Worse than all that, I was falling in love.

I am a practical woman. If the world had not turned upside down, if the sky had not been replaced with the ground, I would never have let that happen.

When things rot all around you, you recognize where your loyalty lies. Joseph was one of the dozen people who helped us. Accepting their fierce kindness—which they would deny required bravery—helped me keep a foothold in the right-side-up world.

I fed my children fairy tales I henpecked from my travels along with their food: stories of our family's history in Galicia, of the starlight above our old house, of our relatives' laughter.

The fairy tales I told myself started containing stray thoughts about Joseph.

In the cave where there was only night, with my bony children curled about me under a *varetta*—the down-filled comforters that helped us ward off the eternal chill of underground—fear could hollow out a body. Under those circumstances, when hope was a specter, holding onto a touch or a kindness, remembering how it felt to be desired, could be a practical distraction. We had to find all the ways we could to convince ourselves to continue to fight.

At least that is the story I kept telling myself.

If you are reading this book now, it is the future. When we were underground, the uncertainty of this future could suffocate us. When we emerged after 344 days, squinting like rats in the sunlight, we didn't think people would believe us. Who would think it possible for thirty-eight people to live so long inside the earth? We barely believed it ourselves.

The longer I lived to retell the story, the stranger it felt in my mouth. As it became a secret in my life, it became precious, often more real to me than my everyday world. Although the story is the stitching that bound my relationship with Joseph, the shoemaker with whom I am living now, we rarely talk about those days anymore. When somebody asks me a question about them, though, I am obligated to answer. I do not speak for myself but for those who no longer can.

Some find it strange that I chose to remain here in Ukraine, so close to the village where so many of my friends and family members were killed, in a city where only a handful of Jewish families are left. Those years taught me that any place where you stand up for yourself is your home. And I didn't stay underground for nearly a year to go live like a gypsy in some foreign land.

More than anything, that year taught me how to go out of my way to help people, to be kind, and to search deep inside myself to find forgiveness. There's always a choice to be human. That's the lesson I try to pass on to anyone who comes to my kitchen. It is the lesson I am trying to pass on to you now.

Chapter One

May 1966

MY FOURTEEN-YEAR-OLD GRANDSON, Valeriy, sits at my kitchen table holding the cool, wide blade of a knife against his bruised cheek. He sits still, like a bird pretending he isn't wounded so other birds won't attack.

"Keep the metal on a little longer. It will keep the swelling down," I say.

He grips the knife tighter. I notice the callus on his pointer finger, the one he strums the guitar with all night. Joseph often laughs to hear how my grandson croons out his favorite Vladimir Vysotsky songs in his gawky voice still caught in that whisker between boy and man. He avoids my gaze and turns towards his cocked elbow on the table.

I turn towards the stove. I pull the door open and poke a large fork into the stuffed chicken necks, inhaling the brothy scent of juices, onion, and dill. This is the healing food that has made me famous, the one that brings everyone to my table, from the church organist to the bazaar workers to the Ukrainian war widows. This dish, like good conversation, can't be rushed.

"Are you going to tell me what happened? Did you get in a fight with another boy, Valerchik?"

I turn around. He opens his mouth to speak and then thinks better of it. His knuckles redden on the knife handle.

"What makes me so different? I just want to know that. I'm good at studying. I'm a good sportsman," he says.

"What happened? Start from the beginning."

The fact that my grandson exists is itself a miracle. He remains silent.

"Valerchik, it makes Granny sad to see you in pain. I'm an old lady. I may just have some advice."

My fat orange cat, Rigik, stretches on the bedspread, looking bored. I examine the brown china cups on the shelf, the needlepoint of the deer on the wall above Valeriy's head.

"Okay, we were playing soccer. Me and Adam Polanski and four other guys. Behind the houses. The score was two–two. I scored the winning goal, and we won the game. Maybe I was bragging, but I swear I didn't do anything."

My legs are swollen again. I sit at the table. The chair squeaks.

"The next thing I know, the guys on the other team are screaming at me," Valeriy continues. "They start saying it again. 'Jew, Jew.' One pushes me. The next thing I know, they are all on top of me. The guys on my own team, even Adam Polanski, are fighting me. They are all screaming it. 'Jew, Jew, Jew.' What did I do to make them hate me so much? I look just like them. All I did was score a goal."

I fold my hands and look deeply into my grandson's green eyes. "You are Ukrainian. Your father is Ukrainian. That's what it says on your birth certificate," I say.

He slams his fist on the table, startling me. "I am Jewish too. Momma is a Jew. You are a Jew. So I am a Jew."

"Yes, you are Jewish too."

"This is not the first time it's happened," he says.

I nod.

"Last month I was watching them play chess—Polanski's father and the others. I wanted to know how they play. I was just standing there.

They got nervous. They started cursing me, yelling at me, shooing me away like the chickens," he says.

I take a long, deep breath. Normally, I am a woman who doesn't have to look in her pocket to find the right words. Along with the stuffed chicken necks, people from all over Borschow come to me for advice. They come to me for my stubbornness, my quick tongue, and my rotten sense of humor. The kitchen is often crowded with them. Some come because we lived the same story. Others visit for absolution, as they would a priest. Still others believe there is a purpose to God keeping our family alive and making us want to stay here. There is some reason we remained.

This conversation is delicate.

I always knew that one day Valeriy would want answers—for why his mother has such poor eating habits, for the way daylight gives her headaches, or for the way her screams while she sleeps sometimes run through the house like the vibrations of his guitar chords.

"You were named after Valeriy Chkalov, the first Soviet pilot to cross the North Pole. We named you that because you are a bridge to the new world." I scrape my tongue against my teeth. "You have sat here at my table since you were a boy. Do you remember the way you used to play with the car I made from the pillow for you? This was before you could walk."

He nods, but his face shows confusion. Stories have been passed at this table. When Jews visited, we spoke Yiddish. When Ukrainians visited, we spoke in code. We tried our best to shield him.

"Does this have to do with the war?" he asks.

I nod.

"What is Popowa Yama?" he asks.

I take a deep breath, fuss with my cuticles. An old, heavy weight cramps my chest. Sometimes it gets so bad that I must bathe in very hot water to breathe freely. How do you explain this story? How do you tell a boy that his momma, his uncles, and I spent nearly a year living under the earth among bats?

"Granny, what is Popowa Yama?" Valeriy repeats.

11

Outside, some sort of bird whistles, a shrill springtime bird. On the table is a vase of cut Convallaria, Lily of the valley. They are tall stalks with tiny white bell-shaped flowers and a strong perfume. Convallaria are bittersweet. They are poison, but you can use them to make medicine to heal the heart. Every spring around the time we left the cave, I have gone to the woods just behind our house and cut them. They remind me of where we have been.

"Well?" he says.

"Start at the beginning," I used to tell my Mania, Valeriy's mother, when something panicked her as a teenager. So that is where I start.

"Priest's Grotto is something not easy to explain. It was not always this way," I begin.

"Before the war, in Korolówka alone, there were almost five hundred Jewish families. We were one-third the population of the whole town. We had a synagogue then, a rabbi. Nobody cared we were Jewish. There were three groups: the Jews, the Ukrainians, and the Poles. We all got along. We were neighbors, even friends.

"Now I can count on one hand how many Jewish families are left: the Shwartzes, the Reitzners, the Fishers. There are practically no Jews left in Korolówka anymore."

"The war was against the Jewish?" he asks.

I push the chair in closer, lean on the back, close my eyes. I open them and then stare at my grandson.

"Listen to me carefully, Valeriy. Listen to everything I'm about to say. It is time that you learned who we are."

———◆•◆••◆———

When your grandfather Chaim Goldberg died from leukemia, we buried him in the old Jewish cemetery. I remember watching the pall-bearers lower him into the grave and noticing how smooth and deep the *chernozem* had been dug. Of course, I had no way of knowing back then that we would soon lose our rights to that soil, to the land our families had helped to farm for generations. And I had no way of knowing that our primal connection to that land would ultimately keep us alive. All I knew then was that I had lost my husband. My three children had lost their father. Your momma, my Mania, was only eleven years old then. Your uncle Dunia was eight, and your uncle Marek was three.

I stood watching the rabbi mouth the prayers. I turned my head up and looked past the cemetery and over the hill where our village was built to the tilled fields down below. The season had turned. Hay covered rows of summer crops. Squashes hung heavy on the vines.

I was hemmed in by the dozens of mourners. Chaim had never been rich, but the turnout made it clear that he was a deeply respected man. I had always known this. Still, I was surprised that so many people had come. This comforted me.

"I'm so sorry, Etcia," a woman next to me said. She squeezed my arm. It was our neighbor Mrs. Wilner. I examined her face. It wasn't cinched in its usual tension, as if she had laid herself bare to share in my grief.

I nodded, thanking her, letting her know our past disputes did not matter.

You see, Chaim and I had spent years fighting a lawsuit the Wilners had waged against us for the rights to build our house and store in the town center where most Jews lived. They believed we were going to build a store with foodstuffs like theirs instead of the leather and tobacco products Chaim sold mostly to families, shoemakers and other craftsmen. We won the lawsuit, but our house was hard earned. We always had to scrape our *zlotys* together. Rooms were left unfinished. Something was always falling apart.

"He was a good man," she said.

I hugged Sarah Wilner in tighter to my chest. I wondered if she knew she was not supposed to say such things until after we left the cemetery.

My family always celebrated the high holidays but otherwise was not very religious. I was pleased with myself for taking care of the arrangements and that all my efforts were successful. Chaim's body had been washed in *mikveh* and prepared for burial by the *chevra kadisha*. He was never left alone. After he died, there had always been somebody by his side keeping guard.

After Chaim's mother died, his father became Orthodox. My Mania was named after Chaim's mother. I owed him the dignity of pleasing his family.

"A loving husband to Panna Goldberg," the rabbi said.

Up until then, the funeral had been a lukewarm dream. I floated in and out without paying much attention. Hearing my name in the rabbi's mouth brought me back and made me feel cared for again.

I thought of my husband, his thick, wavy brown hair and slender frame. Chaim was a few inches taller than me, and I enjoyed how it made me feel to have to tilt my chin upwards to see him. He first met me walking down the street and admired me, complimenting my figure and smile. I was eighteen years old. Chaim was twenty-eight. I liked the way he watched me on the floor of the community dance.

He was the only man I'd ever known.

"A good father to his sons, little Marek and Dunia, and to his beautiful daughter, Mania."

Chaim's sister, Salcia, had her hands on Mania's shoulders. Salcia had the sleeve of her clothing torn on the right side like me and the other immediate family members. The children had their left sleeves torn, symbolizing how distinct the loss of a parent is compared to any other kind of loss.

Salcia looked up at me and half smiled. I tried not to look at her hand. She had already offered to take my girl with her to live with her husband and her in Chortkow to decrease my burden. She had good intentions, yet I vowed to myself that no matter what happened, my children and I would remain together.

"Kindness and compassion towards others. Always, he gave things from his store to those who needed help. He would never deny anyone because they could not pay right away," I heard. The rabbi was wrapping up the *hesped*.

I turned and saw the crowd, noticing families bearing telltale signs of poverty—threadbare clothes, boys with pants that were too short or coats that were too tight around their shoulders, a woman holding the ends of a frayed shawl together. I wondered how many of the children were wearing shoes made of leather Chaim had given them on credit from our store. My face flushed red, the way it always did when I got emotional. I felt proud for Chaim for helping so many people. At the same time, shame burned for having scolded him every time he did so.

I turned towards my left to look at my parents. My mother was leaning on my father's shoulder. She was crying, but I didn't believe she was sad. My family, the Dodyks, was one of the richest in Korolówka. They had many acres of land, a house high up on a hill, a whole herd of cattle, and a restaurant. I grew up in a house that was so large, a horse could turn around all the way in the hallway. We had servants. I was one of seven children, but my mother breastfed only one of us, my youngest brother, Yossel. My parents didn't approve of my marriage to Chaim because he was not from their class.

I tried hard not to be my parents' daughter. I took care of street children. Still, I couldn't really understand Chaim's kindness and compassion towards others. In my mind, we were struggling ourselves and shouldn't have been giving so much away.

"Times are hard, Etcia," he always said. "The children will get sick if they don't have good shoes."

The men moved slowly to make a line to shovel the earth onto the coffin. They wore thick black woolen coats that had been tailored in the city. My husband had known about political matters. He traveled with many of the men in the line, attending rallies and listening to speeches.

Once, Chaim insisted on traveling the two hundred miles from Korolówka to Lvov to see Ze'ev Jabotinsky give a speech. Chaim understood matters of the world I knew little about. As I stood in the cemetery it made me sad to think that the fact that he was gone meant that I never would.

I looked up and watched the men passing the shovel to throw the earth on the casket. One by one, they scooped dirt and covered my Chaim. The *chernozem* was dark, heavy, and cold. I didn't like the sound it made when it fell. I was thankful for the men digging, for their struggle lifting the earth to help put Chaim to bed. Yet it was taking too long to fill up the hole.

My heart dropped like a sack of heavy flour.

Chaim was my first love. He was the only man I'd ever known as a woman. My body already felt the loss of the weight of him, his hands on my hips, his arms around my shoulders. I craved his attention. It was Chaim's protection that had given me strength to fight my parents and marry him.

He had been a good man. A *mensch*. I didn't know it then, but the compassion I witnessed him extending towards others would actually help to save us.

"*Yis gadal v yis kadash shmay raboh.*" I recognized the graveside kaddish through the Hebrew words. This symbolized that my husband was now buried, that we could start moving on.

"Amen," I repeated with the crowd.

I looked up past the cemetery to the forested hills surrounding our fields. The hills were carpeted in bright gold and orange leaves. It was a sight that usually filled me with joy, to see the remarkable way the world was changing, how the trees prepared for the winter.

But now, my husband was no longer alive. I was alone with three children to raise.

And we weren't protected. Nobody was.

I allowed myself one final glance at the crowd. Although they tried to hide it, their faces betrayed their fear.

It was September 13, 1939, less than two weeks after Hitler had attacked Poland.

For months, refugees from Romania, Poland, and small villages along the Carpathian Mountains had been crossing Korolówka and staying in our relatives' houses in the city of Borschow and other parts of Ternopol and Stanislav regions. They shared terrible stories: Jewish deportations, decimated villages, bodies left to float in the river.

In villages closer to Korolówka, neighbors robbed houses, threw rocks through windows, beat Jewish families with shovels. In Korolówka, nothing bad had happened, but some of our neighbors had given us bad looks, or worse, and stopped acknowledging us when we passed.

I was too preoccupied with my own troubles to attempt to make sense of it all.

Salcia grabbed my arm and pushed Marek towards Mania. The other people at the cemetery had formed two lines. We were supposed to walk between them. Wind whipped our dresses and jackets so that they fluttered behind us.

"Hamakom yinachem etchem b'toch sh'ar aveilei." The rabbi recited the final prayer, and we left Chaim behind. We walked slowly, as if backwards. People in the procession mumbled and whispered behind us. I was sure they pitied me, were judging my dry eyes. I thought I might trip over the mud. *"Tzion v'yerushalayim."*

We walked towards the edge of the cemetery and the gates where we would wash our hands.

We were headed towards our house, nestled against the hills. I thought of my dark, empty room. I just wanted to hole up there, to go to sleep until I felt better.

That was impossible. It was partly because as soon as the funeral was over, people would bring food to the house and sit *shiva* with me. It was more than that, though.

As hard apples reddened on trees, danger was approaching us like a slow-moving cloud.

Chapter Two

I WALK TO THE window to clear my head. It's springtime already—the peonies are beginning to pop; the jasmine is twining up the gate. A woman thwacks her rug against the floor, sending dust everywhere. My chickens are out there doing their job, running around like crazies and angering my neighbor Maria.

I go to the table.

"How are you feeling, Valerchik? Is your eye hurting?"

"No."

"Come sit down. You are wearing the floor out."

"That's a good story," he says.

"Well, we didn't even get to the exciting parts yet."

The sun has dropped. The light has moved away from the table. I turn off the stove.

Joseph's heavy footsteps make their way into the room. He has an oily rag in his hand. He throws it in the trash. He looks from me to Valeriy and whistles when he sees Valeriy's bloodied cheek.

"What happened to the boy?" He walks over to me and touches the back of my hand.

"Why are you bothering us? What do you want?"

"I saw Peter leaving the house earlier. What did he have to say? Does he think someone's pinching pennies from the collection plate again?" he asks.

Joseph is greedy for gossip the same way a child is greedy for a plate of cookies. I look at him sternly. He pinches my side.

"I heard you playing last night, Valeriy," he says. "You are getting better. What was that song?"

"'Brotherly Graves,' by Vysotsky," Valeriy says.

I have dreaded having this conversation with Valeriy for years.

"Do you not have work?" I ask Joseph. "Has the great shoe master suddenly become rich enough he can close up shop for the day?"

"Yes, yes, I have work. Stoyko is coming in a half hour."

"Good. Ask him if the coal shipment has come in."

"I hope you got a few good punches in anyhow, Valeriy."

"Leave the boy alone. Go get ready for Stoyko. I'll call you for dinner later on."

Sun streams through the kitchen window, warming my face and the top of my head.

"Okay, okay. I will see you two troublemakers later." Joseph makes a show of leaving, the way men act like boys when they are shooed from a room. He lingers in the hallway, pretending to fuss with some newspapers.

"So, what happened next?" Valeriy asks.

I roll my shoulders back, take a deep breath, and let it back out.

"Things happened slowly at first. The Russians occupied our village for two years until they lost to the Germans and left. Later, the Ukrainian police regained control. A Jewish police was formed. They were all just scarecrows, really. They answered to Germans at Nazi headquarters in Borschow.

"Jews had to register in Borschow and get an armband with a Star of David on it. We were supposed to wear them all the time. The area of the town where Jewish people lived was then called an 'open ghetto.' Soon we were not allowed to leave this area to trade with our Ukrainian neighbors. We were corralled like pigs on a farm, but still we went about our lives. That bothers me. We should have been smarter.

"More refugees came. Then came others, not refugees, no longer free. They carted prisoners on wagons through our town. At first, this was a shocking sight. Then we became accustomed to them. We watched them like migrating ibis."

"But what are these words you always say? *Aktion? Schron?* Popowa Yama?" my grandson asks. "What is *aktion?*"

Joseph drifts down the hallway. He shuts the door to his workshop.

I stretch out my legs and cross my ankles.

"This word you ask about, *aktion.* It is a polite word for a terrible thing. The Germans give orders. Police go door to door. In the streets, they push all the Jews into an open space. Sometimes they tell them to make a hole and everyone to get inside. They shoot them or pour gasoline on them and burn them alive. They cover the hole. That is their funeral."

"I don't understand."

"It's good that you don't."

"What did you do?"

"Prepared. People built hiding spots—in bunkers, in hay bales, under horse stalls. We lived where the animals feces. We traveled the routes the animals did. The dogs were confused when we started sleeping in the same places as them. The dogs had it better than us, though."

I don't know why, but the confusion on Valeriy's face makes me want to laugh.

"Did you know people who were killed during these things, the *aktions?*" he asks.

I take a sip of tea and let the story form.

———— ❖✦❖ ————

One night, I stood with the children and my father in the courtyard of our house. It was one of those clear, cold nights when the sky is littered with stars. It was beautiful. Mania held her youngest brother's hand. Each carried a bag.

"Will we come back?" Dunia asked me.

"Of course, baby," I said.

My father squeezed my shoulder. I looked up at him, taking in his gray eyes and his long, slender body in his overcoat. The hair he had left was uncombed.

"There isn't time. We must go now," he whispered. He kissed me on the cheek, a gesture that surprised me. He didn't even kiss me after Chaim died. The scruff of his beard scratched my skin, and I could smell him, the strange scent I remembered from childhood—one part musty like a horse's neck, one part store-bought cologne. It made me remember how protected he always made me feel. At that moment, I had no choice but to let my father take care of us.

"How did you know, about the *aktion* tomorrow?" I whispered. We cut through people's backyards and gardens. The apple and pear trees that always loomed like large mythological creatures in my childhood watched over us, their heads bowed in prayer.

"It doesn't matter," my father said.

I didn't even think to argue with him. My parents had access to information, a passkey to unlock the heavy doors of politics that blocked our lives.

We walked in silence. I knew the facts. I was dragging my children through people's backyards in the middle of the night. The next day, soldiers with guns and sticks would look for us. If they found us, we'd be killed.

Exhaustion kept me calm. Every so often, I looked back at the children. Marek's sleep-dusted eyes scoured the woods, maybe for wolves or dead birds. Dunia was his usual unreadable self, a quality he inherited from his father. Mania had separated from her brothers. Her thin body poked out of an old coat. She worried me most. She was more sensitive. The night unnerved her.

We finally arrived at my parents' house. My father stopped us in the orchard. I smelled apples in their last phases of ripening, some already rotting in the grass. The children were half asleep. My father looked up at the sky and then at his watch.

"What is it, Poppa?"

"Go up to the house. Let the children sleep. When it is dawn, no later, get some food, and your mother will show you where to go to hide. We made a good spot under the chicken coop. It is deep and clean. You will be safe."

I looked up in the direction of my parents' house. My childhood house had not yet been taken. But it would be. It was too large, too much of a target. The vegetable fields were said to be some of the most productive. The servants had broken down the *chernozem* for years, and our massive cabbage squash and beets were envied all over the village. Even as a child, I had felt how different our way of life was . We had real silver and crystal and embroidered linen tablecloths, things that did not exist in my friends' houses.

Still, I looked as the house as ours. The fact that my parents had managed to keep it confused me. I had yet to truly understand the depth of their worldly connections.

"You children listen to what your momma says. When she tells you to be quiet, you have to be quiet, just like a mouse. Can you do that?" My father's voice was sing-song, and he pinched Marek on the cheek. The boy giggled. My father nodded at Mania and Dunia.

"It is okay. You will be safe, but only if you stay quiet. Sleep well, children. Granny has some good food waiting for you upstairs."

My father stood up to his full height. He was about a head taller than I, but he stood with a slight stoop to his back, as if his body were a violin bow that had been gently plucked for years, the way all tall people generally turn after spending years adapting to looking other people in the eyes. Our whole family had this problem.

"Aren't you coming in with us?" I asked.

23

"No. I will be back soon. Don't worry. I am going to find Yossel, Pepcia, and baby Nunia. The news may not have reached them all the way on the edge of town."

I stood there a few extra seconds, watching his dark figure cut through the trees as he made his way to the road.

He was the first person killed in our family.

Chapter Three

GO TO THE stove and refill the teacups. I take my time getting back to the table. I set the cups down, sit, and stretch my legs so the pressure on my veins isn't so bad. I hold the warm teacup in my palms, blowing into the stream.

"I am sorry that your poppa died. I don't think you ever told me about him before," Valeriy says.

I consider this.

"Why not?" he asks.

"We didn't speak of the dead."

"Why not?"

I take a sip of tea. The warm liquid travels from my gullet to the center of my chest.

"Often we didn't know if they were dead. I don't know if my father was properly buried."

"Didn't they find his body?"

"No. My brothers went looking for him, but they never found the body. They received confirmation that he was shot. There had been several troops of Germans who took Jews into the forest then. Everyone was always running, hiding. It was madness, a time when only *meshuganas* roamed the earth. Sometimes you prayed not to get news. We did not want to know when my oldest brother Zena's wife, Rachel, was arrested and sent to Borschow and then to a camp in Poland. We did not want to learn when, a few weeks later, Zena was caught by the Ukrainian police during an *aktion*."

"They didn't get buried either?"

"We don't know."

"Does it make a difference how they were buried?" Valeriy asks.

"Well, maybe not. But we are taught that the dead must be properly cared for, watched over every hour, and put in the ground as soon as possible. If this does not happen, the dead may get restless. They may try to stay with us."

"The rabbis said this? You mean, like ghosts?" Valeriy says and laughs. He makes a ghost sound in the air, the same sound the man makes in the bazaar when he plays the saw with the violin bow.

I laugh and poke him in the arm. "I told you, I'm not superstitious. I'm just telling you what some believe. But I do believe it's important to die with dignity. When we can't give our loved ones that, it shames us. Maybe this is why I did not speak of my father."

"Oh, I just remembered. You mean you take care of the dead guy like the men who watched your husband after he died? They stayed overnight?"

"You are a good listener, Valerchik. Perhaps you have something besides wind in your head after all." I pat him on the hand.

"Did the *aktions* happen a lot? Did you get to go back to the house?"

"Yes, a lot. After the *aktions*, things got worse. The area was made Judean free. Jews had a choice—they could go to another country or to a ghetto in Borschow. Anyone who chose to stay would be killed or sent to the camps. Any Ukrainian who found a Jewish person had the right to either kill us or to turn us over to police to be killed."

"Did they listen, the neighbors? Did they try to turn Jews in?"

"Some neighbors."

"How could they do that?"

"We gave them the God, and then they killed us for it," I say and laugh. Valeriy squints. "Jesus Christ. He was a Jew. It was a joke, Valerchik. You were looking so serious. You have to have a sense of humor!"

"Why, though? They were cowards," he says.

"No, Valeriy, it's too easy to say that. They had their own families to protect. You know Father Sohatski, the priest in Strilkivtcy village—he used to preach to his congregation not to kill Jews, even to help if they could. He took a terrible risk. Ivan Drobnuak and his wife, Anna, raised a Jewish baby named Sonya, who had been left on their doorstep as their own. There were so many others. So many good and strong people who quietly sacrificed their own safety to help, to protect, people who kept us alive. It is in times like those that you can find how good people are too, how strong and how brave."

Joseph comes back in. He stands at the door with a paper bag in his hand, staring at me. His blue eyes are watery.

"Speak of the devil," I say and wink at him. "I was telling Valeriy about our family, about the war."

Joseph's face is flushed. His walk must have been brisk. His jacket is zipped. It must be getting windy outside. He looks happy. I am pretty sure he has had a few nips on the bottle.

"Kostaski saved us at least a dozen times," I said, calling Joseph by his surname as I did during the days I am now telling Valeriy about. "If it hadn't been for Kostaski, we probably wouldn't have made it."

Joseph looks at Valeriy and shakes his head. "Your grandfather was a good man. Times were not always so easy. He gave me leather, soles, supplies for the shoes on credit. That kept me from starving. We are bound by a scrap of shoe leather," he says.

"And some corn husks," I say.

Joseph laughs, his low, gurgling laugh.

"Why don't you tell it?" I instruct. The telling of this story always makes Joseph happy. It is the truth. It is the reason I trusted him with my children. If it hadn't been for that corn husk, I might not have opened my heart.

I move near Valeriy and cup my hand over his, pressing it gently for a long time, the way we used to do in the cave.

"This happened in wintertime. Your granny was traveling to Scovyatin village. Mania and Dunia had been staying with a nice family for a few weeks, and your granny came to take them to my brother Vladmir's house in Korolówka.

"We were in charge of Marek. By that time, we had built the best hiding spots. Marek was in a back room. It was cold and dark. We wrapped him under a fluffy *pirhyana*. We used to joke that the geese that gave their feathers for those *pirhyanas* were a special breed. Marek knew how to be quiet. We tried not to fuss with him during daytime.

"I was in the workshop, cutting some leather into an old shoe, when the news traveled to me that there was an *aktion*. I didn't have time to even make a plan before I saw Germans banging on a neighbor's door a few houses down. My heart was in my throat. I had just enough time to run to get Marek and practically drag him with me to the barn. He didn't ask any questions. We hid him around the sheaves of corn husks—you know, the way we braid them and lean them against the barn wall for the animals to eat? I told him to be quiet, that the Nazis were coming. Then I went to the yard and pretended to be busy raking hay.

"We heard the dogs. These Nazi dogs were not pets. They made terrible noises. I don't know how they trained them to be so mean. They started towards the barn, and their barking got louder. I could practically feel their breath on my back. I turned around. When I met the Nazis' eyes, I was so scared, I almost threw up. There were Nazis and Ukrainian police yelling in both languages. It sounded like a flock of hysterical birds.

"'Are you hiding any Jews here?' they snarled.

"'No, of course not. I do not hide Jews,' I said. I spit on the ground then, both for emphasis and because I was still choking down nausea.

"Some Nazi barked orders. The Ukrainian police translated. 'If you are lying and we find Jews on your property, we will kill them, and then we will kill your family in front of your eyes. Then we will kill you. If you are hiding anyone, tell us now, and we will spare you,' he said.

"It was like a lump of butter stuck in my throat. 'There are no Jews here,' I repeated.

"My wife, Marta, and my children were in the main house. The children cried. Marta tried to hush them. The men went all over the property, to the chicken and pig house. Sweat was staining my clothes. I stood there with arms folded over my chest. When they got to the barn, I prayed. They made a racket with their rifles. They came out of the barn without Marek. I looked them in the eye when they neared me. They walked away.

"I watched them retreat for a long time before I ran into the barn to get Marek. I'll never forget the expression on his face. He was hollow, in shock. I pulled him to me and hugged him. Then I got down on my knees so that I was eye level with him. 'Tell me what happened,' I said.

"Marek told me. He had stood still but heard the soldiers beating their guns all over the ground and walls. One slammed his gun on two rows of corn husks beside him. *Thwack, thwack, thwack.* They came so close to finding him.

"'You are a brave boy. Your momma will be proud,' I told him. I brought him back to his room and left my wife to tend to him. I went to my room to drink a nice glass of homemade vodka.

"A corn husk. Your uncle was saved by one row of corn husks. It was the closest we'd all come to death," Joseph says. His eyes are bleary, and I see him looking down the corridor towards his workshop. He keeps a secret bottle of vodka between some sandpaper and work boots.

"How did you find out what happened, Granny?" Valeriy asked.

"Well, when I came back, Joseph told me. I was grateful to him for his quick thinking. I was proud of Marek for being so brave. I told Marek that day was his second birthday. We still joke about that sometimes."

Joseph stands there skulking by the corridor. He catches me looking at him tenderly. I never admitted that day was when I started feeling affection for him. He knows, though.

"Kostaski was everyone's friend. Everyone knew his house was a safe place to go, that he would help Jews, that he wouldn't turn anyone in," I say.

"Your granny was the one who sacrificed," says Joseph. "She is a hero. She saved your momma and Uncle Marek and Uncle Dunia by herself, all by herself. She is the one who taught us. Ask her about when she started wearing the man's clothes. Ask her about how she broke all the men and herself out of jail."

I smile. I haven't spoken about that moment in years. It is the moment in my past when I first found my strength, a moment that could teach Valeriy. I start the story again.

———•◦✦◦•———

We had turned into refugees, freeloaders, trespassers in our own village, guests who had overstayed our welcome in our neighbors' homes. We came to know who would help us and who wouldn't. Some hunted us, claiming we stole horses or canned jars of beets from summer houses. Others locked their doors when we came. There were moments those who helped had to let us go.

By the time the bodies rotted to bone in the graves that had been dug in town, the threat of being caught was impossible to deny. There weren't many moments we didn't feel it.

There were unspoken rules: We had to keep moving. We couldn't hide in the same house more than a few weeks. We couldn't eat much of the food offered; whenever possible, we replaced it and looked for our own. We traveled at night mostly, or late afternoon, hunting food.

Marek and I stayed in the house where Kostaski and his wife lived. Your momma, Mania, and Dunia stayed at Kostaski's brother's house. Kostaski's brother told us he had heard that the Ukrainian police suspected the children would have to leave. I begged to let them stay longer. They agreed to three days. If I didn't return, the children would be on their own.

I was walking the back roads from Korolówka to Strilkivtcy. It was just before dinnertime, dark enough for people to slow down but an hour when a lot of families sat down to supper. I had misjudged. The back roads I was traveling branched out past some families' homes and fields. Men were still outside, standing by the side of the road, talking. By the time I saw them there, it was too late to avoid them, so I walked as casually as I could, trying not to draw too much attention. I had a basket in my hand, my headscarf pulled tight.

It was a tough walk. My feet tapped the road, kicking up dust. It tickled my throat. As I passed, I noticed a group of Ukrainian police with the men. My heart dropped to my knees. I kept my clothes clean, but by this point they were already tattered. I had to double up my last pairs of stockings so my legs wouldn't catch cold.

I paid attention to my breath, exhaling like a horse. The eyes of the men faded with the last rays of sunshine. I walked further, concentrating on the way the snow glowed.

Then I made a big mistake. I paused. It took only one moment.

"Why are you letting her go? She's a Jewish. She's a Jew. Get her!" I heard.

I turned around in time to see the police heading towards me. I imagined myself taking off, sprinting like a deer through the woods. Instead I just stood there. I couldn't move.

They captured me and brought me to the police station. Everything became real to me in a way it hadn't been real before. When we were running and hiding, the people we were hiding from weren't men; they were just disembodied parts—the sound of boots and heavy legs creaking the floorboards, voices in the doorway of the house where we hid. Mostly they existed through the stories that were told about them: men who used axes to slaughter our neighbors, men who took our relatives away and put them on trains to the camps. When I actually saw them, they seemed far away, unreal. Even our own lives—Mania's, Dunia's, Marek's—had this faded quality about them. We spent so much time running, trying to make ourselves invisible, it was often almost as if we had.

31

When we got to the police station, this changed. The men yelled at me. I was still a young woman then and had lived a protected life. The men in my life had shown me only kindness. I was not used to cruelty.

"Where were you going?" one of the men asked.

"I was looking for food." I didn't meet their eyes or look up.

"Where?"

"I was going to Strilkivtcy."

"Who were you going to see?"

"Nobody."

"Answer me," one said. He moved in so close to me, he was practically spitting on me. I then did something that surprised me—I looked him straight in the eye. I did not know this man personally, but I knew where he lived. I'd probably interacted with his family on the street, at the bazaar.

It was as if he could tell what I was thinking. His lip twitched, and then he tried to smile. "Where are your children?" he asked. "Answer me," he said.

"I don't know anything. Please," I said.

Before I knew what was happening, the policeman had pulled his arm back and punched me in the nose. I couldn't tell what was worse, the pain or the shock. It felt as if all the bones in my nose had been splintered, as if their shards were cutting my eye. In a split second, the blood started pouring out of my nose. My eyes welled up, but I wouldn't let myself cry.

———◆•◆•◆———

They led me to a barn about two hundred yards away from the police station, where they were holding Jewish prisoners until they received orders from the Germans on what to do with us. I'll never forget that moment when the guard shoved me into the barn and I saw all the men. Some were disfigured and lying on piles of hay against the wall. Others stood, their faces shadowed in dim sunlight. There were ten men and me. I was surprised I didn't recognize any of them from the village.

The guard nudged me in. The prisoners who looked up looked at me kindly, even with embarrassment.

When the guard left, one of the men's expressions turned tender. I watched him walk over to a bucket of water in the center of the room. I heard fabric ripping, then watched him bend towards the bucket to dip the fabric and wring it out. At the same time, he looked around the room, challenging anyone to question what he was doing.

The man walked over to me and handed me the wet cloth. I thanked him. He shook his head, drifted to the other side of the room. I held the cloth on my nose, pressing firmly as I did when Marek had nosebleeds.

I had taken to smoking cigarettes in those days to suppress my appetite so I'd be able to give more of what little food I had secured to the children. I wanted a cigarette to distract me from the pain. I had half a pack in my pocket. I knew most of the men in there would probably like a cigarette too.

"How long have you been here?" I asked eventually.

A long, heavy silence hung in the air. "God only knows," one finally answered.

"What are they planning to do with us?"

It was a long time before anyone answered. "They are dolls waiting for orders from the Germans. Probably they will kill us," one man said.

I looked in the direction of the man who had spoken. He lay on his back in the hay. His face was gaunt and greasy. He hadn't opened his eyes when he spoke.

The man who had given me a piece of his shirt looked at me and smiled sadly.

A few hours passed before the guard came back in. I was surprised that I knew him. His name was Bordetski. He lived on the other side of the village. Mania had gone to school with his children. He was not a bright man, but I had always considered him to be kind. I could, however, guess why the man had referred to him as a doll. Bordetski was the kind of person who was always doing what others told him to do. This was the person who was then in control of our lives.

Bordetski held a half loaf of brown bread in his hand. "Can anyone pay for this?" he asked.

I looked around at the men. I'd given my *zlotys* to the men in the interrogation room and was surprised to see one of the other prisoners hand Bordetski some heavy silver coins. Bordetski tossed the bread on the floor. One of the men picked it up. I knew Bordetski had seen me and knew who I was. He wouldn't look my way.

"Hey, Bordetski," I said.

He turned around and looked at me. He made his eyes go angry and hard.

"How long will you keep us?" I asked.

He shrugged his shoulders and started towards the door. I took a few steps closer.

"Can you not see with your own eyes that I am the only woman in here? What happens when we have to go to the toilet?" I asked.

He turned around. "You call me, Panna Goldberg. Each person who has to go calls me, and I take you out—one at a time," he said.

I was in the barn several days. Time had long since lost its meaning, and I couldn't determine the days. All I could think of was Mania and Dunia waiting for me, worried they'd be thrown out on the street. Mania was smart, but she didn't really know what to do yet.

As the days thickened, thoughts of the children tortured me. I imagined Mania and Dunia roaming the streets, sleeping with dogs, rooting in the field for potatoes. I imagined them caught, the butt of a rifle at their heads, in their mouths. I imagined Marek's tiny hand sticking out of a grave.

The men moaned and slept, their backs turned towards each other. They were like wounded animals, acting as if they were already dead.

Something snapped in me like a tightly pulled rubber band. Anger I had been suppressing all those months we had been hiding rose up from my ribcage and stuck in my throat. A resolve I didn't know I possessed found me. *No*, I thought, *I am not going to let this happen to me. I am not going to wait to be killed.*

I did the only thing I could do under the circumstances. I started talking.

"You know what? I am not going to just sit here like this and wait until they kill us."

Nobody spoke. The silence sealed us. The room was a lidded canning jar.

"I have three children. They are waiting for me. I am not going to just sit here and let them kill me so my children die too. They are just babies. They are my babies. They are not old enough to take care of themselves."

Still the silence prevailed. The thicker it got, the louder I became.

"What, are you just going to let it happen? You are just going to lie down like dogs and wait to die? You can live. Have you nothing to live for? You have to want to live. Wake up. We can escape! We can get out of here! It is our only chance."

I felt eyes on me.

"Shut your mouth, Panna Goldberg, please. You are going to get us killed now," one said.

I turned and saw him walking over from where the guard was posted to where I was sitting. A few of the other men turned around too. They made no effort to move, but a few shifted their bodies around.

"Don't tell me that," I said. "We will be slaughtered if we wait here."

"You don't think we have thought this ourselves? There is no other way," the one over at the door whispered.

"What do you suggest that we do?" another man said.

35

I sat there for a few seconds. I thought about Bordetski. Slowly, I formulated a plan.

"Okay, I will tell you. When it gets dark out tonight, I will ask to go to the bathroom. And if he lets me out, we will attack him, and we will escape," I said.

"That's too dangerous. He has a gun," someone said.

"He has one gun. He is one man. At night he will be the only one here. There are eleven of us here—eleven people who will die if we stay here and wait to be slaughtered."

There was a lot of grumbling. My words sunk in. It was a crazy plan.

"And then they will chase us and hunt us down for days," one said, "and we will get killed anyhow. Not all of us will make it out alive."

There was a long, impenetrable silence. Defeat rested on my chest. I had not eaten in days.

"Please. My children," I said.

"And if we wait here, we will all die," said the one who had given me a piece of his shirt. His name was Melvin. "Panna Goldberg has a point. It is the best chance we have. They will kill us one way or another. If they don't shoot us, we will starve. At nighttime, we are alone; there is only one guard."

"And how do you suggest we restrain him so that we can run? He is not just going to give up his gun. He is not just going to smile and watch us run off."- someone said.

For a while, nobody spoke. They figured, as men do.

"How can you be sure? You can't know that," said one of the men. "Don't pretend that you know."

"It is our only hope."- someone weakly interjected.

This conversation went on for a while. A warmth flooded my chest. We were going to do it. I noticed between the men's words sounds of clenched teeth, of rasping breath. Some of us wouldn't make it. I thought of my children and determined that I would not be killed.

"We can tie him," one man said.

"With what? Hay?"

"Maybe ties from the bales."

"That is not strong enough."

I looked at the men sitting around the room in their tattered clothes. I looked from one to the other, examining them.

"Belts," I said. "We will tie all your belts."

By nighttime, we had our plans set. I waited by the door. The men stood up against the walls. I looked at them all, slowly, steeling my strength. When enough of them nodded, I yelled out.

"Bordetski! Bordetski!" I screamed as loud as I could through the door.

"What?" he grumbled.

"It's Panna Goldberg. I want out. I have to go to the bathroom."

He opened the door. The men descended on him at once, pushing him into the barn. They kicked him and pushed him and punched him. I didn't move right away. I watched the men struggling, trying to exhaust the slow flames of their anger. Someone held a hand over Bordetski's mouth.

"Enough," Melvin said. "Save your strength. Someone help me tie him."

Some men were already out the door, but I stood there with the others, my mind swarming like a beehive. The man who had his hand on Bordetski's mouth spoke slowly. The others tied the belts. The whole time, Bordetski's eyes were fixed on me.

"I am going to take my hand away, but you are not going to scream. If you scream, we will kill you. Do you understand?" the man asked. Bordetski nodded his head, and the man took his hand away.

Bordetski looked at me, disbelief and terror in his eyes. "How could you do this to me?" he said.

I looked at him. "We decided not to kill you. We spared you. Do us the same courtesy. Do not scream. There is one man standing by. If you scream, he will come back and kill you," I said.

My heart was pumping so hard, my legs felt as if they were cushioned in cotton. I imagined them as deer legs, as sturdy and swift. I imagined them helping me fly to my children.

"Go," a man behind me said.

Two men pushed each other to get out the door. When they got out, I took off myself. The cold air ripped through my chest. I pumped my legs through the snowy fields.

I'd never in my life run so hard or so fast. The winter air was cold. It pierced my chest. There was only a sliver of moon in the sky. One hand held the bottom of my skirt in a ball, the other the top of my coat. I pushed and pushed into darkness, feeling my swollen face, the clumsiness of my thick legs, the stockings that were torn and bunched up at my knees.

I ran past the fields to the edge of the forest, forced myself up the hills. I ran through copses of trees, over broken branches and snow. When I couldn't run anymore, I stopped and sat down on the snow, leaning my cheek on an oak tree, feeling the cold bark on my skin.

Something strange happened after that. I started to laugh, hysterical maniacal laughter. The laughter felt removed from me, and I was amazed that this sound was coming out of my body. It just poured out of me, this laughter, cinching my heart, tearing through my chest. It felt so good, and so painful too. I bent into it, laughing and laughing for five or ten minutes until I was spent.

Every bone and muscle and nerve of my body was exhausted. My stomach ached. I think I was shocked that we had done this thing—that we had tied up Bordetski, that we had set ourselves free. I stood up and started to walk.

It's tough for me to explain what the rest of that night was like. I'd barely eaten or slept in the barn. My footsteps were driven by adrenaline, by the voices and hearts of my children. I walked through dark paths, hearing nothing but the sound of my boots cracking snow.

Eventually I rested, squatting with my back against a tree. I breathed deeply, willing warmth into my body. I scooped snow in my hands and ate it.

I wasn't raised to survive in the woods. I curled in the spruce boughs near the trees. I nestled up against the branches. I ate more snow and a few winter berries. I dozed, then imagined waking in the morning with a rifle butt on my chest.

Dawn finally broke, casting a rosy shadow over the snow. I was filled with a mixture of relief and nausea. There were no houses. I guessed I was somewhere in the hills between Korolówka and Urampol. I sat in the snow. I couldn't see any animals, not even a sparrow. Bare-branched oaks and tall evergreens encircled me.

Although I knew I wasn't safe, a new, quiet faith flickered in me like a candle flame. I had done it myself. I'd convinced the men to escape. I'd never before felt such power. This made me believe we had a chance.

Danger kept me moving. The police, the neighbors, maybe even the Germans from Borschow would be searching for us, looking to make an example. They might even kill others in our place. As I walked, I remembered those who had probably been killed: my father, Zena, Rachel, all of those who had mysteriously disappeared.

My feet and hands hurt. The last vestiges of my stockings were still on but provided me with little warmth. I rubbed my legs and hands when I thought about it. I stopped, squatted down, and rested.

A sparrow flew past my face and into a tree beside me. He chirped as he stared at me. I remembered the stories of my brother Yossel, who had been in the Polish army. He was a good hunter, and he had told me of looking for scat and animal tracks on his marches. I wasn't sure what I would do if I found them. If it was wolf or fox, I would go in another direction. If it was rabbit or bird, perhaps I would try to catch it.

I stood up and started walking. When I thought of stopping, I remembered the fear in the eyes of the refugees on the trucks. I forced myself to imagine more horrible things. Women had been made to undress in public. They had been hurt in terrible ways. I imagined what a man who caught me alone would do. I walked, imagining Chaim's arms wrapped around me, keeping me safe. I railed at him for dying and leaving me alone in this kind of world.

Then I became angry at the men: the ones who'd alerted the police, the police who'd punched me, and Bordetski. This pure, sweet anger rose up in me with an intensity I hadn't felt the whole time our lives were endangered. I took hard, angry steps in the snow. *I exist*, I thought. My boots struck the snow like a soldier's boots. *I am still here. I exist. I'm still here.*

Eventually I had to rest. I hated to do that because I was so tired. If I let myself sleep, I might never wake up. When I felt myself slipping away, I thought of the children, imagined them wrapping their tiny hands around my stomach to hug me, imagined spitting on my finger to wipe dirt and dried tears from their faces. I remembered how relatives of one man who had escaped from a labor camp had been rounded up in the middle of the village and made to kneel in a grave.

I was in a sticky trap. I was struggling to return to my children, yet they'd probably been forced from the homes where we had placed them. I had no idea where they were.

I ate snow, but my throat was always dry. Hunger gnawed. I sweat in my clothes. At moments, I put the back of my hand to my forehead. My skin was clammy. My mind became drained. I wanted nothing more than to curl up in the snow and die. As I thought this, a warmth as soothing as I imagined being in the womb might be overcame me. I picked up snow and rubbed it under my eyes. I hummed.

Something happened then that I cannot believe to this day. The longer I sat in the forest, the more noise I heard. Birds called each other. Squirrels climbed tree trunks. Field mice and voles scampered by my feet.

I wasn't alone.

The wind hummed in branches, sending pine cones and needles into the snow. The sun protected us all, casting shadows and false warmth. God was with me. I prayed silently. *Please, God, help the children stay safe. Help them be in the place where I left them when I return. Please, God, help me to find my way back to them. Help me know when it is safe to return.*

I dozed. When I looked up, I noticed an animal—a fox, I think—slinking through the woods in front of me. His sleek, fluffy body moved away from me. It got smaller and smaller until it disappeared.

I stood up. I walked a few yards. I was at the top of a hill. The silhouettes below were familiar—the outlines of a village, stone houses on the edge of the forest. I was not in a fairyland after all. I was five kilometers from our town. I decided then that I would return to Korolówka. I would wait until the sun started to set over the hills.

————◆◆◆◆◆————

When Kostaski opened the door, I saw myself through his eyes. He looked at me at first as if he had seen a ghost, so hard and so long I wondered if I was actually alive. Then he pushed me through the door and into the kitchen. He had me sit down. He came back with a *hummer* in his hand. Marek was with him.

Marek jumped up and clung to me, his fingernails digging into my skin like the claws of a baby bear. I whispered to him words that must have seemed like an incomprehensible language, tears rolling down my face. Kostaski gently pulled him off, telling him I needed to get warm. I must have behaved like an animal, like a child, because I heard Kostaski talking to me in a soft voice. I felt the weight of the blanket he put around my arms, felt him pulling off my shoes and then going to heat some water. I sat there, numb.

"Etcia, we were sure you were dead," he said.

I looked at him, uncomprehendingly.

41

"Panna Goldberg, don't try and speak right away. You are weak. Let us get you warm first," he said.

As if in a dream, I watched him tying a warm cloth on my hands. He wiped my face. An intense gratitude washed over me, a feeling of safety I could never remember having experienced before. I looked at his big hands, the width of his shoulders, and imagined myself curling up against his chest and going to sleep.

Something occurred to me as if I had just woken up. I opened my mouth, but I couldn't form words. "Dunia, Mania," I managed.

Worry crossed Kostaski's face.

"No!" I cried out.

"It is okay. They are safe," he said.

I let out my breath. "I want to go get them."

I could see a struggle in his face.

"No, Panna Goldberg. Don't be crazy. Everyone knows you escaped from the jail. Bordetski named you specifically. He said you were leading them out."

"He didn't know that."

"They have been looking for days. They have been tearing through the village, rounding people up. They are not even digging graves anymore. If you go, you will not be able to help the children."

"I shouldn't be here, then."

He looked at me, meeting my eyes. He touched my hand over the cloth. "Stay. Wait," he said

"They are safe, though? They are still with your brother?"

"I will bring them," he said.

"They are still with your brother?"

He didn't answer.

"What?" I asked.

"The last thing I heard, they were still there," he said.

Panic flapped like a baby bird's wings in my chest.

"I will go now to see," he said.

I nodded and watched him make his way to the coat rack and put on his hat and his coat. He put his hand on the door.

"That was brave, what you did. Escaping."

I shook my head. My chin vibrated. I took a breath, steadying myself. "Find them. Please. Bring them back."

I must have slept hard, so hard I did not even dream. I woke up and heard Kostaski in the other room, puttering around. Slowly, I crawled out of the space where I had been hiding and sat at the table. I didn't have the patience to wait until Kostaski or his wife came to check on me. I picked up the pepper mill on the table and banged it so it made a noise. A few seconds later, he was at the door.

"Are they here?" I asked before he even made his way to the door. My throat became constricted. Hope flickered like a candle flame.

Kostaski's face was ashen, stripped of expression. "They sent them away. They gave them some food, and they sent them away. My brother said it was too dangerous. The police had come by. The Germans too. They suspected the children were there. I am not sure I believe him. I thought it was okay, trusting them with him."

I didn't move.

"It was just yesterday. They could still be okay," he said.

I started to stand. Dizziness overcame me. I put my hand on the back of the chair to steady myself.

Kostaski did not move, but the tone of his voice changed. He had tightened his jaw; the dimple in his chin was visible. He was angry.

"Listen to me, Panna Goldberg. You must not do anything rash. You cannot help the children if you yourself are dead."

"I don't care. Mania is only fifteen. She is frail. They know nothing, these children. They will not survive long."

Kostaski nodded, taking in what I said, agreeing. "It is daytime now. While you were in the woods, they tore apart the town looking for you. They have not stopped looking yet. I already went to find the children. I put the word out you were back to those we can trust. If anyone sees the children, they will send them here. Trust me, Panna Goldberg. You have to be patient yourself. You have to wait, at least until it is dark."

It was as if somebody had shut the lid to my heart.

"Where is Marek?" I finally asked.

"He is with my wife, playing. Do you want me to go get him?" Kostaski asked.

I was vaguely aware that Kostaski was speaking to me in the hushed way you try to quiet a nervous horse. I remembered standing up to the men in the barn, how far I'd come. I tried to get back to that calm place, the place where I could formulate plans.

"Thank you for looking for them."

Kostaski shook his head, as if the words *thank you* disturbed him.

"You did not have to do this. It is not your responsibility," I said.

"It was my brother," he said.

"I know."

I swallowed hard, paying attention to my large, stubby fingers smoothing the wood table.

"Were you able to find my mother, Chancie, or check with my brothers?" I asked.

"No, but I was able to pass messages for them through Kulchitsky. He knows where they are hiding," he said.

"Where?"

"I don't know exactly."

I nodded. There were no windows in the kitchen. I looked at the clock on the wall. Its pendulum swung back and forth. It was only one o'clock in the afternoon. I wondered what was happening with my brothers Mendel and Yossel and their families.

They returned when I was sleeping. I woke up savoring the fragments of a dream I couldn't remember, but it made me feel nostalgic. I knew they were there before I opened my eyes. I saw their legs first—short stick legs reaching just up to the top of Kostaski's wide thigh—and crawled out of the room to go meet them. A sound escaped from my mouth. Kostaski was amused.

The children were on me at once. I bent down slightly, and they clung to me. I allowed myself to quietly cry.

I sat them down. They didn't look good. They were filthy and tear-streaked; their tiny faces were thinner. Dunia kept his eyes averted and appeared to be brooding. My Mania had a bad look in her eyes.

"I will go heat some water on the stove for tea to help clean their faces and for the clothes," Kostaski said.

I nodded. I looked at the clock. It was nearly nine p.m.

"It's okay. They are smart children. They were not followed. Just make sure you don't make too much noise," he said.

We sat for a long time before Mania would look at me. "Were you hurt? Did anyone hurt you?" I asked.

"Nobody even saw us. I knew where to sleep," Dunia said.

I looked at Mania. She nodded. Her chin was trembling.

"I knew that if we could see them, then they could see us. I made sure we couldn't see them," Dunia said.

"Good," I said. This savviness was something my brother had taught him. "Come here, my Mania. Sit with me," I said.

She didn't move.

"They just tossed us out," Dunia said. "They wouldn't even look at us when they told us to go."

"They couldn't," Mania piped in, her voice like a badly tuned flute. She was staring at the edge of the table, one hand slowly twirling her hair. She was tired, so tired.

45

"Kostaski is right. You are both very smart," I said.

Marek ran his hands on his pants, as if he were trying to wash something bad off.

"I was always coming back for you," I said. "I love you so much. I came as quick as I could. I would never let anything happen to you."

Mania looked up at me. "They said you were dead. Kostaski's brother, his wife, they said you were probably dead." The sound that came out of her mouth was terrible. I pulled her to me and kissed her head.

"That's silly. You can see I am sitting right here," I said. I laughed a little. Dunia tried to laugh with me.

Mania looked up. Her blue eyes were wide and rheumy.

"They told us to go look for you," Dunia said. "There was a place where there were bodies on the Scovyatan side of town. We went there. It was the first place we went. They shot them with bullets; they had holes in them. They didn't bury them even. There were so many of them, maybe twenty or thirty people, all dead and puffy like fish. The crows were there, picking away."

"Be quiet, Dunia," Mania said, turning from me. My little warrior.

"I am just telling Momma what happened," Dunia said.

"It's okay, my babies. Sometimes it's good to talk about things that are hard."

"Their bodies were so ugly. They were all twisted up, and they had turned a weird color, and some of them were missing some skin, maybe from birds. They had a bad smell. We couldn't tell who was who," Dunia said.

"I said be quiet, Dunia," Mania said. She was crying. I took that as a good sign.

I went over to her and picked her out of the chair as if she were a young child. I held her against my lap, kissed her on the side of the head, rocked her. I let her sob quietly until she was spent.

"We thought you were there, Momma," she finally said. "We could barely move them, but we kept turning over the dead ladies to look at their faces. We thought one of them would be you."

Hysterical sobs, sharp intakes of breath racked her body. I rocked her, waiting until she had calmed down.

"Shhh…I wasn't there, though, *maidelah*. I was coming back for you all along."

I crawled out from the space we shared behind the stove, leaving the sound of the children sleeping behind me. I walked over to the kitchen table. Kostaski had left the items of clothing I had asked him for: a man's pair of slacks, a button-down vest, and a hat. I lit the candle he'd left me and examined them, holding them up against my body to gauge how they would fit. As I brought them into the dark corner and started to change, a rush of excitement flooded me, both because I was doing something that had always been forbidden to me—not just since the war—and because I believed it might work. I was also proud to have figured it out.

I buttoned the shirt and buckled the pants. They were much too large, so I folded the pants' seam over a few times and safety-pinned everything. Then I took the cord that held the flour sacks I had been tying around my waist and cinched it around the pants. It was snug enough, but I put the belt Kostaski had left me over it anyhow and tied the shirt in a loose knot before I put on the vest. Quietly I jumped up and down a few times, making sure everything would hold. I was giddy, and I tried not to laugh out loud. I was never a small woman. Even though we were not eating much, my big bones could hold those clothes up.

I did not want to, but I put the hand mirror I had asked Kostaski for on the table and peered into it to fix my hair in the hat. If they were still hunting me, I wanted to be unrecognizable. They were hunting a woman named Etcia, not a man. It was a practical costume for this reason, and because, even though men were more valuable for labor, it was easier in those times to pass through life as a man. The time I spent in the barn took its toll, with so many men around me and the pained way some often turned to look at me in the middle of the night. It made me angry enough to dress ugly.

I looked in the mirror. I was already unrecognizable to myself. Mirrors, even the sight of our own reflections in storefront window glass, were luxuries we were not entitled to anymore. Before Chaim died, before the war, I had been considered a pretty woman. But vanity had long since left me. I was lucky if I ran a brush through the children's hair, let alone my own, or if we had a chance to wash our faces, let alone our whole bodies. What use would a mirror have been?

Still, when I looked at the dark circles under my eyes and my concave cheeks, my heart sank. I thought of the way I looked to Joseph Kostaski. It was a silly reflex from my old life. I allowed myself the luxury. Then I listened for the sound of the children's breathing over the stove, buttoned my men's coat, and crept like a man out the door.

My younger brother, Yossel, was waiting for me in the summer house. I watched with amusement as he reared back and looked at me, the candlelight flickering on his silhouette. I could barely see him but could tell he was my brother with the animal sense of a sibling, the scent of his rough cheeks and curly, close-shaven beard. I immediately started laughing. He made his way over and hugged me. His big hand patted my back.

"I don't believe you made it," he said.

I didn't respond, simply nuzzled up to my brother and let him kiss my forehead before holding me out to see me again.

"Look at you," he said, his voice soft but as boisterous as if we were at a family celebration. Yossel and I had always been close.

I waited for him to tell me the names of the people we knew who had been killed and who had been sent to the camps. For the first time, he did not share any information.

"You must be a gypsy fortune-teller," he said.

I looked at him. He blew out the candle and sat down on the floor. I joined him. He took from his pocket a piece of brown bread and split it in half. I split my piece in half, put one in my pocket.

"L'chaim," Yossel said and tapped my bread with his.

I laughed.

We deliberately did not look up, did not notice all the canned goods— the carrots, beets, cucumbers, and eggs all around us.

"I'm not a gypsy; I'm a man. Is my disguise really that poor?" I asked.

"No. It's wonderful. It's wise. And it's good—I was getting ready to punch you," he said.

We laughed a while, then sat in silence, gnawing on the bread. Outside, a night bird, maybe an owl, hooted in the dark.

"I was only saying you are a gypsy fortune-teller because you must know our plan. We did not tell Kostaski. How did you know?"

"What plan is this?" I ate the bread quickly. It lodged in my throat.

"To turn you into a man."

I started laughing again. Yossel joined me. It was sweet to be alone with him out there. I was light-headed. Waves of dizziness passed through me.

"This is not working anymore. We cannot keep on the way we have been. They will catch us It's just a matter of time." I said.

"I know."

"We can't ask to be hidden anymore."

I swallowed. The bread made me hiccup. Yossel laughed.

"We found a place. Me and Mendel and Nisel Stermer. A safe place to live."

"What place?"

49

"It is underground. It is a cave as big as a palace."

"We are to live down there? In a cave?"

Of course, over time, I had heard of families living in all kinds of strange places—in the sewers, in bunkers, in crypts underground. I tried to imagine a cave we could climb into, dark and fetid and swarming with worms and blind bats.

"Nisel and his family lived in another cave just like it in Bilche-Zolote called *Vetebra Grotto*. They made it nearly six months. It was good down there for them. They had comfortable beds. They didn't have to move from place to place. Nobody knew they were there."

"Why are they not still there, then?"

"They were caught."

I started hiccupping again. I reached into my pocket and picked out two cigarettes and some matches, then lit them and handed one to Yossel. He looked at me strangely, at first, then shrugged and took a drag. I did the same.

"Still, they lasted a long time down there. It is safer than here. It is one spot, and we will stay there and live...until this war, until all this nonsense, is over."

I took a long, deep drag of my cigarette, quieting the hiccups. I stretched out my leg, which had been spasming ever since the nights in the barn. I clenched and unclenched the muscles. In the pants, I could see it was slightly more swollen than the other.

"Tell me about this place," I said.

"It's a grotto, a *schron*."

"Who will go there?"

"The Stermers, our family, you and the children, Momma, Mendel's family, sister Meimel with her four children, sister Fradel, and some others. There is plenty of space. It is seventy-five feet under the ground. You look up, you can barely see the top. So deep, nobody can ever hear us. It's all rock and earth, but it's like a real house down there," he said.

I tried to imagine this space so deep underground that nobody would find us. I imagined breathing full gulps of air, sleeping for real. I imagined a space big enough that the children and I could stretch out our arms and our legs, snuggle against each other, and have room to walk around.

"How did you find this place?" I asked.

"The fox showed us."

I raised my eyebrows.

"You know how Nisel and I served in the Polish army together, right? Well, you trust the people you serve with like no others. Nisel approached me and asked me if I knew somewhere like the cave they had left where we could hide. I thought for a while.

"I knew Munko Lubinetski. He was a forester, and I thought he might know somewhere. We went to him. He said he'd seen a sinkhole in the middle of the Popowa field. He guessed there might be some caves around there or some animal dens at least because he'd seen some foxes disappear into the ground there.

"We went to this valley, good sturdy earth. For days we walked. There were a few places to enter, but none was so good. Then one day, when we were just about ready to give up, we looked and saw a fox, a beautiful red fox. We saw him running, and we saw where he disappeared. We followed him.

"We found the sinkhole. We dug around and found the entrance to the cave. We didn't know what it was like in there, though. Two days later, we brought some shovels and picks and lanterns and string. The earth was slick and hard at the same time, and it took us a while to dig. When we finally did, we slipped into the cave and looked around. We couldn't believe what we found.

"We stayed there all day, looking around. It is named after the priest who lives there, Priest's Grotto. It is a *schron*, a natural house, as I said."

"How will we eat?" I asked.

"This, my dear Etcia, is why I said you are a gypsy fortune-teller," he said.

"Tell me."

"Each family will take care of their own. One member of each family will go out every few weeks, always at night, and bring back supplies: potatoes, flour, corn, beets, whatever you can find out there."

I never liked the idea of stealing.

"Each family has a man to do this. Now yours does too," he said and laughed. "Do you think you can do this? It is our only shot to stay alive."

I nodded. Not only was it the only plan I had heard, but there also was no question in my mind that I could do it. I would make good on my promise to myself to keep my children alive.

"Nobody else will take care of them for you. You have to provide for your own family if you are going to come down with us. I just want to make sure that you are clear about this."

"I am clear. I will be the one to go out."

"You are the *only* one from your family to go out. The children will stay safe inside," Yossel said.

I nodded. I still didn't know if it was going to work, but we were running out of choices. I had already burned our bridges at Kostaski's. The people who were left in the village, even the good ones, were too vulnerable. There was nowhere left to go.

"Etcia, you were always the smart one. Tell me, why are you hesitating?"

"Tell me the dangers."

"It is cold so far down. The children can catch cold. There is only one exit. If anyone notices us, we are trapped."

I tried to imagine this cave, a place so far underground that nobody could hear us. I remembered the *chernozem* from Chaim's funeral, how deep it seemed even though it was only six feet under the ground. I thought of how cool the rock was that I had pressed my ear on when I went to sleep.

"We will just have to be careful not to be noticed," I said. Outside, a mourning dove began to coo. "It won't cave in on its own?"

"No, Etcia."

"It's a good place to live?"

"It's perfect. The more we explored, the better it got. There is a place we can cut the logs at night and pass the wood down to burn. But the best part, Etcia, is there is a lake, a huge underground lake down there, maybe ten feet deep and thirty wide." His enthusiasm made it seem possible. "There was no water in the other cave. They had to catch what dripped from the ceiling. They were always parched," he said. "We will be together, but each one will be separate. One man from each family will come together to make decisions. You will be the man because of course you are already dressed the part." He laughed and used his fist to rub my head. "What do you think?" he asked.

I did not know what to think.

"We will not have to move, Etcia. We will not have to run anymore. We can just stay there and wait. When the war is over, we will be the lucky ones. The children will live again. It's the best shot we have."

"Okay. When do we leave?" I asked.

Yossel sighed beside me. For a while, we just sat there, imagining what would come next.

Chapter Four

May 5, 1943

THE CHILDREN AND I sat on chairs at Kostaski's kitchen table. A small lantern illuminated the children: Marek's head lay in the crook of his arm on the table. Dunia sat on his hands, forcing himself to stay nailed to the chair. Mania looked nervous, her face pale and shadowed like a little old lady's.

Only a few bundles remained on the floor. Those were the last items we'd take with us after Kostaski and Yossel hitched our things to the wagon. It was a moonless night.

I am a woman who likes to keep busy. My strength has always been in my swiftness, my ability to move through a problem. Even though the Ukrainian police had caught me, I escaped on my two legs. What worried me most about this place we were going to beneath the earth was that if they found us, we'd be trapped.

"How much longer, Momma?" Marek whined.

"Hssh," Mania hissed.

"Not much longer, baby. Close your eyes; rest a while. Momma will wake you when it is time."

The clip-clopping noise of the horse and wagon shook me. We'd been waiting so long. Dunia and I exchanged a glance. He was as worried as I was.

The door to the house opened. Kostaski stood in the kitchen.

"It's time," he said evenly. I picked up the bags, gestured for the children to do the same. "Pick up your bag, Marek. Remember how we planned, like a mouse," Kostaski said.

We walked towards the threshold. Kostaski patted Dunia clumsily on the back and tousled Marek's hair. "Be safe, children. Mind your mother." He walked over to me, squeezed my shoulder. "You will need to come out for supplies, Panna Goldberg. When you do, come find me," he said.

We were almost the same height. I looked into his deep blue eyes and opened my mouth to protest. He was a good man. He looked so solid, so strong. He was a man allowed to walk upright in his own house.

"No arguments. I expect to see you back here."

I started to walk, guiding Marek in front of me.

"Etcia," Kostaski said. I turned around. He took a step towards me, bent slightly down to my ear. "Stay alive," he whispered.

The seriousness of his gaze, the way that he nodded, left me no choice but to agree.

<hr />

We stood silent in moonless wheat fields, waiting our turn. There were thirty-seven men, women, and children. My mother, Chancie, was one of the eldest. She was seventy-four years old and allowed to go down with the first group. The rest of us waited. I stood there with my arms crossed over my Marek, Mania pressed against my shoulder.

It was dark, but we could make out the rough outline of the place we would be descending into. It was a gaping hole in the middle of the ground. We barely saw the lumps of people climbing beneath the field, down rungs of rock and logs into the underground palace. Every so often, we heard a child's smothered cry.

Yossel stood on the edge of the field with his wife, Pepcia, and their two-year-old son, Nunia. Pepcia was a short, pretty woman with short brown hair and a thin frame. She was so unlike the women in our family, the opposite of my mother. Her nature was quiet, delicate, and sensitive. My brother regarded her with the same gentleness he did the birds in the forest that he was so fond of. There was a privacy about her, a secret language that few people could read. My brother tried hard to understand it. He appreciated the fact that he could never emulate her mannerisms, that there were things about her nature he would never know. And like those birds, he would defend her with his life.

They were some of the first to go down. There was a line of women waiting for Pepcia and the baby—they had found a place for them to sit while they waited.

Pepcia held Nunia to her chest. He was unbelievably quiet. I'm sure he was heavy. Yossel had his hand in the small of her back. He scooped his son out of his wife's arms, and they started making their way to the opening. Just then I saw my little brother in a different way. He was a strong man with his own family.

I prayed that little Nunia would survive. He was one of the youngest children we were bringing down. I watched Pepcia turn around, then climb down. Yossel handed the baby down. They disappeared.

I turned towards the direction of the village. At my feet, raindrops glistened on blades of grass. I did not remember having heard rain.

"Almost. We are next, Momma," Dunia said.

I took a deep breath. The warm spring air smelled faintly of mint. We were completely exposed.

Yossel came over and guided us to the sinkhole.

"I will go first, then Dunia, then Mania, then Marek, and then Momma," he said. "When it's your turn, go just like I told you—hand over foot. It will be slippery and dark when you get down. Don't panic. We have made lanterns. It takes a few minutes for the eyes to adjust."

As we approached the opening that would carry us down to the belly of earth, I smelled it—the stench of some rot, mud, and old grass. Yossel and then Dunia descended. There was a straining sound. I approached the edge with Mania and kissed her on the head.

"Now, Mania," I heard from below.

"You can do it. Like in gym," I whispered as my girl descended over the side. She climbed down. Rung after rung after rung, I counted her steps.

There was a sound almost like a splash down below. They were safe inside. I picked up Marek, then positioned him so he was facing backwards over the hole. "Momma is coming after you," I whispered. He started to climb down; then I did the same. I was surprised that he didn't seem to be scared. It was like a game. I tried to follow his example, my thighs and arms bouncing each step down, holding the rocks, balancing on the wet logs. Finally, I was with everybody else, gathered at the entrance.

"It is very narrow. You must crawl through. Do not be afraid," one of the men from the group instructed.

We moved forward. The previous months had turned us into animals, reacting to threats out of instinct. Still, the darkness in the narrow entrance we crawled through assaulted me. It was like entering a tomb.

We walked carefully. The men held lanterns they had made from old bottles and kerosene. These were lit along the walls of the cave in a line. We finally gathered by the spot they'd picked. The large room was dimly illuminated by the rationed light.

The rock ceiling above us arced like a tunnel. The men had worked all day leveling the floor so we could sleep there.

I looked around, glimpsing the bodies of my children, my mother, my brothers, sisters-in-law, and my sisters. I let out my breath.

"Do you see, Etcia?" Yossel said. His voice was strong, no longer a whisper. It shocked me at first. Then I realized other men were talking loudly too. A child, a girl, howled and another giggled, as they used to do before it was illegal for us to exist.

"Nobody can hear us?" I ask.

"No, Etcia. We are too far below."

"Are you sure?"

"Yes, Etcia!" he shouted, his voice echoing through the cave. Marek screamed too and then laughed. The bottom of my spine clenched.

I looked up. The cave was illuminated only enough for me to see the surface of the rock walls, which sweated dampness like a human body. I could see neither ceiling nor sky.

Even after the walk, it was ice cold. I glimpsed around for rats, for blind, angry animals that scurried or flew. The air was fetid. It was hard to breathe.

To me, this freedom was false.

<hr />

We slept fitfully that night, huddling against each other on top of the blankets and the thin layer of straw each family received from the bundle. I didn't worry about Dunia as much. His constitution was strong like his father's, and he never complained. Marek had always been sickly, but as the youngest children, he seemed to regard the cave as a game. He was six years old. We'd been hunted for one-third of his life.

I worried most about Mania. She had always been a beautiful girl, and she had always been frail. I used to blame her sensitive nature on my mother, Chancie, who had fawned over her when she was a girl. But it wasn't my mother's fault, and there was nothing wrong with delicacy. The boys were already fighting over her at fifteen if the world had continued right side up, she would have had a charmed, beautiful life.

What worried me most was that Mania didn't have the same sense of self- preservation as her brothers did, and I might not have time to teach her how to be strong. The first time we hid under the chicken coop haunted me, the time when Mania had fought us to try to run out, even though if she did, we would die. That memory kept agitating me, like a bug bite.

My own brothers had been up for a while, talking in solid man voices, making plans. I was a man too and vowed to pull my own weight.

I bent down near Mania. She breathed steadily even though she'd sobbed herself to sleep. I kissed her on the head and slid her onto our makeshift bed, praying that she would sleep for a while longer.

I sat up slowly, then raised myself up from the floor. Moving too quickly was still dangerous. The darkness was pitch. We barely knew the floor from the walls.

I padded across the room to where I heard my brother's plotting.

"It's me, Etcia," I said. "How can I help?"

Chapter Five

TWO WEEKS AFTER descent into the cave, the men had to place their lives on the line to get the necessary supplies. They left the cave under the cover of the night to cut down trees. Their risk paid off. Yossel's body was silhouetted in the candlelight. He was crouched down, setting the wood to make Mania and Marek's bed. His broad chest and arms were still muscular. His black hair swept over his eyes. He was grunting and sweating despite the cold cave air. Yossel hadn't slept much since we'd arrived. The slow, determined way that he worked made me worry. Responsibility weighed heavily on him. If we were caught, he'd never forgive himself.

Mendel was on the ground, measuring how high up the beds would go, trying to figure out what kind of plank we needed to raise the platform high enough that we wouldn't catch a chill from the mud floor.

Marek, Dunia, and I sat on an already-constructed bed. Marek and I stretched out on the *varetta* we laid over the straw. The bed was a luxury compared to the crawl space at Kostaski's.

The candlelight flickered, casting shadows of my brothers on the cave floor. I put my hand over Marek's, anchoring him. His head rested against my arm. He still hadn't gotten over the dizziness. He didn't know back from front, up from down.

"Are you almost done?" Mania asked. She was standing somewhere just beyond the edge of the bed. Even disembodied, her voice was filled with teenage rebellion.

"Mania, be patient," I said sharply.

"There are no stars," Marek whined.

"No, baby," I responded. Marek was starting to act much younger. It made no sense to try to explain it anymore, how the top of the cave our heads faced when we lay on our backs was also the ground that the tree roots grasped and that people walked on up above us.

"It's not the sky," Dunia said, then snorted. Yossel laughed. He loved Dunia because he was a strong boy, as Yossel had always been.

I felt there was a dead, wet animal lying on my chest. I reminded myself the air filling my lungs was free.

"Are you almost done?" Mania asked again, her voice strained.

"Almost done? We have to make it right so it lasts," Yossel responded.

"Mania, come here and share our bed," I instructed.

"What do you mean 'lasts'? How long?" she hissed.

"Mania, sit down," I said.

Her breathing was very fast, almost like a dog pant. I released my hand from Marek's, gently pushed his head to the pillow, and rolled off the bed.

"I can't. No. I can't do this. We can't do this!" Mania shrieked.

Even that close, it took me awhile to figure out where she was, to find her shoulders and put my hand on one of them. She shook it off.

"Momma, we can't live down here. This isn't a house; it's a grave!" she screamed. I took her arm just as she slid to the floor. She cried, hysterically at first. Then slow sobs racked her body.

Someone made a *shhh* sound.

"It's terrible, like we're being buried alive!" she shrieked.

"Mania, it's okay. Hush," my sons or brothers whispered—I couldn't tell who was speaking or where the voices were coming from.

I sat down next to her. I didn't touch her, but she knew I was there. She'd pulled her knees into her chest. She rocked, comforting herself.

"It's okay. Everything is going to be okay." I reached over instinctually and pulled one of her hands from the ground. She let me take it. Her fingers were moist. I rubbed around the nails. There was blood there from where she had clawed at the mud.

I stood at the edge of Khatki, as we called our sleeping area, with Yossel, my hand on a clammy wall. The children and I were taking turns learning to read the contours of the cave like blind people. The bottom of my shoes had worn thin already. The cold floor seeped through them. They were flat women's shoes, which put me at a disadvantage.

"It might be smart to save my shoes for when I go outside, to go barefoot until we go for the food," I said. My voice sounded hollow to me, like the cobs of dried corn.

Yossel grunted. He was tired. "Maybe. You don't want to catch cold, though," he said.

"It would be a miracle if we don't catch cold here," I responded.

Yossel squeezed my shoulder, indicating we should walk. "Did you count the steps, Etcia?" he asked.

"Fifty-six."

"Good. This is the water. You can sit on the ledge. Come sit."

I lowered myself down clumsily until my rump banged a ledge. I laughed to cover my anger. The cave was like a foreign planet. It made our bodies clumsy, lumpy things.

"Are you settled? Behind you is the water. Don't touch it, whatever you do. Make sure to tell the children. The water is our salvation. The worst would be if we contaminated it with germs."

My eyelids fluttered. The air was thick, syrupy. I wondered if our lungs would ever adapt to this, if we would turn like the bats. Even the thought of them made me shudder. The previous night, I'd heard the undercurrent of their terrible screech.

"I'm not sure I can go too much farther today, Etcia. These are the most important things—the water, the latrine, the stove."

Yossel was being kind. My brother had a gift for allowing people their dignity. For a man, he was sensitive. It surprised me because the way my mother doted over him his whole life could have made him selfish. He was not selfish, though. He appreciated the gentleness in things— nature, animals, Pepcia.

"This is good. But tell me, Yossel, how far does this cave go?"

"We don't know. It is big, though, the size of Lvov maybe. It is a city. There are no signs, no traffic lights, no street names. We don't know how strong it is, if it is infested with rats, if there are sinkholes or areas where the walls or ceilings can collapse. So for now, we stay in Khatki and the areas we just saw. Khatki is our village. We stay there."

I pushed my palm into the flat, cool stone. Did I imagine the air was fresher here, clearer, the way it was at a lake?

"So they can get to us here, through other tunnels, in this city?" I ask.

"That's the beauty of it, Etcia. It is so big, we are invisible. Even if there were rumors we were down here, unless they find our entrance, we are safe."

I pushed my feet into the floor. The cold mud tickled my soles.

———————

Who knew a straw mattress could be so comfortable? The pillows and *varettas* seemed luxurious, even though they were musty and used. Those were the real first beds we had slept on in many months, beds that we were free to move and stretch on.

The children felt how special the beds were too. Marek slept, his body curled against his snoring brother's back. Mania lay on her side, turned away from me. I turned towards her quietly and touched her on the shoulder. "Are you feeling better, *zise maideleh*?"

"It's warmer tonight," she responded.

"Of course. We are off the floor. It will get easier. We will improve things down here. I know you don't believe it now, but it's a good place."

She sighed deeply. I remembered lying beside her on the giant bed Chaim had built us when she had been just a girl. She was a little princess then, with a fancy nightgown my mother had tailored for her.

"You know, this reminds me of when you were a little girl, maybe six or seven, and you used to come into my bed. Remember? You used to wear that nightgown Granny brought you. It was your favorite color. Blue. You were so stubborn. You refused to go to sleep until I told you a story."

Mania moved her arm so close to me, I could feel the downy hairs.

"We have to be stubborn now, Mania. We have to be brave."

I pulled the cover a little bit higher. *This is how I will hold them, then. This is how I will keep them safe*, I thought. We always have memory. We always have stories.

"We are trapped," Mania said.

I didn't argue. I never taught my children to lie.

"We are together. You, me, your brothers, your uncles and aunts, Granny. That's a true miracle. We are all stubborn. As long as we stay together, we will live."

She kicked her leg up in the air, then let it fall near me. Her rough dress brushed my skin.

"Yes, but Momma, how do we know we can live here? We aren't bears. We're people. People aren't supposed to live here. So how do we know we can?"

"We have no choice."

I touched her forehead with the back of my hand. It was clammy. I held her around the waist. Her slight frame chilled me. The women in our family all developed early, our full breasts and thighs a staple of our clan. Mania's body was still prepubescent, her chest lanky and flat, all hips and elbows and knees. I worried that she would never mature, that she would never fall in love or raise her own family.

Worse than that, her sensitivity, which would have made her a great mother, was a hazard to us all in the cave. She'd never been able to stand darkness. She understood more than her brothers how bad things really were.

"I need you, my Mania. You must stay with me. You will help me with the laundry, the cooking. "

"No. I don't want to. Why should I have to do work? I didn't ask to come down here. I don't deserve to live in the dark," she whined.

I took a deep breath. In that breath, I took in what was happening—my anger for Mania for being a spoiled teenager—and let it out, relief for her being a spoiled teenager. This was normal. This I knew how to deal with. And dealing with this would save her.

"Now, you listen hard to me, little girl. None of us asked for this. You are not special. You are lucky to be alive, with us, your family. You are older than your brothers, and you must set an example. You cannot act like a spoiled brat," I said.

She recoiled as if I had slapped her. She didn't run away, though. She also didn't breathe.

"Mania, I love you. I speak to you this way because you are like me. You are a young woman. You more than anyone understand that this life isn't fair. But it is temporary. God gave us the water and this cave to protect us. Maybe with God's help, we will survive."

"What God? What kind of God is it that takes my father, that murders all of these people?" she said, words wrung out of her belly like water from a washcloth.

Cautiously, I moved closer to her. I smoothed her hair, her beautiful brown hair, working the knots out with my fingers. I remembered that I had brought a comb down.

"It was disease that took your father," I said, lifting and fluffing her hair, drawing it down to the small of her back. "As for the rest, God didn't do this. It was man. I can't tell you why." I gently brushed the section of hair that was smooth, letting my fingertips trail on her neck.

The women in my family had always been pretty, and our money allowed us to be vain. In the cave, there wasn't even a butter knife in which to glimpse our reflections. Mania had always been defined by her prettiness. Without it, she might be unsure who she was. "You get your beauty from your great-grandmother," I said.

She sighed and leaned her head back a little more, letting me brush her hair.

"What was she like, my great-grandma?" Mania asked.

The future was better left unspoken. It was a good idea, I thought, to talk about the people who had lived and died long before, to tell stories from the past when the land was still ours. If they were reminded of all the ways we were bound to Galicia, maybe they would fight for it if they had to.

"She was pretty. Like you. She had your eyes," I said.

"Really?"

"Do you remember Grandma's estate? The vegetable gardens and barns and the forest? The foyer that was so large a horse could turn all the way around in it? That was your great-grandparents' land first and their grandparents' land before them....When your granny wakes up, we could ask her about her momma. Would you like that?" I asked.

"I don't know."

I continued to comb her hair with my fingers. Her body shuddered. As I spoke, I drew the blanket up to her neck. Her heartbeat seemed to slow down.

———◆◆◆◆◆———

Mania and I sat on the edge of my momma's bed, waiting for her to start speaking. Her breath wheezed. She covered my hand with her own, and I was surprised, both by the strength of her grip and by the fact that she knew where my hand was. I nodded. I was glad I had brought Mania to see her.

We'd all been worried about Momma. It was partly her age, but it was more than that. When the war had first started, I was surprised at how well Momma, who had always eaten meals others prepared for her and slept on sheets others washed, had taken control. She knew things, drawing on her secret network of social connections to keep us alive, trading her jewelry for our safety. It was as if she were a different person. The war made her feel useful, respected, as if she still had high status in the village. After our father was killed, she shut down again, fixating on flimsy things, like the loss of material items. She lost her footing. Everything Momma believed in was gone.

"Mania wanted to know about your mother. I told her that is where she got her beauty," I said.

My mother coughed, then pounded her fist on her chest. "Well, of course she does. My momma was beautiful like Mania," she said.

"Can you tell us about her?" Mania asked.

"We have some spare time," I said.

Momma laughed. She coughed again and pounded her fist on her chest. "It is good she remembers where she came from," I coaxed my mother. My mother grunted. She understood.

"My maiden name, before I was a Dodyk, was Krikenfield. I was the fifth child in the family. We were nine. My mom, your great-grandma, was Sara. My poppa was Rudolf, but people called him Rudik.

"When my parents were young, it was a good, peaceful time. Where we lived, it was called Austro-Hungarian Imperia. We had money. We had culture. In some other European countries, there were revolutions. People wanted to change the monarchies into republics—but things were quiet for us.

"My mom lived in Korolówka in Galicia—our own village, Mania. At that time, Korolówka was small. Six hundred families lived there; maybe eighty of them were Jewish. There were no problems. It didn't matter if you were Jewish or Polish or Ukrainian. They did business together.

"My mother grew up more religious than we did. Marriages were mostly arranged by the parents, always within the community."

"Those eighty Jewish people all married each other?" Mania asked.

My mother wheezed in the bed. Her arm banged something, and then I heard her drinking a long sip of water.

"If you are tired, Momma, we can come back," I said.

"Nonsense. Mania, there were more people to choose from than you may think. Those families were big. Most had between seven and ten children. Everyone was close. People knew each other from the time they were toddlers until they grew old."

"Sara, what was she like?" Mania asked.

"Shhh," I scolded her gently.

"Well, she was a beauty. She was tall with black hair and those strange dark blue eyes like you have, Mania. Everyone was impressed by her beauty. She was a magnet for the Jewish boys. They all dreamed about marrying her."

My mother coughed a few times. The sound was phlegmy. We waited.

"How did she find her husband?" Mania asked.

"You can tell the rest of the story later, Momma, if you are tired," I said.

"The Kershners were a successful family. When Sara was sixteen years old, the boys started to get anxious. This was around the age they married back then."

It was tough for me to imagine Mania in a year or so fending off suitors for marriage.

"The Kershners were a successful family. Their eldest son, Shlomo, was attracted to Sara. He was twenty-six years old, nine years older than Sara."

"Really?" Mania asked.

"That was usual back then," I said.

"Shlomo was an attractive man. He had a good build. But his eyes were always dark. He always had a pinched, serious expression.

69

"Rudik was Shlomo's brother. He was twenty-three years old at the time. He was a handsome young man with dark, curly hair. He had soft brown eyes and a gentle smile. He was a few inches taller than Shlomo.

"Often when they were in the synagogue or at a festival, Rudik and Sara would talk. She was more attracted to Rudik than to Shlomo. She was falling in love with him."

My mother's voice trailed off. She was tired. She probably hadn't spoken so much since we'd come down.

Mania yawned.

"Why don't we let Grandma rest, and she can finish the rest of the story another time?" I said.

"*Yes, zise maideleh.* I will tell you later," my momma said.

I woke up in the aftermath of a terrible dream. I lay there willing my breath to slow down. I didn't know if the children were nearby. I tried to pull the details from the throat of the nightmare. One good thing my mother had taught me was that if you could name what you feared, then you could see its real shape and you wouldn't be scared. There was something foul, rotted near me, a scent something like thin sour milk. I imagined the milk came from an animal that had blue veins. I tasted something like hair and flesh in my mouth.

Then, for the first time since we'd entered the cave, I heard the bats.

It was a sound you wouldn't notice if you weren't paying attention. It was a high-pitched, half-plucked sound that bounced off the walls above us. My brother had told me that was how they communicated. He had also told me that we had to be careful. The bats were blind creatures, and they spread disease. We were in their home now, their darkness. The world was inside out. We were the invaders, not them.

"Momma, are you awake?" Marek said. He touched my arm. I didn't move right away. Instinctively my tongue ran over my teeth. They were solid, smooth, jagged at the tips. I remembered then what I had dreamed. I dreamed that I had lost all my teeth.

Chapter Six

MOST OF US had gotten our bearings and were making a real effort to make the place into a home. When I lay down for too long, I felt like an animal was on top of my chest. I kept busy replenishing our water stores from the lake and piling sticks by the fire in a nearby chamber. Somehow, by the grace of God, the smoke we used for cooking did not concentrate in on place above the cave. It is impossible to explain, but smoke was not visible above ground. The smoke could have been spreading into various crevices of the cave, instead of leaving the cave in one specific place. We will never know how it was possible.

The cold was ever present. Darkness made us imagine strange things. I swore I heard the beating of the bats' wings. I imagined them, their hairy little bodies squirming, roosting in our beds or our hair.

I also saw the good in the place. It was nice to walk upright without fear, to laugh out loud with my family and to manage our own paltry food.

My sister Fradel and I stood in the kitchen, cutting potatoes on the large stone we had turned into a table. We lit the wick in the neck of one of our lanterns. Food was more precious than light. We couldn't afford to lose one crumb.

"Are you getting used to it here, Etcia?" Fradel asked.

"Yes, it's a great palace," I said.

Fradel didn't laugh. Her rounded face was illuminated enough to show her frown lines etched deep into the corners of her mouth. It was nice to see her after so long in the dark. It was hard to read her, though.

Fradel had always been loyal. When my parents refused to sign a security letter to the bank to get Chaim and me a loan for the house, Fradel often visited me. She told me our parents were stubborn for holding a grudge for so long.

I'd lost track of my sister for several months before we came down. She'd always had an anxious personality, but the war had made it worse. Her nervousness infected people around her, made them uncomfortable to be near her for too long. I didn't know exactly what she'd been through.

"I'll start the fire," I said.

I walked to the far end of our stone table and pulled kindling from the basket. This I put underneath the *triniszka*, the Polish tripod oven like our mother's mother had used. I felt in my pocket to make sure the matches were still there.

I picked the copper-bottomed pot and ladle from the floor. I walked to the small pool of water at the edge of our kitchen. This pool was part of a chain of pools that led to our main water source, where we got water for laundry and drinking. It was crystal clear. The water sloshed loudly in the metal when I scooped it.

I filled the pot, then took it back to the stove and lit the wood. The strong scent of the fire brought me comfort. I tossed a cup of barley in, and Fradel tossed in the potatoes.

"Thank you for helping me cook, Etcia."

"If you could call this cooking."

Fradel laughed in an uneasy way.

"But we will make a good porridge" I said.

"Yes. And it's good to have company," she said.

I nodded, trying not to look at the food inside the pot. It would be hours before it was my turn in the kitchen.

"Maybe we should blow out the lantern," I said.

"Where are you, Etcia Goldberg? Fradel Dodyk?" our brother Yossel said in a sing-song voice.

"We're in the palace, and Fradel's the queen," I said.

He walked to the side of the stone. Fradel had not yet blown out the lantern. It was a relief to see my brother's rugged face.

"How is Mania?" he asked.

I didn't respond.

"The supplies won't last," he said.

Fradel groaned.

"I know," I said. While the children slept, I ran over and over our food stores in my mind. Even with the harshest rationing, it will barely last another week and a half.

"We will go first for the firewood," he said.

It made sense. There was no sense getting food if there was no way to cook it.

I blew out the lantern.

"A chance to check for danger," Yossel said. His voice was gruff, but underneath I could hear the childlike timbre of my little brother.

"When?" Fradel asked.

"Tomorrow night. Before the moon gets too full. To the closest part of the forest so we can bring it back quickest. We have axes, rope, pulleys."

"You are still strong," I reminded him.

He sighed. He understood. The longer we were in the cave, the worse our health got. When we worked, the sweat chilled our bones. It was different from what we'd been taught. We'd always learned that we work to survive.

"How are you going to get it down through that hole?" I asked, remembering the narrow passageway.

"You are still a gypsy fortune-teller, Etcia," he said.

I remembered the fortune-teller I'd gone to see to help to prevent Chaim's death before I knew any better. Yossel had helped me move the stove to the other side of the room as she had instructed. Still, Chaim had died. Looking back, in some ways, his death was a blessing. He didn't live to see the world turn upside down.

There was no room for foolishness anymore. I prided myself on being a practical woman. This is the way I kept my children alive.

The steam from the water warmed my face. Soon it would boil.

"Mendel thought of this. I agree. Dunia is a sturdy boy, yet he is still small. His hands are strong enough."

I cringed. "He is only twelve, still a child. I can't allow him to go outside."

Yossel waited. Silence pulsed, like the lungs of an animal. "We don't need him outside," he said eventually.

"Then what?"

"He and Yohna would stand at the entrance inside. We'll pass the wood to them. They'll move it into the cave. Later we'll all move the wood into Khatki."

I was risking my life to save the children. It wasn't supposed to be them risking their lives to save me. The passage into the inside was so long—at least five yards. If the men were caught, Dunia wouldn't stand a chance.

"He isn't a man yet," I said.

"That's true. The boys are the only ones small enough to fit there."

"I don't know, Yossel."

"It would be dangerous. He'd have to move quickly. If we are followed, the boys would be exposed. He'd be cold. He'd be standing in mud."

I imagined my baby's legs frozen raw.

"But Etcia, we'll treat him like a man. He will gain courage with us. These are not usual times," he said.

An odd warmth flooded the back of my head. Thankfulness towards my brother welled inside. It was true. The boy needed a father. My brothers were the next best thing.

I found Yossel's hand and patted it. "I will tell him," I said.

Dunia and I met my brothers in front of the kitchen where the other men had gathered. I'd insisted on walking him down even though it humiliated him. My brothers lingered outside with me and Dunia.

Mendel held a lantern. It jiggled, bouncing light off the wall behind us. It brought me comfort to see the faces of my brothers and son.

We'd been standing awhile. Time was so slow. I didn't know what we were waiting for—more men to come? A sign that it was safe to go up? The men might have just been steeling their nerves.

"I'm fine, Momma. You can go," Dunia said.

Yossel and Mendel both laughed. Dunia's shoulders rose.

"Your momma must stay for a minute. We want her to hear this. She's one of the men too," Yossel said and then poked me in the arm. I whacked him back.

"First, Dunia, I have a gift for you. Here," Yossel said. He reached behind him. Metal clanked against a rock. "It is a hand shovel. It will be important for you to keep your area of the cave clear."

Dunia's expression was prideful, the same way it had looked earlier that evening when his brother and sister and I had given him an extra ration, a half of our hunk of bread, and insisted he eat it.

"You must take good care of it. We have only a few tools. The men keep them clean. You give them to Mendel after we are done, and he'll give them back when we return. Understood?" Yossel asked.

"Yes," Dunia said.

It occurred to me that the work would be good for Dunia because it would keep him grounded in reality. He was twelve years old and already restless, spending too much time with his cousin Yohna by the lake. I wasn't so afraid of their causing mischief as I was of their passing on rumors. I didn't want him to worry about imaginary things.

"It's a very important job you are doing," Yossel said. "We need the wood for the fire, for cooking and warmth. Without wood, we cannot cook the potatoes and grain your mother will bring. Without wood, we won't survive."

"Do you understand?" Mendel snapped.

My elder brother had a temper that frightened most people. I was the only one who could keep him in line.

"Yes, sir," Dunia said.

"Good man. We'll show you what to do," Yossel said.

"If they catch us, the Nazis, the Ukrainians, we will die," Mendel continued.

It was good that he heard it.

"We have a plan. Don't worry, Dunia," Yossel said. "It's hard work. You'll get used to it. Working together, all of us, we are strong," Yossel continued and clapped me on the shoulder.

Behind us, the men were starting to move. It was almost time for them to go up.

"Be careful, Dunia," I said. I wanted to hug him.

"Momma, I'll be fine. Trust me. Go and take care of the others," he said.

Yossel had the lantern close to his face. He was smirking. I whacked him on the shoulder, then turned, put my hand on the wall, and started counting my steps back to our room.

I woke up when Dunia came back. I heard the distinct shuffle of his feet dragging across the floor, the way he banged into the bed with his shins.

Thank you, God, I thought. My son was back safe. If he was back, so were my brothers.

"It's okay, Momma. Nobody else was out there but us. We weren't followed."

He was learning.

"Well, don't get the bed wet. There are dry pants on the end. Change into them first."

He did as he was told, silently. He lingered, hovering above us as if he weren't sure what to do.

"Why don't you sleep next to me tonight?" I said. Mania had rolled to the other end of her bed and there was room.

Dunia sat down without saying a word and climbed in. I hugged him to me. He let me. His body was shivering, just slightly, but it was enough to worry me.

"What did you do with your shovel?" I asked.

"Uncle Mendel," he said.

I closed my eyes. My brothers were taking care of my son.

"Is everything dry? Did you change everything? Even your socks?" I asked.

"My shoes are no good anymore. Yossel says everyone has to go barefoot now."

It was true. Our shoes were torn into bits by the rock and clay. Like the other heads of household, I'd already stopped wearing mine. I kept them on a makeshift shelf behind me and would use them when I went out. The shoes were important. I sometimes touched them to make sure they were still there.

I didn't speak for a while but pulled the blanket so that it cocooned Dunia. I held him as close as I could without his resisting. It was morning, I thought. He'd probably been working for hours.

"Enough wood for several weeks," he said.

It took me a minute to understand what he was talking about. Then I remembered my brother's words: "They catch us, we will die." To conserve mental energy, they had begun speaking in clipped sentences. Thought had to be rationed, like the bread. Or maybe we were just forgetting how.

"Were you scared?" I asked Dunia.

He didn't respond but snuggled up slightly closer to me, just enough for me to notice. I pulled him close, wrapped the blanket as far under him as I could.

"It's a good job. It's important," he said.

I fell asleep feeling his heart beat in my arm.

Chapter Seven

June

ALL NEWS, BAD or good, crackled in the cave like burning wood. You sensed it but were reluctant to get out from under the covers and walk barefoot over cold mud to receive it. When you got to the source of the news, you did not know whether it would warm you or burn you, or whether it would be a fire so weak it disappointed.

That night a woman cried; she had received bad news. I listened until her sobs quieted and the night was broken only by an occasional gasp of the ones she'd choked down. I fell asleep thinking about how lucky I was to be surrounded by my whole family, with the exception of my father and Chaim.

When I woke, I knew the woman was gone, that she'd moved through the cave to the water. She wasn't my family member. I picked up the bucket as an excuse and slowly followed my steps down to the lake, tracing the grubby walls with my palm. I still walked slowly, imagining scurrying rats, the glint of fox eyes in the dark.

When I arrived, two women were speaking quietly. They heard me approach and went quiet.

"It's Etcia," I said hoarsely. It was as if I'd gone tone deaf to the sound of my voice.

"We're here," my older sister, Meimel, said.

"And me, Fridzia," Fridzia Kittner said.

Fridzia was a young woman, about twenty years old, Shimon's pretty sister. We didn't know each other well, but she always seemed sweet to me.

"Just down here, sitting on the ledge. Follow this," she said. She rapped her fist on the stone—*rap rap, tap tap, tap tap*.

I heard their breath, the sulky labored breathing of women. Our constitution was different, even in the cave. I moved slowly. Dizziness capped my head. I eased myself onto the rocks next to Meimel. My sister cupped my icy hand with her own.

We sat for a few minutes in silence. Conversation was also rationed.

The water was comforting. The lake was the lungs of our house, close enough to remind us that we still had access to a precious life source, yet far enough away that it wasn't contaminated by smoke or disease. The women and children were responsible for hauling. We had to be cautious not to spill even a drop, to make sure we were clean when we handled it. For that reason, the water was sacred. We tended to gravitate towards it when we needed reassurance.

"Who?" I asked cautiously. I rubbed my fist on my chest, loosening the suffocating feeling.

"They found my aunt, her husband, Sarah and Benny Reisner, and their fifteen-year-old son, Ezya, in a basement," Fridzia said. "Ezya ran. He was shot in the back. Benny and Sarah watched. They took them away."

I grunted. I knew the family, but I didn't know them well. Benny was a good tailor who had done business with Chaim. They were close. They had traveled on the train together to Lvov to see Ze'ev Jabotinsky speak. The men's voices boomed when they spoke about politics in the shop. After they finished debating, their laughter was slow and easy.

I imagined the scene Fridzia described, remembering Sarah, her tall, skinny frame, the stoop with which she walked to disguise her height. It was probably daytime when they took them. Her son had run out on the road.

At least it was quick, I thought. My callousness surprised me.

We rarely spoke of the dead anymore. This was for the same reason we didn't keep Yahrzeit candles burning. Sentimentality was a luxury we couldn't afford.

"Where?" I asked.

Meimel laid her head on my shoulder. Sweet, gentle Meimel. She was my older sister, but she always seemed younger to me. She'd always turned to me for guidance.

"In Korolówka. They didn't go to the ghetto," Meimel said.

I let my head cover my sister's. Meimel had watched her husband, Yakov, get murdered in the ghetto just a few weeks before we went down to the grotto. Her heart had gone soft like a boiled egg.

"I'm sorry," I murmured.

Meimel's breathing was labored. She was a little smaller than I was but not in as good shape.

Silence coated my throat. I was ashamed to admit, even to myself, that I was relieved I didn't know too many people outside the cave anymore. Then I remembered the pharmacist, Mr. Shwartz, and his wife, my old friend, Fucia. I remembered her face, soft brown eyes, and wide forehead framed by short, curly hair.

"How did you find out?" I asked.

"When Shimon went out to get food. They found out from Munko," Fridzia said.

"Last night?" I asked.

"They are sleeping now," she said.

I listened to the remnants of the woman's sob, cradling my sister's head.

Jealousy for the men who went out curdled. The previous night, I'd snuggled Mania, and her hip bone poked my hand. Our food would last us only another few days.

———————◆◆◆◆◆◆———————

Later, I went to see Yossel in his family's section of the cave. I wove around the barriers of the other families' rooms, working the numbness out of my feet. In the rooms where our bodies pressed together, our breath added some humidity. It was slightly warmer.

"Who is it?" Yossel asked.

"It's me, Etcia," I said, moving towards the sound of his voice.

He hummed a low, sweet dirge, and I followed it, finding him sitting up on a bed. Then there was a sharp, long grating noise.

I stood. The swirling dots in the darkness changed from red to green, and then I could make out the shape of the bed and of my brother's arm moving back and forth. He was sharpening a blade on a rock.

I crouched down and sat near my brother, the planks creaking under my weight. I pressed my palm into the *varetta* blanket and waited. My brother was close enough that I smelled him, the scent of wood smoke and unwashed clothes.

"I saw Meimel," I said.

"Mmmmm," he said.

"She is sad." The rhythm of the metal continued. "Some men went out last night," I said.

He didn't respond. I gripped the blanket in my hand. It wasn't right that they hadn't informed me.

"We must go too, Yossel," I said.

"Soon," he said.

It annoyed me to have to wait for my brothers to go out. I felt it'd be easier to slip through unnoticed, and Mendel always had heavy steps.

84

I'd agreed to go with them because it was the first time, and that's the way the other families in the cave did it.

"Not soon. Tonight. If you don't want to, I'll go alone," I said.

The stone sharpening stopped.

"Etcia, don't be unreasonable."

"Reason is why I choose this. We have little left. My children need food," I said. I meant to whisper, but my voice grinded, surprising us both with its intensity.

It did not matter that Yossel had been a soldier. I was indebted to him for finding the cave. Still, he was my younger brother. He needed to listen.

Yossel exhaled loudly. The wooden planks creaked as he shifted. "There is a rock blocking the entrance. When we are ready, they will move it for us," he started. "The men are still at the entrance with the axes. We will continue to keep them there. You remember we came down feet first, like backwards babies. We figure this is good for us. If the soldiers come, we can chop their feet before they can get down with their rifles."

The picture of the foot chopping made me laugh.

"This is dangerous, Etcia. It's nothing to laugh at."

"You think I don't know this, Yossi?" I said. I poked his arm.

"There is a password—7835. It keeps changing. You have to tell the men this when you get back so they don't chop your legs." He poked me back. "After the stars come out, we will go."

<hr />

We were sitting on the floor near our beds, eating the last of the soup. It had been a quiet meal. The candle was lit. The children lifted their spoons to their mouths slowly, as if the effort hurt their wrists.

"I am going outside the cave tonight. I will bring us food," I said.

Marek's shoulders hunched. Mania blew on the soup in her spoon to cool it off.

"We can't go outside, Momma. There are bad people out there. The air is poison," Marek said.

"No, Marek, the air is not poison," Dunia said. "You're not going, only Momma."

Marek's spoon banged, then bounced onto the floor.

"I'll get it," Dunia said. His body dipped down effortlessly, and his hand swept the floor. Utensils usually disappeared into the mud, but he was quick. We were shocked when he rose up with the spoon in his hand.

"You will be shot," Marek said. He was crying.

I went over to him and put my face close to his, breathing his sour scent. I kissed him on the forehead before returning to my own soup.

"We knew she'd have to go out. Remember, she told us," Mania said. Her dainty voice trembled.

"There is nothing to worry about. I am your momma. I will be careful. I will always come back."

Nobody responded. The last time I had left them before we went down to the cave, I wound up in jail. I imagined Mania and Dunia standing on the edge of the river, flipping the women's bodies, praying none of the bloated faces was mine.

"It doesn't matter how careful you are," Dunia said.

"We don't even know what it's like up there anymore," Mania continued.

"Children, finish your soup."

The way they scraped the sides of the bowls with their spoons gave me chills. The soup was already gone.

"Now, stop this foolishness. There is no choice. I'll be careful. I promise. You will go to sleep and have good dreams. By the time you wake up, I'll be back in the bed snoring next to you," I joked. The children always teased me about snoring.

I watched Mania move closer to Marek, rub against him with her shoulder.

"Momma loves us. She will not leave us alone," she said.

She brushed Marek's bangs with her fingers. Her hand shook.

<hr />

My brothers, Yossel and Mendel, and I sat on Yossel's bed in his room. Pepcia, Nunia, my children, and our sister Fradel left for the common room to leave us alone to plan.

"You remember the wheat fields we must travel though to get to Yasinovaty Woods?" Yossel started. "The moon will be full, bright. We must hurry. The wheat field is only four hundred yards away."

"Are we nitwits?" Mendel asked. Mendel's temper got worse when he was scared.

"Don't be smart," our mother wheezed from the bed.

We all laughed.

"It's bad out there," Yossel said. "The other men didn't see one Jew. Nazis, police posted everywhere, even night. Not too much has grown. They planted fields with potatoes for the troops. Don't waste time. Go to the houses; find people you trust. Get everything: kerosene, matches, candles, grain."

"We need grain," Mendel said.

"And you, Etcia. Will you go to Kostaski's?" Yossel asked.

I hesitated. Showing up would put Joseph in danger again. As the war intensified, his services as a shoemaker had become even more valuable. Jews showed up at his house for his kindness for the same reason they showed up at a doctor's for medicine. I considered that he had a similar belief as we Jews did—that performing *mitzveh*, or good deeds, while we were here on earth was our responsibility to God. Also, I'd promised Kostaski before I left that if we survived, I'd visit.

"Yes," I answered.

"Once we climb out of the cave, we will walk together," Mendel said. "After we pass the fields, we will split up. Etcia, you tap us each on the shoulder. Then you go first. Go to the big birch. It has a white trunk and it glows, even with just a little moonlight. The trail is straight, four kilometers south to Kostaski's. You will be well covered in the trees.

"Walk the path the wagons rode in. You remember? Mendel and I will travel past you to the far right corner and wind our way in slower. After that, we are on our own.

"Remember, come back when you see the Big Dipper's clock hand pointing back towards the cave," Mendel said. "The password is 'black mountain.'" His breathing was labored. It was a lot of words.

I thought back to the nights that I had spent in the woods after escaping jail, how bright everything was with the moon on the snow. There were dark, shadowy roots by the tree trunks. I'd clung to them and watched for animals in the light.

"It will be bright out there, brothers. Make sure you stay close to the tree trunks, where it's darkest. They can't spot us there," I pointed out.

Mendel snorted.

"Etcia is right," Yossel said. "That is why it's important that we clear the field quickly. That is where we are most exposed."

In the bed, Momma made a half-strangled sound. Yossel touched me on the shoulder. In the next room, the voices of my children, my sister, and my brother's wives gurgled. It was like music. I could sense it, but I couldn't quite make out the sounds.

Sliding up and out of the cave through the mud that stuck to our clothes was like being born. I stood up, taking my first sweet gasp of air. The fields were still green, the young wheat just starting to poke out of the ground. There was almost no wind. The cool night tickled our cheeks, reminding us of childhood—summer nights in a world half-forgotten. As my brother predicted, the moon made the whole field glow. The dizziness was inside out. As opposed to that black nothingness we had dropped into, the space where we stood now was almost too solid. There was too much to take in.

A sour taste rose in my throat, and I swallowed hard, then looked towards our right at the stand of trees we would run to. I tapped my brothers' shoulders, as we'd agreed. They tapped me back, and we took off, Yossel to my right and Mendel on my left.

It wasn't a long field. Our steps were quick, tense, but it felt as if we were moving so slowly, we would never get there. It was like in a nightmare—any step we took seemed to have no effect.

I was slightly hunched, the mud on my shirt and body encasing me, my heart pumping so hard that it physically hurt. My brothers' breath was labored. I felt the imaginary soldiers at our backs pointing guns, in the woods waiting for us with snarling dogs. We walked, side by side, our shoulders pressed close to each other's. I remembered walking with my brothers the same way when we were children to pick up something like a letter from the post office or bread from the store.

My father was a strict disciplinarian, and we were never idle. In our family, he always threatened to have Momma sew up our pockets so that we would remember that our hands were always to be busy working. Our pace had that intensity then, the threat touching the same nerves as our fear that our father would give us a beating. We walked and walked, crushing new wheat until we reached the dark, patchy woods and could finally leave the moonlight behind.

We stopped. I tapped my brothers on the shoulders as we agreed. Then I ran to the glowing white birch.

I leaned my back against the tree, catching my breath. The trunk was not really protection, but I felt safer with my back covered. I allowed myself the luxury of staring upward. The stars were brighter and closer than I ever remembered seeing them before. Outside was like a dream, like the world inside the cave was the real world and the one outside was fake.

My brothers' footsteps stopped. I turned towards the wheat fields. The thick, empty moonlight illuminated even the slight bend of stalks that we'd crushed when we ran. I scanned the field. I didn't see any soldiers.

The woods were blessedly dark. The animals made a racket. Yossel was the only one who could speak their language. He would know if they were that noisy all the time or if it was a special occasion because the moon was out. After all that time we had been sealed underground, the racket was overwhelming.

If the animals are out, it's probably safe, Yossel had said before we left the cave.

I looked towards the curving path through the woods that would take me into the village. My thigh was still swollen. It throbbed. We had to pass through only a few yards to get to Kostaski's.

"Please, dear God, get me there safe. Help me get back to my babies," I whispered.

A few creatures called wildly into the air, smothering the sound of my prayer. I took it as a good sign, a protection, then breathed deeply and bolted down the path through the woods.

<hr />

I stood at the door to Joseph's house, locking my knees to keep them from shaking, and tapped our secret four-beat knock on the door. I put my hand on my chest and attempted to catch my breath, praying silently that somebody would answer. With my hair in the cap, the skin on the back of my neck was exposed. I closed my eyes and counted backwards from ten. Ten, nine, eight...

On seven, I heard a creak from the house, and somebody moved behind the door.

"Come in," Joseph's rough, sleepy voice murmured. He touched me on the shoulder to guide me into the dark house and closed the door. I followed him. We reached the well-lit windowless part of the kitchen. Joseph's wife, Marta, stood there, nodding her pale face, indicating I should sit at the table. Marta was partially deaf. For ease of communication, she and Joseph frequently used sign language instead of words. Marta smiled sadly at me. I sat down at the table. She busied herself putting sticks in the stove, then lighting the fire to boil water for tea.

Joseph and Marta pantomimed a silent conversation with their hands. It looked even stranger than it had before I went to the cave. In the bright light, they had hands with no voices. In the cave, we had voices but no hands.

"Thank you," I said to Marta. She shook her head as if to say there was no need for thanks. Her expression was pinched and her body thin. Harboring Jews had taken its toll.

Joseph sat down at the table. He bent his barrel chest into the table and studied me with his pale blue eyes.

"Panna Goldberg, it's good to see you." There was tender awe in his voice. He stared at me, almost as if he were embarrassed.

"I'm still here," I joked.

Joseph rubbed his fingertips back and forth, back and forth, like sandpaper.

"How are the children?" I asked.

Marta made a racket in the kitchen getting the mugs from the cupboard.

"They are well. Lunducia is getting mouthy," he said. He looked at Marta and laughed. Her head was bent, pouring tea into mugs. She sensed him looking at her, looked up, and smiled faintly. "And your children, Etcia?" he asked.

"Adjusting."

We sat for a while, listening to the firewood crackling.

"What's your life like down there? "

"In some ways, it's better. We have built beds out of wood, a cooking area. There is fresh water, firewood. Dunia has turned into a little man.

He helps pass the wood from above. He's a hard worker. The cave is a gift from God. It's home now."

Joseph cleared his throat. He wasn't fooled by my cheery description.

"The danger down there is less," I said.

Joseph, better than most, understood threats above ground.

Marta walked to the table and set two steaming mugs down on the table. She touched Joseph's shoulder, smiled at me again, then left the room.

"She's sleepy. Little Victor is teething," Joseph said.

He took a sip of the tea. I took a sip too. The hot liquid slid down my throat.

"I've been collecting supplies for you since you left. They should last you."

"Thank you."

Joseph made the same *don't say that* motion with his head that his wife did. The war had exhausted him too but probably for different reasons. In my opinion, Joseph was wounded by what was happening to us all because it went against his nature. He couldn't understand how men could behave as his brother did.

His mouth twisted, as if he were trying to get rid of a bad taste. Then he looked up. His eyes bored into me.

"There was another *aktion* last week. At least seven hundred killed in the ghetto in Borschow, many from Korolówka. There were no more Jews left here than I understood. They dug their own graves, made them climb in, shot them, set fires."

I waited. My body tightened, my ribs pressing into my back.

"Do you know if the Shwartz family was there? The pharmacist?" I asked.

Joseph walked across the room and tapped his wife on the shoulder. He signed something to her. She shook her head sadly. She didn't know.

At least seven hundred. I heard Joseph's words in my head. *There were no more Jews left here than I understood.*

I put the mug down, looking at the mud that I'd missed cleaning from under my nails. It didn't feel real, sitting there in a chair in a lit room sipping tea. I imagined Mania holding Marek in her lap, trying to convince him to dream.

"I have to get back," I said suddenly.

"Rest a little longer," Joseph responded.

"Thank you for your kindness," I said.

He nodded and stood. I followed him solemnly through the dark house. He picked up some bags. When we got to the door, he put them down.

"Be strong. Take care of the children. Survive," he half whispered. He brushed the side of my hairline with his finger, so lightly it could have been accidental.

"Come back," Joseph said and then opened the door. He handed me the bags, and I hoisted them. They weighed my arms down, anchoring me. I took a few steps into the dark night.

Joseph lingered at the door behind me for a second before it clicked closed.

<hr />

As I climbed down the rungs of the rock wall into the cave, the dawn light disappeared from above. I held the tattered bags of food and supplies. They were heavy and got heavier as I traveled through the four-hundred-yard tunnel to get to our living quarters. It was so narrow in places, I bruised my knees crawling through. Still, I had made it. The closer I got to the children, the faster I could move.

When I was a few yards from our bedroom, I stopped. The stale air cramped my chest. I took a breath. Relief spread over my body, and I left it behind—the world above ground that had gone so crazy it was unrecognizable, where I might be welcomed to somebody's table one minute and have a gun pointed at my head the next. I descended deeper into the fetid darkness, yearning for the love of my children, the only thing that made any sense.

It was true that we lived as the dead do, sealed under the ground. Our bodies were part of the earth. But in that deep cavern where the light had been snuffed out, we were free. They didn't believe we existed. And so we were left alone in peace.

I wound quickly down the corridors, counting my footsteps, reaching for rock walls like a blind woman. When I saw our living quarters, I held up the lantern. The three bodies of my children were curled around each other under the blankets. For a brief second, they looked more animal than human, small lumps of fur in a nest.

Marek saw me first and bolted up. Dunia and Mania turned slowly, their small eyes squinting in the darkness. I dropped the bags on the rock ledge, collapsed on the bed, and opened my arms. They surrounded me, their cold skin clinging to the folds of my stomach and sides. I squeezed them, feeling them—sourness, clumped hair, one small, sticky hand gripping my thumb. I willed my heartbeat to slow down, reminding myself that I was back at home, that my children were safe. It took a long time for me to readjust to the utter darkness and to convince my body that we were all together again, that we still drew our breath.

"We thought you weren't coming back," Marek said. His words had the weight of a heavy stone in a river.

"Shhh," Mania said. The lantern was off and I couldn't see her face, but I knew she was looking at me, that her small prepubescent body was reaching for her youngest brother, and that she was trying to take some of the burden from me. At her age, I had been practically a woman. I tried to imagine how different her dreams were from my dreams as a girl. Did she imagine that she would marry, have children and a small house and fields?

I reminded myself that I couldn't afford to think that way.

"I will always come back for you," I said.

I wanted nothing more than to sleep, but I pulled Marek to me and propped myself up on my bed. He clutched me, his fingernails biting into my back. His heart beat triple time and his breathing was labored, reminding me of the colic he had had as a baby. He had started acting like a much younger boy again, sucking his thumb and clinging to me while we slept.

Mania and Dunia gathered at my sides. Mania shyly touched my hair, perhaps feeling in it the cool air of the night above. She pressed her lips to my cheek. They were eager for stories, my babies, anxious to know what the world was like above ground.

I waited until my eyes stopped watering, until I had grown used to the heavy weight of the children. We tried to be considerate of our neighbors. We rationed our words like our food.

"What was it like up there, Momma?" Marek whispered. He was still young enough to believe in fairy tales.

"There were many stars out. Horses grazed on grass in a farmer's field. I brought something special for us too. We will dine like kings."

Dunia laughed a deep-throated boy's laugh. "Momma is tired. Why don't we sleep for a while longer?" he said.

"What did you bring, Momma?" Marek asked.

"It's a surprise," I said.

Already, they knew not to ask about food until later, when it was our family's turn again at the stove.

"Did you see our house?" Marek asked.

The children all turned towards me.

"Of course. It looks fine. We will maybe have to clean the weeds in the yard when we get back. The apple tree has blossoms," I said.

Marek gasped and touched my face with his clammy hand. I put it to my mouth and kissed it until he pulled it away.

"Can you tell us a story, Momma?" Marek asked.

My tongue was a dead thing in my mouth.

"Why don't you tell me a story?" I responded. "Tell me about what you dreamed."

"I had a dream of a beautiful country," Marek said. "There was a tall man, and he was singing and dancing. There was a sun you could rub with your hands and it made you warm, but it didn't burn you. There was an orchard filled with nice apples. You could run and sing, and the apples tasted so sweet. They were delicious."

"That's a good dream," I said.

"When can we eat, Momma?" Marek asked.

"Shhh," Mania hissed.

"Marek, we'll eat at the same time tomorrow that we always eat—when it's our turn in the kitchen. The food I got needs to be cooked."

Marek sighed heavily; then he was quiet. I couldn't blame him for being anxious—I knew that hunger gnawed on his belly. I wanted to tear open the bags then, to look for something to tide us all over. I was afraid I'd be disappointed, though. And right then, exhaustion was more urgent.

It had required a lot of effort to be above ground. It wasn't the running, terror, or carrying that wore me down—it was the exposure. As sweet as the air had tasted, the feeling of being cloistered and the darkness had become almost an infatuation.

"Panna Goldberg, it's good to see you," Kostaski had said.

Looking straight into his kind blue eyes and at his large hands when he set the soup bowl down was so foreign after being unable to see the faces of my neighbors and family for so many weeks. His gaze had been so gentle, it hurt. It reminded me of the way he had looked at me when I was a girl, respectfully admiring my form. He'd always been a good man. We'd been so innocent back then.

"Your turn, Momma. Tell us a story," Marek said.

"She's tired," Dunia scolded.

"Listen, children. I have a good story. The best story. But it's a story that's meant to be told properly. Let us sleep now, and I'll tell you all about it tomorrow. How does that sound?"

"Okay," Marek said.

Dunia grunted. He was a man now, too old to be interested in stories.

I pulled Marek to me. He nuzzled so close to me, his eyelashes fluttered against my cheek like a butterfly wing. I didn't need to be told to sleep.

One or many hours later, Marek stirred. I thought about lighting the candle to look at the clock, but its numbers were meaningless then, the candle too precious. The only hours important to measure were days until I had to go out.

"Momma, are you awake?" Marek asked.

"I am now."

"Momma, do you need help with the cooking today?" Mania chimed in, as if she too had been waiting for me to wake up. There is only so long you can trick your body into staying asleep.

"Is Dunia awake?" I asked.

"He went to see Uncle Yossel," Mania said.

I knew the older children would hear the news about the *aktion* eventually, but I'd expected to be the one to break it to them. I was grateful to my brother for taking such good care of Dunia. I promised myself again that I would repay Yossel someday. It was another reason to make sure that we stayed alive.

"Momma, the cooking?" Mania asked.

I thought about the bags that I'd hung off the ground, taking stock of what I'd collected. I too wanted to rush into the kitchen and look at our treasures. But there was a schedule we had to stick to.

"Not yet, Mania. Soon."

"What about the laundry, Momma?" Mania asked.

97

I smiled inwardly, pleased that Mania was taking an interest in work. It had been a good move to ask her to help with the laundry.

"We just did the laundry. We'll have to work hard to get more clothes dirty first," I said.

There had been no noise from the families in the rooms beside us for a while. There were hours to waste.

They made them dig a hole. They shot them. Some did not die right away. They closed the hole, buried them.

I was sure my brothers had told their wives. I would meet Yetta, Mendel's wife, in the kitchen to knead dough and cook as we sometimes did. I needed another adult to confide in. That was not a burden I wanted to pass to my daughter.

"I don't need help with cooking, but later, after dinner, you can help me straighten, Mania," I said.

She didn't respond. My eyelids were starting to close.

"Come closer, children. Lie under the covers with me. We'll pretend it's a holiday today. There's no school, and we can spend the whole day together under the covers."

Immediately Marek rolled over and was by my side.

"Come on, Mania, you too," I said.

"I'm fine here," she grumbled.

I drew the covers up over Marek, and he rested his head on my stomach. I cupped his forehead with my palm. As usual, it was cool.

"Well, okay, then. But you will listen to a story, right?" I asked.

"I will," Marek says.

"Mania?" I asked.

She didn't respond for a while. I waited, smoothed Marek's forehead.

"Yeah," Mania said.

"Good. You don't have to come on my bed, but come closer. I don't want to wake anyone. Momma's voice is tired."

I waited until the bed creaked next to me, and I began.

"Your father used to visit Vienna to sell cows and buy leather for the store. He was more cultured than I was. He liked to visit fancy places like operas, theatres, and museums. He liked to stroll down the streets in the cities.

"One day he was standing in a square near the hospital, just enjoying the sights and the sounds. He watched one man who was feeding the pigeons and a woman who was planting some lovely yellow flowers. There was even a lady walking a dog on a leash. In the cities, they walk dogs on leashes so they don't run away."

Marek's ribs rose, and I was sorry I mentioned the dog. To him, dogs were the ones who helped the soldiers catch us, the strays who ran alongside us when we were hiding.

"Anyway, your father sat on a bench, and one man came up to him and started talking. He introduced himself as a Mr. Zabradone. What a funny name, huh, Marek?" I said. I poked him in the ribs, and he started laughing.

"Well, Mr. Zabradone, he tells your father his story. He says he works as an accountant for a publishing company. He makes a good living and has a good reputation. Mr. Zabraaaadoooone," I say, poking Marek again, "talks to your father for a while about all kinds of things, about politics and art and science. He is a very smart man this Mr. Zabradone. Your father could tell that because he was a smart man too. Oh, your father knew everything. He read everything and always was debating with the men who came into his shop about smart things.

"So your father is impressed with Mr. Zabradone, and he likes him. Mr. Zabradone tells him that he can't figure out why he is in the hospital. He asked your father if he would come to the hospital and ask them to discharge him because they must have made a mistake keeping him there.

"Your father never turned down an opportunity to help someone in need. The man told him his doctor was named Dr. Rosenblatt, and he told him where the office was. So your father visited this Dr. Rosenblatt.

He told him, 'Dr. Rosenblatt, I just talked to your patient Mr. Zabradone, and I think it may be a mistake that he is still in the hospital.'

"The doctor smiled at your father. 'Was Mr. Zabradone standing up when he was talking to you, sir?' the doctor asked.

"'Yes,' your father responded.

"'Well, please do me a favor and ask him some more questions, but ask him to sit with you on the bench first. Then, if you think Mr. Zabradone doesn't belong in the hospital, we can talk more,' Dr. Rosenblatt said.

"'Okay,' your father said, and he went off to the square to talk to the nice gentleman. Mr. Zabradone was excited to see your father and hear what the doctor had said.

"'I have some more questions for you about your family, but I am a little tired. Can you please sit with me on this bench?'

"Suddenly, Mr. Zabradone changed. His face got very pale, and he looked scared. 'No. No, no, I cannot do it!' he exclaimed.

"'But I don't understand. Why not?' your father asked.

"'Well,' Mr. Zabradone said, 'I have a butt made of glass, and it is very fragile. There could be a disaster if I sit down.'"

I paused, waiting for the children to get it. I poked Marek in the ribs. My throat was parched. I hadn't spoken that long in a while.

"A butt?"

"A behind. A tushie," I said and patted Marek on the behind.

Marek giggled. Even Mania chuckled a little.

"Naturally, your father was embarrassed that he'd bothered the doctor, and he never went back to see that doctor again. But much later, on his way home on the train, your father thought about this encounter with Mr. Zabradone, and he laughed and laughed and laughed. So he turned to his seatmate on the train and told him the story, and then he told it many times afterwards."

"What's so funny? That the man thought his tushie was made of glass?" Marek asked.

"Yes, that the man thought his tushie was made of glass, and that the man tricked your father into believing he didn't belong in the hospital," I said, tickling Marek until he nearly screamed.

I couldn't see Mania, but I felt something in her relax, and I knew that she would stay a few more hours in bed.

Chapter Eight

STOOD IN THE kitchen with Mendel's wife, Yetta, kneading flour into dough on the wooden board. We worked in silence, shaping the dough into balls, then flattening it and using a steady rhythm to press into it with our fingertips. It was familiar, this rhythm. It felt like home.

"I wish we could have some of your famous *latkes* in here," Yetta said. "Or *pierogies*, or chicken necks, stuffed chicken necks. I would give up my rations for a week for some of your famous cooking."

An old pride blossomed in me like a flower. It was kind of Yetta to remind me.

"It's strange, but I've stopped thinking about good food," I said. "When we were first here, all I could think of were pickled cucumbers. I wanted them so badly I could almost taste them; it was almost on the tip of my tongue. Do you know what I mean?"

"Yes, I know exactly. Sometimes I can smell frying onion and garlic in my dreams," Yetta said.

"We had better stop now. This is a dangerous conversation," I said and laughed. Yetta laughed too.

Preparing food was one of the rare times when we left the lanterns lit. We stood there working. I looked at one of our most precious possessions—the heavy millstone Nisel Stermer had stolen from a local farmer and carried on his back for three miles. I watched the men use it once, pouring the grain a handful at a time through the center hole while the other turned the top stone to grind the bottom rock that Nisel had chiseled with a railroad spike. The flour fell out and got pushed to the edge, landing on a tough cloth, fine to the touch, like gold.

I watched the way Yetta's tiny hands pressed on the dough, compared them to my own larger hands. Yetta was my age, and we had a lot in common. She had also rebelled against my parents and her own to marry Mendel, and she seemed unbothered most of the time, even though he had a temper. Unlike me, she was extremely meticulous. Everything she did had a quality of exactness about it, even the way she kneaded the dough.

"At least they had the decency to bury them this time," she said, with a vulnerable stare in my direction.

Her wide, brown, deer-like eyes were clear and flecked with gold. It softened me. Even my breath slowed down.

"Not decency. They don't want contagion," I said.

We started to knead again, working the stretchy paste with our hands. The scent of the raw dough rose around us. All scents, pleasant and unpleasant, were stronger in the cave because we were so closed in. The dough smelled nice.

"Did you get any names?" I asked.

"Nah."

She slapped the slab of dough down on the board, flipped it over and over again. I did the same.

"You went to Kostaski? Everything was okay?"

"Mmm hmmm."

"He's a good man," she said.

I swallowed hard and started the next phase of the bread making—braiding the dough into something like *challah*.

"It was strange being in his kitchen," I said. "I wished I had a hair-brush, that there was some way to clean better, to take a bath."

Yetta laughed a high-pitched sound that startled me. "Panna Goldberg, are you being vain?"

I smashed the braided bread and started over, feeling the heat rush to my cheeks. It surprised me. "I mean that we are living in different worlds now. Their lives are civilized. There is no way for them to understand what it's like," I hissed.

Yetta kept her eyes downcast on her bread, the perfect braided loaf she'd nearly finished. I regretted snapping at her. It made me feel like my brother.

"I worry for them," I said. "It's not right to keep going back there. We put them in danger. It's not only Jews they are killing."

Yetta took the loaf and put it on the second board, then dusted the surface with flour again. "Oy. That's stupid," she said.

I looked up, surprised. There was a mischievous smirk around her mouth, a glint in her eyes. The light bobbed, casting shadows on the table and on the stone walls.

"They choose to be brave," she said.

I nodded, dipped my fingers into the water bowl, dripped droplets on the flour. "At least we are self-sufficient," I said.

She laid out more dough. Her palms moved rhythmically, kneading upwards,

"Maybe we should have sold our gold watches and immigrated to Canada," I said. "We'd be speaking French, strolling the streets in our fancy dresses and parasols."

Yetta laughed lightly. Her breath wheezed. Her eyelids fluttered. I hoped she wouldn't fall asleep like a horse standing up.

"Or maybe we should all attach this millstone to our ankles and drown ourselves in the river." She picked up my train of thought. "Then the Nazis would be happy, and we wouldn't have to trouble our old neighbors."

She laughed then, hysterically, ridiculously. I joined her. There was nothing but absurdity about the war, about our situation. There was nothing to do but laugh.

We both stopped laughing abruptly, almost guiltily, and started again on our work. My ribs actually hurt from the strain.

"Each man who helps has his own reason," Yetta said. "If something happens, that decision is between him and his God."

I paused for a second, considering what she'd said. She nodded, then looked at the table and continued to roll the dough.

Chapter Nine

MANIA AND I sat on the edge of Momma's bed. Behind us, Nunia babbled. Pepcia and Yossel were curled in each other's arms. I could not see this, but I could tell by the slow, womanly way Pepcia laughed. It was the sound of a woman who found comfort and protection in the arms of the man she loved. It made me feel lonely.

"We're sorry to interrupt," I said. "We came for the rest of the story, Momma. About Mania's great-grandmama Sara. Is it okay?"

"Oh yes. I know. I've been waiting so long for you to ask. It's a story about love," she said.

I laughed. My mother had become sentimental in her old age. I would never have predicted that could happen. My mother had been stern, almost unaffectionate towards my father in front of us children growing up.

"Where did I leave off?" she asked.

"Sara was in love with Rudik, Shlomo's brother," Mania said.

Momma's voice seemed to strengthen as she spoke.

"Yes. And Shlomo was very in love with Sara. He told his parents to arrange an engagement, and they did. They hired a *shaffer* named Zina to start the process.

"The *shaffer* visited Sara's parents to inform them about Shlomo's intentions to marry Sara. Sara's parents brought Sara into the kitchen and told her. She looked embarrassed and confused. She didn't look happy.

"Sara's parents understood their daughter was a private person. They saw she was upset. They told the *shaffer* they'd talk to her later. When they were alone, they asked Sara what she thought about the marriage. She didn't want to talk about it. She confessed that she didn't want to marry Shlomo because she was in love with Rudik, and Rudik was also in love with her."

We were silent for a while, soaking in all the words in the darkness. Sitting so close to each other listening to stories made us peaceful. It was a special feeling, comfortable but different from real life, even before the war. We were three generations of the same family sitting together, sharing our lives.

"My grandparents were devastated," Momma continued. "It was tradition that parents were supposed to support the eldest son's marriage first. They were angry with their daughter. Later they saw how much she was suffering. They loved her very much and respected her feelings.

"They asked the *shaffer* to find a solution. The matter was delicate because two families were emotionally invested in the situation. The *shaffer* decided to ask the rabbi for advice.

"The rabbi acted as a mediator. After many discussions, he told them it was better if two are laughing than three are crying. He gave his blessing for Rudik and Sara to break tradition and get engaged.

"Of course, Sara and Rudik were thrilled with the rabbi's decision. They had true love, which was not so common in the Jewish community in Korolówka at the time."

"What happened to Shlomo?" Mania asked.

"He signed up for the Austrian army and left town right after the wedding." Momma laughed, a tinny laugh that seemed false somehow.

Pepcia was tickling Nunia. He cooed, like a regular baby who didn't live in the dark. To him, it probably didn't make any difference.

"That's so strange, that parents can pick who you marry. They don't do that anymore, do they?" Mania asked.

"Yes, of course they do. It's just not as common," I said.

"No, they don't," Momma said.

Anger cut me. It was unexpected. It annoyed me.

"You did, Momma, but it's okay. None of that matters anymore," I said. Yossel groaned.

"I did not. Why would I do that?" she whined like a petulant child.

"Momma, I don't want to argue," I said.

"Who's arguing?"

"I just can't understand how you can say that. You opposed Mendel's marriage, my marriage. It's the exact same thing as that story. Chaim wasn't good enough. He was beneath you." I spit the words out. I had no idea that was in me.

"Etcia, calm down," Yossel said.

"I'm calm. I'm calm. But Chaim is gone. After all that we went through."

"You children are the ones who always had to do everything in secret, getting married without our consent," Momma said. "If you hadn't done that, my own husband, your father, would still be." Her voice was ragged, like a tightly stitched patch ripped off her heart.

"Momma," Yossel started.

"You didn't have to rent that house, Yossel. We would have bought you something by us," she said.

Everything stilled. Even their baby, Nunia, was silent.

I touched Mania's shoulder, indicating we should get up and go.

Chapter Ten

MANIA CAME BACK from the latrine. She collapsed on her bed, then hunched over with her knees drawn into her chest. She let out her breath loudly, a sound that might have been a sob. I sat up and carefully touched her forehead. It was clammy.

"Come," I whispered into her ear. She followed me. We sat down on the planks with the pillows on them across the room behind the stone wall. We were too far away for anyone to hear us. "Baby, did your menses start?"

"What?" she said in a snotty teenager's voice.

"Do you have blood?"

"What? No."

I waited for a minute. She turned her back to me at an angle, but her shoulder and the top part of her arm brushed against mine. Her skin was soft, the fine downy hairs raised.

"You were in the bathroom a long time."

Her back arched. She was revolted. She mumbled.

"Speak up, Mania."

"It's nothing. It's just hard to go," she blurted out.

I touched the back of my hand to her forehead. Constipation was a big problem. The lower our food stores got and the less we moved around, the more people struggled at the latrine. It was another humiliation we attributed to our attackers. They might not have caught us, but their cruelty had wormed into our bodies.

The one place I wouldn't let it get into was my mind.

"This is a problem for me also," I said. "Drink more water. Walk more. It may help."

I took the comb from my pocket and gently started to work the knots from her hair. She let me.

"It must be hard, Momma, to live all this time like a man," she said after a few minutes.

The first section of hair I had combed through was no longer tangled. I ran the comb along that section for a few strokes so she was aware of its smoothness. I started on the next section.

"Your hair is still beautiful," I said.

I had of course seen it only by lamplight. She leaned her head back in response, spilling her long hair over her shoulders.

"I don't live like a man, my Mania. I dress like a man only for practical reasons."

"You carry the food like the men. You risk everything."

The knots in that section untangled more easily. Mania enjoyed the attention. She tossed her head slightly from side to side, like an actress. Even though here, in the dark earth, we had no idea how we looked, I was happy to allow Mania the luxury of her prettiness.

"I risk nothing. If I stopped, I would be risking you."

"I don't understand."

"Well, the secret, Mania, is that women have always been stronger than men. We go through childbirth, and then we do anything to protect our babies. I'd do anything to protect you, Marek, and Dunia. Men don't have the same determination."

I started on the third section of her hair. It was badly knotted. I put my palm against the top of her head and clasped the section, then carefully worked through the tangles. She leaned her head back to help me.

"You will see someday when you have children of your own."

For a long time, we were quiet. I worked on her hair, taking long sips of dark air. I put the comb back in my pocket and swept her hair back with my fingers, pulling it away from her face. I parted it into three sections and started to braid it.

"This place is a miracle, the reason that we have survived," I said. "That's a miracle too. We are meant to live."

I braided the tail tight down her back, then let it hang for a second. I took the thread I had saved from the button that had popped off my sweater and tied it to the bottom. I pulled the braid off her back and let it fall down so she knew it was done. She swung it against her back. Then she turned so we were both facing front.

"Dens are for wolves, not humans," she said.

I smiled. It was her catchphrase. It comforted her to repeat it.

"Maybe. But you know, Mania, we may not be the only people who have lived here."

"What?"

"Well, when I was about your age, Granny told me a story her mother had told her about ancient people who lived in the caves outside Korolówka. It was just how people lived then, maybe to protect themselves against wind and storms. They cooked with fire just like us. They made their own tools. That's all I remember."

"They lived in this cave?" she asked.

"Maybe this cave. Maybe there was another magical spot. There could have been another entrance into this place."

"Why would anyone crawl into this pit if they didn't have to?"

"I don't know the answer. Maybe they thought it was cozy," I joked.

"Maybe they were afraid of the sun," she said. She giggled then. The weight on my chest eased. *As long as we can laugh, we'll be okay*, I thought.

"Who can tell?" I said. "Maybe it was a very nice place back then. Maybe they built nice things down here. It could have been as fancy as Granny's house is."

I paused, waiting for Mania to ask about Granny's house, to ask if the Germans were living in it.

She sighed. It didn't seem to matter anymore.

<hr />

That night, I heard my mother crying. It was terrible—a gurgling, underwater cry. I don't know how I was able to distinguish it from the sound of any of the other women or children, who all cried every once in a while. There was never any particular reason for it except for all the reasons in the world. They cried out of grief, grief that had burrowed down deep into their hearts. It was indescribable, this grief. It made us believe terrible things about ourselves. It made us believe terrible things about each other.

Although I had never heard this sound before, I knew instinctively it was my mother crying. I had never talked to her about the death of our father. As far as I knew, nobody had.

I reached back to the shelf behind my bed and felt for the form of my two shoes. It had become a strange habit. I needed to remind myself they were there, that they hadn't been swooped up by a bat or chewed to bits by imaginary rats. I felt them, nodded, and pushed myself up on the bed.

Slowly, I walked across the room, counting the twelve steps to the barrier. I felt the barrier, then counted the twelve steps to her bed. I kicked the wood by accident. Shards of pain shot from my toe to my knee.

"Who's there?" my mother asked.

"Etcia." I sat down on the bed. Yossel touched my back. He was already with her.

"It's not his fault," my mother said. "I shouldn't have blamed my boy."

I sighed. My mother could always hold resentment towards me like a heavy locket around her neck, but Yossel could never do any wrong. It had shocked me that she blamed him for his choices, for marrying Pepcia in secret, for going to live so far away on the edge of the town. It hurt her being so far away from her baby. I didn't know for sure but believed it was Pepcia who'd insisted they build on the outskirts of town. She was smart—she could see that my mother fawned over him as if he were a child. Momma might have even viewed Pepcia as competition.

"It's nobody's fault," I said.

The crying eased. Her breath heaved irregularly.

Nobody moved. There was a thickness to the people sleeping around us. Even though the darkness was constant, I believed that outside, it was night.

My mother's hand covered my own. It was bony, clammy. She pressed it into the bed. "Chaim was a good man," she said.

That night was a small blessing I would never forget.

Chapter Eleven

THE CHILDREN WATCHED me as I came back from the pool where I had tried to wash, smoothing my hair, bending down to gather the bags. Marek whimpered a little, pressed in the crook of Mania's arm.

"Go to sleep. I will be back before you wake up."

"Momma, don't go!" Marek cried. Mania shushed him. Dunia's big arm gently thwacked his younger brother.

"I'll always come back."

"Be careful," Dunia said.

The children never left the cave. The world outside had become a story to them. The memories that were branded in them—Mania and Dunia lifting the bloated women's bodies on the edge of the river, Marek being prodded with pitchforks in a corn crib—became stronger the longer we lived in the cave.

I pulled my hair up and secured it with the bobby pins I had saved in the waistband of my underwear, then shoved it into my brother's cap. I straightened the buttons on my outside shirt, pulled up my trousers and suspenders. I had bug bites, and it was impossible to tell if I smelled decent.

I struck a match and lit a candle. I took in my children's anxious vole faces, a smudge on Marek's baby face. I put my calmest expression on, then moved the candle towards the clock. Eleven p.m. I blew the candle out.

"Come give me a hug," I said

"No, just wait a little while longer," Marek begged.

It was like the countdown before an execution. I'd never had respect for hesitation. If something needs to be done, you put one foot in front of the other. Begrudgingly, I opened my arms, and they surrounded me. I squeezed them, feeling bones and hard angles.

"Stop being silly. Go to sleep," I said.

"She will bring roasting potatoes," Mania whispered, unhinging Marek's claws from my hips. She walked him back to the bed. *Little Momma*, I thought and in my head repeated the prayer that one day she'd have children of her own.

I relit the candle and snatched one last look at my babies curled up under the dirty *varetta* like a litter of puppies. Marek sobbed.

It was a good reminder. I had no choice but to keep from getting slaughtered. The men were going out less for their own families. There were more fights. The children's terror was real. None of the adults ever discussed what would happen if one of us died.

"I love you. I'll always come back," I said. I blew out the candle, turned my back to my children, and counted my footsteps, extending my hands, remembering the winding path past the other rooms through the cave and back up and into the world.

After the chill of the cave, the warm outside air took some time to get accustomed to. It shocked the lungs, like plunging into a cold river shocks the skin. I tipped back my head, allowing myself to find my bearings in the sky. After breathing stale air laced with bat feces, being outside was a guilty pleasure. At least the air outside moved.

The awe dissolved. I took a few uncertain steps on the flat ground through the grass, then started running—first at a slow clip, then, after I was sure that my legs had stopped shaking, faster, fast enough that I didn't feel the exposure of being in the field under the bright sky. I couldn't imagine soldiers pointing their guns at my back. I ran until I couldn't run anymore, until I reached the Yasinovaty Woods.

I stopped in the shadow of an evergreen tree, holding my bag in one hand, and I placed my palm over my fast-beating heart. The sound of a bird screech anchored me. The soles of my shoes had worn thin enough that I could feel dampness in the earth. It must have rained. I walked between bluish shadows underneath the evergreen trees. My heartbeat slowed.

I walked until my stomach cramped. This often happened once I had stood upright for a while. I leaned up against a tree and bent into my stomach. The confusion that clouded me seemed to last longer than the previous time I had gone out. I willed myself not to think about how the last time two men had ventured out of the cave, soldiers had opened fire on them while they were in the fields stealing potatoes.

"*Whoo, whoo,*" I heard. It was coming from somewhere in front of me, a low, throaty sound. The sound of an owl. I scanned the branches of the trees. I couldn't find it. Still, the fact that it called was enough to shake me out of my fog.

"The animals have not yet forgotten," Yossel had said.

"*Whoo whoo,*" it called again.

The sound was definitely coming from in front of me. I followed it blindly. I cursed myself for stopping, for losing my way, and then forgave myself. I kept walking, doing what I had to do, reminding myself who I was. *I am Etcia Goldberg,* my footsteps bellowed as I walked on the ground. *I am from* Korolówka. *This is my land. I am Etcia Goldberg. I am a mother. I am going to feed my children. We are going to continue to live.*

As I walked down the narrow country road leading to Strikivitcy village—the road we had traveled as children to visit our relatives, to eat supper, to go swimming in summer—memories returned and flooded my senses with every step. It was faint at first, the scent of wild herbs and brush released from the dry earth with rain, the smell of the brackish river. I began detecting scents I had never taken notice of before—night flowers blooming, the ripe, fecund scent of field mice. These smells guided me, kept me from being afraid. I would never have known the world was so beautiful if I hadn't been forced to leave it.

I turned off the narrow country road to the main road and stopped to scratch insect bites on my arms. Something had shifted. The main road was wider. In the dark, every step I took felt foreign, more foreign than Korolówka had become. It was too wide, too open. It was no longer the road we knew as children. Instead it was a road marked with graves where people had been maimed and bludgeoned and thrown into pits. I imagined bodies dropped in the ravines where frogs screeched, twisted in the choked weeds.

The hot air caressed my cheek. The sky was flooded with starlight. I stuck close to the dark side of the road.

I walked as swiftly as I could, pacing myself to keep from getting muscle cramps. I walked until the trees and weeds receded, until the road thinned. I stood at the crossroads of Ivasiuk's village. He was a kind man, renowned for helping Jews. Then I saw something that made me stop short, as if I'd been hit with a plank across the chest.

On the road in front of me was the shadow of what appeared to be a medium-sized man.

If I can see him, he can see me, I thought.

I couldn't tell what he looked like, only that the top of his cap appeared squashed. His silhouette showed a partially untucked shirt hanging from his pants. I couldn't make out a weapon. He was not a soldier or Ukrainian police. The way that he stood, stock-still like me, and his ragged appearance made me believe I made him nervous too.

I couldn't take any chances. I treated him like a wolf. I hoisted my walking stick into the air, stood up tall to make my man's appearance look more imposing. I took a few steps. Then I stopped, holding the stick in the air. Everything slowed down: my breath, my heart, my mind.

The man turned and started walking away from me. My frozen arm slowly lowered the stick to the ground. I stood there, looking at the place where the man had been. I picked up his shadow walking down the hill. I talked my feet into moving. I followed slowly at a distance just to make sure he was gone.

I followed Grigori Ivasiuk through the narrow corridor of his house to a small side room. He lit the lantern and indicated I should sit on a red chair next to a table and lamp. I noticed a mattress that had been shoved against the wall, a few more books on an overturned crate. I had picked the right place. Other people had hidden here.

He left me there for a moment while he went to go fetch something. The safety of the dank room relaxed me so much, my body practically melted into the chair, and I had to keep my eyes from closing. The man from the road was practically a figment of my imagination. At the same time, I was in awe of the strength I had found while standing there, of the imposing figure I must have cut on the road. It was good to be reminded that courage hadn't left me, that if I needed to, I could fight.

"I hope you like dried plums, Panna Goldberg," Ivasiuk said.

He entered through the side door, turning sideways through the cramped room to join me. He straightened to his full height. He placed a sack on the floor next to me and a plate of bread, nuts, crackers, and dried plums on the table in front of me. It was good, rich food. I didn't know if my stomach could take it.

"You are very kind," I said.

He sat on a cushion across from me. He was smiling, his face as jovial as ever, as if I were a regular visitor. His skin was flushed red, healthy. He didn't have trouble getting good food. He didn't look directly at me.

"The man's clothes are smart. I almost didn't recognize you," he said.

"I think I saw a man on the road. He saw me; then he retreated. I circled around many times. I wasn't followed," I said.

"A soldier?" he asked.

"I don't think so, no."

He nodded. I had to tell him. The men in the cave trusted him. He was one of the few people who knew where we were.

"How are things in Strilkivtcy?" I asked politely.

"Not good. I was able to collect some supplies for you, Panna Goldberg—some bread, red beets, beans, cheese, jam, and some candles and matches if you have need for those."

I smiled. I couldn't help myself. Those were luxury items. Still, they wouldn't keep us too long. I quickly went through the list of supplies in my head. I'd collected just a few ears of corn and potatoes from the nearby fields. I vowed to leave soon, to hit some more fields or summer houses on the way back. If that didn't work, I'd have to make a new plan.

"We are thankful," I said.

He didn't respond right away. His appearance was sad despite his neatly combed brown hair, beardless cheeks, and neat clothes. Ivasiuk had always looked like this. It was comforting to notice this familiar trait.

"Your children?" he asked cautiously.

I squinted my eyes when I looked at him. *They are alive*, this look said. *They are still with me.*

"This is a terrible time," he said.

I took a plum from the plate and put it in my mouth, chewed on its gummy surface. Its dry, pungent flavor rushed to my head. I took a sip of the water he'd brought when I first came, forcing it down.

"You aren't alone," he said.

I looked at him seriously and took another bite of the plum. He stared back directly, his gaze settling me. There was something almost peaceful about him. He remembered me as an old family friend.

"Father Sohatsky is telling people that if they come across Jews, they should not turn them in, but they should help if they can," he said.

"He says this openly?"

"At service, at church, whenever he can."

A slow smile formed on my face, and I put my hand on my heart to indicate that I'd heard.

"He is brave," I said.

"He is respected. People are still afraid of God. Nobody will turn him in."

I took a nut from the plate and nibbled it.

Ivasiuk hadn't had old neighbors try to kill him. He hadn't run with the dogs in the night. He hadn't seen all the bodies. He didn't realize that nobody was safe.

The part of the forest I stood in was strange. It was darker and lusher than the side I was used to. The leaves on the trees were small and shiny rather than dull. I walked stealthily until I couldn't ignore the pains anymore. My wrist felt as if the bone had been turned backwards. My stomach ached. I slowed down, entranced by a sweet scent filling the forest. When I realized I was losing my bearings, that traveling any farther might get me lost, I stopped at a tree trunk and kneeled down.

I waited, as if in a dream. The sweet warm air caressed my cheek. I rubbed my hand on the bark, grounding myself in night the air. My eyes caught a pocket of flowers—tiny stalks of white bell-shaped flowers with oblong leaves. I knew them, but the name had been lost to me. I knelt there. Their sweet perfume cloyed. It was so strong, that scent. Was I imagining their scent, which I knew from my childhood? It irked me that I couldn't remember their name.

The longer I sat, the more disoriented I became. The greatest danger was getting lost. The night would soon turn to day.

I almost stood, but something stopped me. I cocked my head upwards to scan the trees. The sight of something large and shadowy gathered in the branches to my right. Slowly I turned. When I saw him, I nearly screamed.

A dead man was lying in the bushes near a copse of trees. His skin was a strange color. His tongue hung out of the side of his mouth.

I collected myself, stood, picked up the bag, and started running back. My heart beat throughout my whole body. As I ran, I paid attention to it, allowing it to root me. Visions of the man were lobbed in my mind. It wasn't him exactly, more the absence of him, the terrible weightlessness of his body.

It occurred to me that during the terrible years we'd been hiding and fighting, with all the deaths that had been described to me, I'd never seen a murdered man or woman up so close before.

This was one horror that my children hadn't been spared.

Once I was safely back in the cave, I sat on the bed with the children, praying that they would soon tire. The bed was ripe with the scent of yeast. All three children were delicately gnawing a small chunk of bread. I hoped having something in their bellies would make them quieter, maybe even help them fall back asleep. I wanted nothing more than to close my eyes and return to the safety of dream.

After going outside, my body was so tired, it was melting into the mattress. I was readjusting. Even though the world outside was terrible, the fresh air and rhythm of walking and breathing like a normal person made me feel acutely how smothered we were.

"I'm finished, Momma," Marek said.

"Not me. I'm making it last. It's so delicious, Momma," Dunia said.

Mania was silent. Eating had become a delicate matter.

"Yes, we are fortunate," I said.

I lay down, pulling the covers higher up to my chin, trying to keep my eyes from closing. The bloated face of the man, his dead weight, had not left me.

"Children, I saw some beautiful things while I was out there," I said.

"What did you see, Momma?"

"Well, I went to another part of the forest. It was a place I'd never been to before, not even when I was your age. And in the forest, there were strange, white flowers shaped like little bells, and they had such a sweet scent. It lingered everywhere."

"Really?" Mania asked.

"Convallaria. Lily of the valley," I remembered. "Your granny used to keep a vase of them in the kitchen. They were written about in the Bible, in the Song of Solomon."

"What did they smell like?" Mania asked.

They smelled of the past, I thought. "They smelled like heaven," I said. "And they were beautiful. They were bright white. Even though it was dark, I could see them."

"Did you see any men with the guns?" Marek asked.

"No, baby."

"I wish I could see those flowers," Marek said.

"Well, you can, Marek. Just close your eyes. Have you closed them?"

"Yes."

"Okay, now imagine you and Momma and Dunia and Mania are sitting in a nice safe place. It is a forest, like the one I have been to, but it is in future times. We're allowed to be there. Each hour, the sky turns more brilliant blue. The air is so warm and fresh and nice, it makes you feel like someone is touching you lightly, brushing fingers on your cheek. And the sky is lightening. It is getting brighter.

"Imagine a scent, the sweetest scent. You can almost taste it, like sugar cake, like frosting. It is coming from these tremendous white flowers. And the flowers are so pretty and delicate. Like your sister, everyone wants to be near them."

When I finally heard Marek's heavy breathing followed by his baby snores, I stopped talking. I yawned.

"I think he's out," Mania whispered in a motherly tone.

I smiled, patted her on the hand. "You would have appreciated their beauty."

Chapter Twelve

July

I HEARD MOVEMENT, THE sound of somebody pacing back and forth on the floor around our area. It took me a few seconds to wake. It was neither a sleeping dream nor a daydream, but something on the edges of both. As I sat up, I imagined a short, burly man with a bald head and kind eyes sitting at a kitchen table coming towards me. It was Kostaski, but not Kostaski as he appeared now—the Kostaski I had known when Chaim was alive. His expression was respectful, almost humbled, the way he had looked at me when I was a young woman. The expression told me he admired my beauty from a distance. It was the same way he'd looked at me when I met him outside.

It was natural I thought about Kostaski because he was my main connection with the outside world. He represented real life, stability, myself when I was a young girl too naïve and spoiled to think of anybody but myself. Kostaski linked me to our untroubled past. That past was a better place.

As I remembered where I was, I brushed away the thought, like a stray leaf caught on my clothes.

The slapping of feet on the mud floor and heavy breathing continued. It took me a few seconds to recognize that it was a girl's breath and anxious walk. I put my hands on the edge of the bed and stood up.

"Mania, is that you?" I asked.

The footsteps stopped. She was silent. I walked over to her. Her breath was thick and phlegmy. It took me awhile to locate her.

I stopped near her and gently touched her shoulders, grounding her. I found her face, feeling fresh tears on her cheeks.

"What is it?" I asked.

"Nothing. You know. It just hurts."

"Come sit down," I said and guided her to the board with the pillow. "I am going to bring you some water. Wait."

I heard her sitting down and went to the bucket, filled the glass, and brought it to her, pressing it into her hands. Then I sat down.

"Drink it slowly, but drink the whole thing," I said.

She gulped the water.

"This place is terrible," she said.

"It is," I agreed. "Did you finish your water?" I asked.

"Mmm hmm."

"Turn your back. I will brush your hair."

I took the comb from my pocket and started to brush her hair. It had become another ritual for us. Even though it soothed us both, it had also become dangerous. The comb had lost some of its teeth. Our poor diet had done strange things to our hair. At first Mania's hair had been greasier, as if her body were overcompensating for the lack of fat in our food. Now it was drier, more fragile, and the knots were worse. I brushed carefully, often using just my fingers instead of the comb.

"It's like being stabbed," she said.

I nodded and continued to lightly comb her hair. "Is there still blood?" I asked.

"Uh-huh," she mumbled.

"Is it more than before?"

"Who can tell?" Her voice was ragged, the voice of an old woman.

I had no words. My daughter was suffering. There was nothing I could do. It was the worst feeling a mother could have.

"I'm sorry, Mania," I said.

As I continued combing her hair, I held back a gasp when a clump came out in my hand.

"Momma, do you think maybe the monsters that Marek and the other children see are ghosts? I don't mean from the Jewish people now. I mean maybe the ones you said came before us, the ancient people Grandma talked about."

I realized I was clasping the lock of hair that had fallen out in my hand. I reached back and put it on the floor behind us. Instead of touching her hair again, I hugged her from behind.

"Mania. Do not entertain the ideas of monsters. You are the sensible one. You know what's real. It's your gift," I said.

"How do we know what is real anymore?"

"We know."

"How?"

"We know we are still safe here in this cave, that God is protecting us."

"But Momma, I keep thinking about that. How would God let this happen? He wouldn't. They took God from us. The police, the soldiers, the people who live in the houses without us, they took him away."

"No, Mania, they didn't. They tried, but they didn't succeed."

"I don't understand."

My mind was garbled, but I knew in that case, a story could be as helpful in moving Mania past her pain as water or rest. In the cave, focusing on pain made it latch onto you tighter. It was best to find some distraction. It could be anything: running down the list of clothes to be washed, keeping a tally of the food I needed to secure, imagining the path I would take on my next trip out. If I didn't find something to divert Mania's attention now, the thoughts would haunt her worse than any monster or ghost or ancient cave person.

"Do you remember when you used to visit your father at the shop where he sold the leather?"

"I think so,"

"That shop always smelled so good, like leather and tobacco. I always thought of it as the men's place even though I went there and helped out. You, my Mania, were in love with that place just as you were in love with your father. He encouraged you to visit him there. Sometimes he'd give you something special to do, like cut some leather for him or look for something he'd misplaced. Mostly, though, you just watched him. He gave you sweets. You'd sit there for hours when the other men were there talking. You'd always been sensitive even then, and when you looked at people, they always had the feeling you could understand everything about them. That was what your father said about you. He always thought that you, more than your brothers, could understand his true heart."

I paused, remembering that version of Mania, who was so unlike this fragile teenager terrified of the dark. That Mania roamed free in the sun, touched the ground with both feet. She was like a bird back then—slight and beautiful, and she knew how to soar. No wonder she was having so much trouble in the cave. Her wings had been clipped.

"You did, Mania; you knew him. Your knowledge kept you strong like it does now. You were your father's little pet. You more than anyone knew his true heart.

"Your father's heart was courageous. He was a fighter. He believed in defending other people, standing up for those unable to stand up for themselves. He used to go all over Poland to see leaders speak. I was too young to understand the importance of these things. It makes me ashamed that I used to try to talk him out of going on these trips, or of helping people in need by giving them free things. I didn't know any better. I was young, and unlike you, I had never had to face hardship. Before this all happened, everything seemed easy. Everything made sense. Nobody ever threatened our safety or freedom," I said.

"Nobody ever tried to kill you?" There was a glassy clarity in her voice that made me believe the worst of the pain had in fact passed.

"That's right, my Mania. The world was right-side-up then. Nobody tried to kill us. And I didn't know any people who suffered like we do now, though people, especially Jewish people, had always suffered all over the world.

"One of your father's heroes was Ze'ev Jabotinsky. I am ashamed to say that I don't know too much about him except that he believed that the Jewish people have a lot of enemies, and that they need a safe place to live, and that they should fight. Your father used to repeat these lines from his hero all the time. I heard them so many times, I guess I memorized them. Please forgive me, Mania. I don't have the exact words. He said, 'Jabotinsky said Jews live on the edge of volcano these days. Anything can happen to them anytime, any moment in Europe.' And that has turned out to be true—look what is happening now."

Mania moved in closer to me, scratching her head. "I don't understand, Momma. What does it mean? What is a volcano?"

"It's a big mountain, like the Carpathians, but it erupts and spits poison all over the place. It can kill people."

"I don't understand."

"Well, he said that lots of people all over Europe have tried to hurt Jews—but that we are an old people who have survived a lot of persecution, that the only way to survive is to stick together."

"Underground? Like the rats?"

I took her and put her head on my shoulder, then scraped my nails over her scalp.

"Mania, my darling. We do what we are capable of. For each of us, that is different. We are alive when so many others have died. That is because we are fighters. We are fighting now."

Chapter Thirteen

August

THE BARRIERS WE put between the families' compartments in the sleeping quarters weren't sufficient. They gave us the illusion of privacy, and when we spoke in low tones, most of what we said was muffled enough that it couldn't be understood. Though I liked conversation more than most, and in the old days I did appreciate a little good gossip, in the cave, listening too closely gave me a headache. It was terrible to lie in bed unable to sleep, hearing the hiss of voices and trying hard not to eavesdrop and make out what they were saying. Sometimes I tuned them out by imagining the voices getting drowned out by the sound of a flowing river. At other times, I couldn't help myself; I tried to pick the words out, like stones in a sack of grain.

The night that Yetta and Mendel fought, I couldn't tune them out. My brother's temper raged. Yetta was embarrassed and tried hard to keep him quiet. I couldn't completely make out what they were saying. I pushed my hands into the sides of the bed to control my own temper. Not only was their argument interrupting what might have been a sweet, harmless dream, but the anger was also aggravating. My brother was as stubborn as an ox. Mendel would never hit Yetta, but it was terrible to hear him bullying her. There was enough hatred in our lives already without my brother having to bring it down into the cave.

Truthfully, I was also a little afraid. The longer we were down there, the more violence seemed to infect some of the men. There had been a few minor skirmishes between them. I often thought it was more terrible for the men—to feel so powerless against the people who fought us, to be unable to protect their families. Their anger was more likely to be turned outward. They were less used to feeling powerless than we women were. They were more likely to lash out.

The raw intensity of Yetta and Mendel's fighting was clearer than any of their words. I turned my head towards the ceiling, closed my eyes. I heard Yetta crying hysterically. Then I could I pick out her words clearly.

"You're a coward, Mendel," her voice hissed.

There was a bang, then more crying, and then the sound of my brother stomping away to seek privacy in another part of the cave.

When it was clear that Mendel was gone and when Yetta's crying had eased, I stood up and went over to her room, thirteen steps and two rock walls down from our own, to comfort her.

"Yetta, are you okay?" I asked, reaching to the shoulder-height edge of their wall where three smooth sticks jutted out, then walking the six toe-to-heel steps to her bed.

"Who's that?"

"It's me, Etcia," I said. I then kneeled where I heard her voice and eased myself onto the edge of the bed. My back hurt tremendously. I pressed my hand into my spine, seeking to quell the pain.

"Yetta, I heard fighting. Are you injured?"

"What? Oh, Etcia. No. Mendel would never put his hands to me. Thank you. You don't have to worry about that."

The evenness of her voice told me what she was saying was true. "Good."

The cave was silent. Everyone was either asleep or lying quietly, listening for gossip.

"What happened?" I asked.

"I need your help. You are the only one who can talk sense into Mendel. You are the only one who can stand up to him," she said. Her breath wheezed. She continued. "You are his big sister. He respects you. He always talks about how you helped him avoid being drafted into the Polish army. He knows you are strong, what you can do."

She moved on the bed, gulped some water, then put the glass down on something stone.

"This is about my nephew, Ulo Barad," Yetta continued. "When the men went out, they found he's still alive. He's suffering, though. He's only a teenager, Mania's age. His parents, my brother and his wife, were murdered in the second *aktion* early on. He's all alone. He's the only family I have left," she said. Her voice tore. "I want Mendel to go out and find him and bring him back. I want to take care of him. I've heard he is sick."

"He refused?" I asked.

"He doesn't mind if Ulo comes to live with us. He agreed to provide for him too. But he's afraid to go out there now. He thinks it's too dangerous," she said.

I rubbed my hand over my hair, thinking. I remembered the dead man lying between the bushes, the terrible feeling I got looking across the now-barren wheat field.

I'd noticed the men had been going out less lately. I was sure they'd seen things, that they'd brought back their own stories. Returning to the place where we'd been sealed in was a constant reminder that our enemies were still out there, that they knew who we were.

"You want me to try and convince him to find Ulo?"

"He's all alone, Etcia. He's just a boy, Mania's age. Anything could happen to him out there. He could be shot or stabbed or burned. The wild animals could eat him. They can probably smell he's sick. They could be watching him, waiting for him to die."

I didn't know if the wild animals she was talking about were the Nazis, the Ukrainians, or the wolves.

"Etcia, please. You are the only one who can talk sense into Mendel. You don't know what it's like with everyone gone. You have Yossel, Mendel, your children. Ulo is my brother's child. He'd expect me to help him. I'd go out myself if I could."

She picked the glass of water up again, gulped down more sips, coughed.

"Okay, Yetta. I will do my best. I promise, I'll try."

An hour later, I met Mendel in a rock alcove near the kitchen, the area men went to smoke when they could find cigarettes. I was surprised to smell cigarette smoke, to hear him taking a long, slow drag.

"It's me, Etcia. Is that you, Mendel?"

"It's me."

"Have I died and gone to heaven, or are you smoking a cigarette there?" I said.

He laughed lightly. His fit had passed.

"Would you like to maybe share a pull with your older sister?"

"You don't smoke, Etcia."

"When I'm hungry, I smoke. Don't be greedy."

I sat down next to him and touched him on the thigh. Reluctantly, he gave me the cigarette. I brought it to my mouth, took a long, slow pull, and drew the smoke into my lungs. When I handed it back, I was dizzy.

"Smoking was partly how I bought my freedom," I explained. "When the police had me locked in that barn with all those men, I had a few cigarettes. I shared with the men. It helped them to trust me. It helped to convince them to take down Bordetski."

Mendel laughed, just barely, but he laughed.

"That must have been a sight. The old lackey fool."

"It was. But it was also terrifying. The only thought in my mind then was getting back to the children. I've sacrificed everything to make sure they are safe."

He inhaled the cigarette. My stomach dropped, and I felt slightly nauseous. Still, the tobacco smelled good, familiar.

"It is her brother's child, Mendel. It isn't safe."

"Leave me alone, Etcia. I've already been through this with Yetta. My decision is made."

"What if it were me who'd been killed and Dunia alone in the forest?"

"It wasn't."

"But what if it was?"

"It's a ridiculous argument. It isn't. Talk sense. You know what is real."

"What's real is that your wife's brother is dead. Her nephew is alive, and he is in danger. It's a miracle he stayed alive this long, but he won't last out there. She's asking for your help."

He jerked his body, made a move to stand up, then decided against it. "It's too dangerous. You know that."

"I know."

"What if I get caught out there? Then who takes care of Yetta and my daughter? What happens to Regina? Yetta doesn't think about that. She thinks only about herself. She doesn't see reality. She lives down here in a fantasy place. She doesn't know what's real!" He was yelling.

I waited for a while. Mendel's temper was a fire. If you fed it, it could cause an explosion. But if you let him sit with it for a while, it burned steady and eventually went out.

"Getting caught is a risk you take every time you leave the cave, Mendel."

He took a long drag, then exhaled. I think he snuffed it out, then put what was left in the top pocket of his shirt.

"And what if he is sick? He can infect everybody," he said.

"That is a risk. But if he's survived this whole time, his constitution is strong."

"They don't know exactly where he is. You don't know the difference. You always go the same routes. You always have a safe place to go."

"That's not true, Mendel. I know."

He was silent. We knew better than to ask too many of these kinds of questions. He rocked slightly, the way he had when he was a little boy and upset. Nobody except me would have noticed this.

"The boy must be smart. If he survived this long, he must be in a safe place," I said.

"It isn't where he is. It's where he isn't, all the places I'd have to look first to find him. You keep private, Etcia. The men don't tell you everything they have seen. It's bad out there."

"You think I don't know this? Tell me, when in the last two years has it been good? We have to choose our battles, but when we choose them, we must fight."

"This is not my battle."

"It should be."

"That's not for you to determine."

"Okay, that's it. If you don't go out there and find your nephew, I will do it myself."

"That's not going to happen. You wouldn't be able to find him, let alone carry him even five or six yards. Who knows what kind of condition he's in?"

"Exactly! Who knows what kind of condition he's in? We should take care of him. Mendel, he is family."

Mendel sighed. I waited until he stood up.

"That's all we have left, Mendel. Family. It's what keeps us strong. It's why we still live," I yelled in a voice so raw it surprised me.

"We are alive because we are lucky," he countered.

"There is no such thing," I replied.

"Well then, it's a fluke. You're right, Etcia. There is no luck. There's nothing to believe in at all anymore. There are no more rules."

"Exactly, Mendel. All we have left is who we are. We believe in ourselves, in our family and our heart. It's how we remember what's real."

"For God's sake, Etcia! Can't you women just leave me alone?" he screamed. His voice was shaky, though. I knew I had won. I leaned in and went for his throat.

"I don't care what you say. If you don't pick Ulo up, Mendel, I will. I'm serious."

Something, maybe a rock, rebounded off the wall. I wondered if Mendel had thrown it.

"Fine. You made your point. I will go pick up Ulo. But Etcia, if something happens, remember, I warned you."

He made a lot of noise shuffling down the corridor

I sat there for a while, trying not to think about what he had said.

I'd been sitting with Yetta half the night after Mendel had left, waiting. We were on a bed in a private nook just beyond our own sleeping quarters where we had prepared space for Ulo.

We had set a pot of water and one of the *triniszka* up in the corner so Yetta could treat his sores and boil his clothes without infecting anyone else. We had scissors to cut his hair. We even had a salve one of the men had obtained from a peasant on one of his journeys outside for his wife's sores..

Yetta and I sat side by side, each with a corner of her *varetta* blanket pulled up to our necks. We'd been waiting a long time. We didn't speak much. Yetta and I had never been that close. I liked her, though. She wasn't the kind of woman who wore her nerves on the ends of her skin. She hadn't lost her bearings.

"It feels like in the old days when somebody was ill and you stayed up praying for them, hoping they would pull through. It feels like that," Yetta said.

"Yes. It does."

We waited awhile. Yetta had prepared a special supper for Mendel before he went out. She gave him extra portions to keep him strong. The scent of wood smoke clung to her clothes.

"Two months. Just as long as we've been in the cave. How could he have lasted so long?" she said.

It wasn't a question that required an answer.

"He would be proud of you for looking after his son," I said.

She shivered once, then pulled the *varetta* higher over her neck.

"It is Mendel who is looking for him."

"Yes." I ran my hand over the *varetta*, using it to massage the palm of my hand.

"He's been gone a long time," Yetta said.

I rubbed my palm clockwise and counterclockwise. The matted fur tickled. I rubbed my palms together, then clasped them, put them on top of my belly. "Don't worry. Mendel will find Ulo. He will bring him back."

"I was wondering what it must be like for Nunia, for the other young children, who have been in the cave just as long as they walked the earth," she said.

"Maybe easier. They don't know anything different."

"Do you think so? Even babies must know how cold this place is. Imagine taking your first steps, barefoot, on this cold floor, living only in darkness."

I must have let my eyes close for a minute. I opened them and heard a sound like a heavy animal dragging a hurt leg. It took me awhile to decipher the voices: Mendel's and Yossel's. From in between them came the moans of an injured young boy.

"Ulo!" Yetta shrieked. "Oh, my Mendel, you did it! You brought him to me. You brought him back."

There were some half cheers, some laughter, and some concerned voices coming from different areas of the cave.

"For God sakes, clear the bed, Yetta! Move out of the way, woman; he's heavy. He needs to lie down."

We rolled off the bed and moved back to the wall while the six-legged animal—my two brothers holding Ulo between them—moved past us. They groaned and strained and lowered him onto the bed.

"Oh, my poor nephew," Yetta said. "You are so brave. Your father would be proud."

I lit a candle and put it by the bedside. Yetta was bent over her nephew. The light was bright enough to make out his face, which was covered with cuts and masses that could have been injuries or sores. His eyes were swollen so badly, it almost looked as if they were shut. His neck and chest almost sloped inwards.

He choked. Yetta raised his head up and put it on the pillow. I reached up and handed her a glass of water,

"Not yet," she said. I put the water back on the shelf.

I looked up at my brothers. I couldn't make out their faces, only the awkward way they were hunched over, as if they were ready to collapse themselves.

"Etcia, we are going to need hot water. Can you boil some? And some bandages. We need bandages. Do we still have those clean sheets we were saving? Can you tear one into thick, wide strips?" Yetta asked.

"Of course," I said. "I didn't know we had a nurse among us," I joked.

Yetta wasn't listening to me, though. I glanced at the bed where Ulo's body was twisted so badly, it almost looked like his elbow and knee joints were turned the wrong way. He was barely moving. He was half dead. I wondered how Mendel had found him and if he had had to walk him like that the whole way.

I stood up and walked towards my brothers. I reached over to Mendel and hugged him tightly. He reacted as if he were paralyzed at first, then gave in and relaxed.

"You did it. Good job," I said.

He patted me awkwardly on the back. "I will help you, Etcia. I know where there is some good dry wood," Mendel said.

"Me too. I think I know where there is some ointment. We can clean the cuts out," Yossel said.

Chapter Fourteen

T WAS PROBABLY midafternoon when I felt Dunia's body jerking beside me. I sat up, positioned my legs in front of me, and talked softly.

"Is something wrong, Dunia?"

"My damn hands."

"Don't curse."

"Sorry," he said and banged his hand hard.

"Don't do that. What is it?" I asked, then pulled his hand towards me and held it. He shook me off.

"It hurts. Like it fell asleep but never woke up. Damn!" he said, shaking it in the air so I heard it like a bird's wings beating and cracking bone. "It did it all last night. I couldn't get back to sleep. I didn't want to wake anyone, so I kept it still under me. Damn!" He kept whacking the hand on the side of the bed.

I sat up straighter, relieved. Finally, a normal problem to deal with.

"Stop doing that. You're going to wake your sister. It's okay, my boy. This is normal. Give me your hand. I know what it is."

Reluctantly, he came to sit near me. I took his hand in my own and held his wrist. I clamped my thumb on his palm and my middle finger on the back of his hand and pressed down hard, working my way out towards the knots. His hand was limp like a dead fish. As I rubbed, the sensation would return. He was silent as I worked.

As I felt his hand, I was surprised that his skin was no longer the soft baby skin I remembered. His hands were still as small as a boy's hands, but thick callouses lined them.

"Your father used to have this problem when he was building the foundation of our house. He was not used to working construction. His hands were too gentle. It comes from making the same motion over and over, or squeezing muscles. It went away but acted up sometimes. It was very painful to him, I remember. Sometimes it kept him up nights. It is a man's problem, my Dunia. Your hands are a man's."

His breath wheezed through his nose. I kneaded his palms and worked out each finger, relieved to have something practical to do. If oil had not been so precious, I would have rubbed some in the cracks in his skin.

"It was like pins and needles?" he asked.

"Sometimes, yes. But sometimes, your poppa said it was like shards of glass in his hands. It went numb. It was painful."

"What is it?"

"I forgot the name. It's not important. It may bother you for a while. It's nothing to worry about. But you should be proud. It is a man's problem. You got it because you are strong and working hard to help others, like your poppa. He worked so hard on that house and the store so that we'd have a good place to live. Did I ever tell you the story of how he built it?"

"Not really."

"Well, he had such big dreams for that house. Secretly I think he was building it to show off to my parents. You know, your granny and grampa didn't want me to marry your poppa at first. He was from a different station in life than we were. "

"What do you mean, 'different station'?"

"He didn't have as much money as we did. These things don't matter now, of course. They never really did. But your poppa and I fought to get married. We loved each other, and I really respected your poppa.

"We had to fight for rights to everything. Even the neighbors, Mr. and Mrs. Wilner, tried to sue us. They didn't want us to build there because they thought we would compete with them for customers. So when your poppa and I finally started to build, he got a little carried away. He built everything large. He worked hard his whole life. He wanted to have a place to provide for his family and for others in the community—it didn't matter if they were Jewish, Ukrainian, or gypsy, rich or poor. He did not discriminate with his kindness."

My throat was dry. It had been a while since I had spoken so much. I reached behind me and took a precious sip of the water we kept in the mug.

"We are still fighting now," Dunia said.

"We are still fighting. But your poppa paved the way. His generosity made us many friends. Those friends have helped us stay alive."

I put my hand on Dunia's forehead to steady him.

"Do you miss him, Momma?" he asked, his voice already drowsy.

"Of course. He will always have a place in my heart," I whispered. I kissed Dunia's forehead. Instead of squirming or pulling away as he had ever since he was Marek's age, he let me. His breath thickened.

I rolled onto my side on the mattress, just close enough so he didn't lose my body heat.

Chapter Fifteen

Y CHILDREN AND I sat in the common room on the stone benches, eating our food quietly. I lit a candle and placed it on the table, an act that might have invited criticism, but I didn't care. The children had to see me. I had to see them.

The candle was a small luxury I hoped would distract them from the bland food. The watered-down soup contained only a few pieces of potato, and our bread ration was getting smaller.

We ate in silence except for the sound of the slurping. I examined the children, trying to memorize their faces. Mania's blue eyes had a more serious set. There was a precision in the way she lifted the spoon, ate, and then brushed the sides of her lips with her fingers, pushing stray morsels back into her mouth. She was more self-possessed than I'd ever seen her.

Dunia was skinny, but his body had broadened like a tree trunk. His calloused hands tore the hunk of bread purposefully, making it clear his work had toughened him.

Marek still worried me. He was frail and in many ways such a baby. His deep lack of understanding about what was going on seemed impenetrable. He woke up sweating and got more chilled than the rest of us.

"Momma, can't we have some more soup?" Marek asked, then hunched his head down, deeply ashamed. He knew he couldn't. He hadn't asked that question in months.

I looked at him sternly. He flipped over his palm, then used his whole tongue to lick up the bread crumbs.

"How is Ulo Barad?" Mania asked, tactfully changing the subject.

"He isn't out of the woods yet, but Yetta is taking good care of him," I said.

Mania nodded and stared at the candle, formulating thoughts. "He's just two years older than me. He lasted months outside on his own. It's amazing," she said.

Marek was carefully eating his bread.

"He's a strong boy. A fighter. Like you," I said.

"What's wrong with Ulo?" Marek asked.

"You know, Marek. He got a skin infection when he was hiding in the woods. This was dangerous because the infection eventually poisons the blood. Your aunt Yetta is taking care of him, making sure that he gets better."

"Yes, but where are his mom and dad?" Marek asked.

Dunia clucked his tongue at Marek. "Don't be so nosy," he said.

"I'm not being nosy. I just want to know."

"They died, Marek," I said.

"How did they die?"

Dunia knocked the spoon. It bounced on the table.

"Dunia, don't be so clumsy. That's our only damned spoon,"

"Mania, don't curse," I said.

"I'm sorry. It's just the spoon. It's our only spoon. We have only two."

"How did they die?" Marek asked.

"They got sick," Dunia said.

"No, they didn't," Marek said. "Parents don't get sick anymore. The Nazis killed them."

Mania met my eyes. Neither of us was really surprised. Some of the young kids had been caught playing a made-up game in which some pretended they were Nazis and some pretended they were Jews. We couldn't make out the rules. We only knew they chased each other, that some kids ran and the others hid. Some of the parents were angry, but it was nothing to be angry about, really. The kids, like the rest of us, were finding their own strange ways to cope.

"Hey, Mania. I've got it. Your spoon. Now we still have two," Marek said.

"Thank you, Marek," she said. She poured the tiniest bit of water into her cup. "Why don't you use it before your soup gets cold?" she said and handed the spoon to Marek. He took it and greedily dipped it in the bowl.

"Mania, the next time I go out, I will bring us more spoons," I said.

Mania didn't respond. She was looking at the candle, deep in thought, as if the spoons were irrelevant to her now.

"Momma, do you think Aunt Yetta needs help taking care of Ulo? I'd like to help her if I could."

I smiled, broke off a hunk of bread, and put it in my mouth. It was tough. It hurt my teeth to chew. I swallowed,

"I will ask Aunt Yetta, but yes, I think that can be arranged."

Chapter Sixteen

I DON'T KNOW HOW I found myself lingering on the road outside our old house. Nobody was out, but it was still a fool's move. I stood like a ghost staring into the courtyard, at the wooden grape arbor Chaim had built himself, the bare twining vines spotted with snow. First, I recognized the yard had been cared for. The walkway had been shoveled. Then I noticed that the light was on in the kitchen and that a large-bodied woman was hunched over a stove.

Finally, I noticed the dog. He was a big black dog. He didn't look very aggressive. The proud way he was sitting on the bricks stunned me. An old primal anger pressed inside me—not that someone was living in our old house but at the dog. I stepped into the anger. It validated me. It was not right that the dog had more rights to live in my village than I did. It was not right that he was free.

As if he had been listening to my thoughts, the dog turned. He cocked his head towards me curiously. Everything inside me slowed, but I walked swiftly, forgetting to be afraid. When I got to the end of the road, my heart beat inside my ears, and my knees jellied. I followed an old childhood route, cutting through the downtown to the edge of the river until I finally made my way to Kostaski's yard.

———◆✦✦✦◆———

Joseph opened the back door and took a step back to let me in without a word. It was only when we got to the kitchen table and he moved the chair back for me to sit down that I worried I'd made a mistake. I didn't really have a choice. There were no summer houses on the way back to the cave. The fields had been picked through.

His eyes were tender. I wondered for a moment if it was because he was feeling sorry for me. But his look didn't reveal pity, only warmth. His gaze felt almost too intimate.

He glanced once towards the door, then down the hall where his wife slept. For the first time, I wondered if her inability to hear well gave Kostaski a certain kind of invisibility too. They must have used words sparingly, as we did.

"I didn't know where else to go," I said.

He closed his eyes, shook his head as if the statement were irrelevant.

"I wasn't followed."

He nodded. His blue eyes were watery, pained even. His face was still round, but worry pinched his forehead. What was happening hurt him, possibly in many of the same ways it hurt us.

"How are the children?" he asked.

I nodded, took a long sip of the water. His blue eyes shined at me in a way that looked almost embarrassed. I cupped my hand around the hole I had made in the elbow of my shirt from scrubbing it so hard, then slyly scraped some cave mud from my wrist. The shirt didn't fit anymore. It hung off my body.

"How are the shoes?" I asked.

"Not so good, but we get by. I wish Chaim were still around. Nobody's buying shoes, but at least he'd be able to repair our shoes, make them last longer."

Chaim and Kostaski had been friendly. Although Chaim was older than Kostaski and more educated, to me they seemed like equally important men.

We sat in silence for a while. Joseph brushed my hand lightly without meaning to and then got up. He spent a while fiddling at the stove, then brought me a cup of soup and a spoon. He put it down in front of me. He lingered long enough for me to feel the solidity of him, then allowed me my privacy.

"Thank you," I whispered before he sat down.

The soup was watery, like ours, but there were vegetables in it—carrots, parsley, and potato. It smelled so rich of onion and dill, it made me dizzy just to lift the spoon. I did so anyhow, blowing on the liquid like a polite person and trying to resist the urge to gobble it down. If I ate too quickly, I'd probably be sick.

"The soup is wonderful. Please thank your wife for me," I managed.

He nodded. He was a quiet, thoughtful man, who showed how he thought through his actions. "I had a feeling you would come soon," he said simply.

The curtains were drawn, and there was no noise coming from the road. I hadn't seen any soldiers on the street or motorcycles.

"I saw our house, mine and Chaim's," I finally said. The words barely made it past my throat.

Joseph rubbed his beard scruff. He'd spent hours in the shop talking to Chaim about current events. He knew how important the house had been to Chaim.

"Bastards," he said. His jaw tightened.

I closed my eyes, put my hand on the tabletop, and pressed my spine against the back of the chair. Without trying to, simply by speaking the truth, Joseph gave me dignity. Being around him always made sense.

The light flickered in the kitchen. Despite the bright blue paint on the table, the room seemed gloomy, almost distorted.

"I'm sorry. I don't have much time," I said. These were not times to mince words.

He nodded and went into the other room. The sound of cans banging and bags rustling both soothed and humiliated me. The war had made me a different person. By that point, I'd rather have stolen than beg.

Joseph came back with a bag and left it discreetly on the floor next to me. I started to get up.

"Sit down, Etcia. Please, relax. You have time."

It was not really a request, so I sat down. I always knew Joseph, like my Chaim, was a good man to customers and friends. I never really knew what he was made of, though, until the war. I saw then that Yetta was wrong—Joseph didn't see risking his life to be kind to us as a choice.

I examined him, his bald head and broad chest. He was solid and calm. He made sense. I realized how much safer I felt simply being around him.

"I care for you, Etcia," he said, as if reading my thoughts.

I looked up, surprised. He stared down at his hands, then at my own. His cheeks reddened. Dizziness rushed me.

"I have to go now," I said and rose, hoisting the bag from the floor. He stood up too, pushed back the chair, and followed me out to the door.

Chapter Seventeen

STARTED WORRYING ABOUT the boredom. It was true that the children had to sleep long enough to forget about food, but I didn't want their minds to soften with their bodies. When they slept, they lived in their dreams. When they woke up, it was easy for them to lose touch with what was real. I appreciated time alone with my own thoughts, but the hours when we were awake together could be precious. I was determined to use them to build up their minds.

"Mania, are you awake?" I asked.

She grunted. I thought of Mania's frailty, of her bony hips and clammy skin.

"Later I will ask you to help with the laundry," I said.

"Why?"

"You are fifteen. You must pull your own weight here. Everyone helps," I said. Mania's moods moved in and out of hopelessness, frequently coming across as teenage temper tantrums.

"What can I do?" Marek said.

"Are you awake?" I asked.

"We are all awake," Dunia snapped.

I was surprised. We slept close together, almost as if we were one organism, and I had not noticed I was not the only one with my eyes open.

"Of course we are. Isn't it lovely?" I bluffed. "Tell me, my Marek, do you remember what it was that you dreamed?" I asked.

Marek was slow to respond. The darkness was sticky.

"I don't remember," he said.

"Try, baby. Did you dream about your old friends?"

"No."

Dunia made his horse-snorting noise.

"Maybe I dreamed I was outside. I miss it there," Marek said.

Grief is most terrible when there are no words to describe what is missing.

"What do you miss most?"

"What do you mean?"

"Well, think back to your old life. Tell me what you are most missing. Do you miss the stars, or maybe the way the grass feels when you walk in your naked feet?" I said, tickling him. Marek giggled.

"The sun. I miss the sun," Mania piped in. "The way that it feels on my hair and turns it red when we play outside in the summer."

"Yes, I miss that too," I said. "What do you miss, Marek?"

"I miss the trees. I miss getting fruit off the trees in the orchard and going to play with the boys at the river, catching those little frog fishies," he said.

"Tadpoles," Dunia said in a scolding tone.

"And what do you miss most, Dunia?" I asked.

"Nothing."

The silence that followed his answer was broken by the sound of a draft seeping through. It sounded like someone pressing a piece of folded paper to their lips and whistling. A creature in the cave made that sound.

"What's the use pretending?" Dunia said. "There is nothing here. Just darkness. If I touch someone, it's like they are a ghost."

"There are no ghosts here. Right, Momma? You said!" Marek exclaimed.

"No, Marek," Dunia said, "I don't mean a real ghost. There are no ghosts. I'm sorry."

"There are no ghosts, period," I said. "We are here. We breathe and walk and eat and talk and dream. We always remember who we are."

"Dunia, tell me," Marek said. "Tell what you miss."

Dunia sighed heavily.

"Please?" begged Marek.

"I miss playing ball in the school yard," Mania said. "I miss walking wherever I want. I miss having my friends sleep over and eating real food and seeing my brothers with a real light. I miss looking into a mirror and brushing my hair. Don't you miss those things, Dunia?"

"Yes, Mania. You are right. I miss those things too," he said.

<hr />

In the cave, I learned that there are certain senses human beings have that can be felt but not really defined. You don't use them often. One is the sense of love. When I heard my children still breathing, I was reminded why I still walked the earth. There was also the electrical sense of threat, of present danger. That sense jolted me when I heard our men's voices crackling in the air. There was no question. Something had happened.

I was already standing up before I realized I had moved. By the time I'd counted the twenty-eight and a half steps from my bed to the narrow corridor, I wanted to get the news first, to have a few seconds to figure out a way to break it to the children.

I heard the men's footsteps and whispered, "Yossel." His heavy hand pressed down on my shoulder.

"The entrance is blocked. We stand in a grave," a woman moaned down the corridor.

"Get the children, Etcia. Keep them quiet. We will holler if you need to run."

"Yossel, what do you mean? What's happening?" I asked.

"Mendel discovered it when he tried to go out. The entrance has been sealed, blocked with rocks and mud."

"The entrance to the cave is blocked! We will all die here of starvation!" Mendel screamed.

A sigh escaped from my lips. It surprised me. We all knew this moment would occur. Of course they had found us. Somebody probably had always known where we were.

"I knew somebody had seen us," a man's voice jittered in the distance. "They have known for a while. Ukrainians, the soldiers, who knows? Somebody who wants us to die."

Someone else laughed uneasily.

"Etcia, sit down. Are you okay?" Yossel asked.

"What time is it now?" I asked.

Yossel touched my shoulder and squeezed it. "We think they have left. The hole has been sealed for a few hours," he said.

"Yossel, why didn't you wake us?!" I said.

"We are looking now for another exit," Yossel said.

His voice, laced with fear, sounded so young, there was almost a sweetness in it. It woke me out of my stupor. The person standing next to me was no longer the grown man who had served in the Polish army, who was a father and husband. It was my younger brother. He had worked so hard to find the place, to bring us down here. He was so hopeful we'd live. The last thing I wanted was for him to be disappointed.

A bitter anger rose in me. *How dare they disturb us now?* I thought. *How dare they?!*

"Go," I hissed. "Go, Yossel, now."

———◆•◆••◆•◆———

I didn't know how much time had passed. I knew only that the children had dozed off. Sleep had become their safety net. They slept most ferociously when they were afraid, almost as if it were a rebellious childhood act. With the terror shut out, they could retreat into their dreams where they were free to lie in the grass and stare up at the moon and the stars.

I was marveling at their ability to protect themselves by retreating into sleep, at the even, undisturbed sound of their breath, when Mania shuddered beside me and began tearing at her hair and screeching.

"Mania, what's the matter? What's wrong?" I asked.

"No, get out! Momma, make him stop!" she screeched.

"Mania, what's wrong?!" I was screaming by now.

There was a long, painful silence. Then Mania started laughing. She laughed so hard and loud, even Marek woke up, rubbing his eyes.

"Mania, stop it," Marek whined.

"What's wrong? Come here," I repeated to Mania.

"Sorry. No. It was dumb. I thought there was a bat in my hair. When I woke up, it felt like there was a bat in my hair. It must have been a nightmare. It's okay, Marek. Go to sleep."

It was a terror we all shared, especially the women. Someone had spoken of the way bats could get stuck in your hair by accident because they couldn't see. If they flew into your hair, they became tangled and then terrified, screeching in your ears and clawing your head. So far this hadn't happened, but it could, and we all knew it. One of the women had even sheared off her hair to prevent it from happening to her.

"Do you want me to brush your hair, Mania?" I asked. My own head was heavy, like a leaden weight supported by my neck. I wasn't sure I could lift it.

"No. I want to get out of here,"

"We will." Yossel's voice beamed like a flashlight into the dark space behind Mania's head.

Mania shrieked, then laughed. "Uncle Yossel!" she cried and then laughed again.

"It's okay, Mania. You have to be brave and stay calm. We found a place for a new entrance ten yards from our old entrance. There's a space between two rocks. We are digging. We are taking shifts."

I sighed. "Isn't it too close?" I asked.

"Yes. If it works, we will hide it. Then we'll look for another," he said.

"Shouldn't we just leave? They know we're here. What's stopping them from coming down?" Dunia said.

Things had changed. It was no longer fair to keep secrets from the children.

"There are two factors in our favor," said Yossel. "One, the old entrance is too small. You have to enter feet first, one by one. We have men standing guard. If someone tries to come in, we will clobber him before he has a chance to squeeze in."

"They can shoot down," Mania said.

"To their feet, yes," Yossel said. "They can't get the gun in before their bodies."

"We shouldn't stay," Dunia said.

"We shouldn't stay," Marek mimicked.

"Hush. It is not your choice," I said.

"They can give their opinion. It's okay," Yossel said. "You aren't wrong, Dunia. We all thought about it. We all gave our opinions. Even your momma. We decided it's the best thing for us if we stay here. The ones who found us will grow bored. They will assume we have died. The fact that we have lasted so long down here means it's a safe place. Others are not as lucky."

Nobody responded right away. We each remembered stories of all the people gunned down in their houses, burned in the fields. Many of the children's friends had been killed. There was no place left for us up there.

"Can I help?" Dunia said.

"Etcia?" Yossel asked.

I hesitated for only a second. "Okay, Dunia. You go."

<hr />

If the Christian idea of hell is real, we were in it. As we waited for the new entrance to be dug, the cave truly felt like a grave. The suffocating feeling I had felt in my chest when we first arrived returned, but it was worse. It used to be I could loosen that feeling with my fist. After the cave was sealed off, it was as if concrete had hardened there. There was also a lump in my throat. It was hard to swallow or speak, even to the children.

I tried to keep it together. There is only so far a human being can be pushed. And we all fed off each other. When one of us panicked, we all were in danger of being infected. That's why we always tried to provide comfort, to talk others out of their fear.

"How is this possible?" a woman wailed.

"Shhh," came the voices of her neighbors. "You must stay calm. Be quiet. For God's sake, shut up."

This is how the time passed. We sat in our spots, fear pressed against the small of our ramrod-straight backs, slithering on us like a clammy snake. We barely slept. Someone cried out. Someone else vomited.

It infected us all. I lay next to the children, railing on the inside against the others. I knew my anger was misplaced, but that didn't make it go away. The rage was toothy, ever present. It gnawed on me at night.

Other strange things happened. The scent of sour animal milk returned. I put the back of my hand on Marek's forehead, and it was so clammy, I thought he was dead. Before I knew what I was doing, I'd physically shaken him, startling him awake. The sound of his cry was the greatest blessing in the world.

Sometimes, when it became too much, I stood up and paced. Movement, even within a limited area, seemed wise. My legs were heavy, though. The ground was so cold that it hurt my feet. My body was as lumpy and misshapen as clay. My mind wasn't clear. I lost count of the number of steps. And I wasn't alone. Often I bumped into somebody else pacing, somebody else who had lost his or her footing, forgotten how to count the steps. We were prisoners, penitents, wild animals pacing our cells.

We moaned, ghosts left in an in-between realm, a place where our bodies withered, where the air suffocated us. In this place there was no God.

Calm down, Etcia. Stay calm. For the children. You've been through worse, I told myself, pressing my palm into my chest.

It wasn't true, though. Hope was almost futile. Death felt more real.

I forced the children to lie down again, tried to get them to relax. Mania and Marek lay on either side of me. Mania was facing the corridor where her uncle had first emerged. Her body was a gnarled stick. She wouldn't allow herself to turn back around. Her determination not to move was ferocious. It was a new quality I'd noticed in my daughter, and it brought me hope. I prayed her determination would keep her fighting.

Fear ran in cycles, unnaturally, like the sunless days. It would seize our bodies for a while, terrorizing us until it ran through our system and we became numb to it, hollow. Emotions accompanied the fear—shock, disbelief, anger, sadness, rage—magnifying all our worst qualities.

After a while, though, a funny thing happened. Gradually we became accustomed to the fear. Our reactions were barely human anymore. We no longer cared.

My mind changed. I started thinking I'd rather be murdered than to have to watch my children die from starvation. Images of their concave bodies, of Mania eating her hair, of Dunia trying to rip out one of his ribs, of Marek drinking his tears haunted me. Exhaustion did funny things to the brain.

Those odd thoughts floated through my mind while I lay there rubbing Mania's back in small circles to keep her warm. Marek fell in and out of sleep. Every so often, I felt Dunia staring at me. He wanted to join the search party. He was like me. He couldn't stand being still.

"Mania, come closer," I said. Her body flinched once. I ran my fingertips over her hair. "You are safe, baby," I whispered.

After a few seconds, the wood creaked. She'd finally turned.

"Why do you say this? Why do you lie?" Mania hissed.

I considered scolding her for her fresh mouth. I decided against it.

"What if they never make another exit? I don't want to die here. I don't want to die!" she exclaimed.

"Then you won't."

Mania's lips smacked. She'd gotten in the habit of wetting them with her salvia because they were so dry. It just made them drier. More than once, I touched blood on them where they cracked. Correcting her just made it worse.

"They will make another exit. God will show them a way," I said.

Dunia made a noise like a horse's snort. He was taking after his uncle Mendel, imitating the raw, angry way he railed at the world. *Let him*, I thought. He, more than any of the children, suffered without having his father around. At the same time, his bitterness suited him in the cave. I thought the fire in his belly might save him. It might even help us.

———◆❖◆———

Each hour brought a new level of despair. My mother woke up screaming, having dreamed of a Nazi with bad breath and a beard pointing a gun at her temple. It took us awhile to convince her he was gone. A child cried for so long, he lost his voice. His mother was obsessed with the idea that it had been stolen, that it would never come back. One of the men who was digging had passed out. It took the other men a long time to revive him. Collectively, we had practically stopped eating. That one fact alone made me believe we'd survive—despite it all, we were thinking ahead.

For the first time, real fighting occurred. A man slapped his wife. The other men pulled him away before he could hurt her. For a long time, we had to listen to the wife's strangled sobs, the husband pleading with her to forgive him.

We were not ourselves.

We were becoming who they wanted us to be.

I vowed not to let that happen to us.

Mendel came back reeking of sweat and desperation. He glugged water loudly. His breath was tearing in his chest. His panic seized me.

"Nothing yet. Every time we get close to the surface, the earth falls on us. It is like being buried alive. I don't know what we're going to do."

Mendel sat on the edge of the bed, catching his breath. Fradel poured more water.

"You are doing the best that you can," I said, though I no longer believed it. I could think of nothing worse than being sealed inside this cave forever, watching my children starve. What would happen to us?

"Our best isn't good enough," he screeched.

"Mendel, calm down," Fradel said.

He slammed his hands into the bed and stood up. His footsteps plodded down the hall. We heard him calling to the other men, "Hello. It's Mendel. I'm coming in." Someone's holler in the distance echoed back.

I sat on my sister Fradel's bed, close enough to the children that I could still bolt over there if I needed to. Terror was a poison we were afraid to breathe in. It hollowed us out, exhausted us. I put my hands on my thighs, slapping them every few minutes to remind myself they were mine. The cave was filled with the raspy sound of snoring, a woman panicking, the swallowed gasp of the end of a good cry. Among those crying women was my sister Fradel.

"We will die here," Fradel said.

I found myself getting impatient with her, even angry. I knew it was because deep down, I believed the words she was saying. At moments, the weight on my chest was so heavy that breathing hurt my chest.

The place where we had created Khatki, our home in the cave, had been far enough away from the sinkhole to help us forget that we were trapped. We saw neither moon nor uniforms, could hear neither wind nor the sound of boots tromping the ground.

We got updates of news from our travels outside, a pamphlet, an old flier, a report from someone who knew we were alive, but the puzzle would always have missing pieces. We didn't really know whether Hitler's army was advancing or retreating, whether the Russians had burned down the countryside, or if there were any Jews left in Ukraine or Europe at all. Up until now, we had tuned out our terror like a station on the store radio with bad reception. But now there was no longer any option of changing the station.

I was reminded of how vast the cave was. It would be a miracle if the men who were exploring the cave with their axes, the little bits of colored string they used to mark their steps, found their way back.

"We can't think that way," I said. "There is always hope. When I was in jail with all those men, we didn't stop fighting. We will find a way. We have to."

Fradel sighed. My kind, sweet sister was always so loyal.

I touched Fradel's hand. We had always been close. It was not right that she might never marry, never have children. It was her right to do these things.

"I sometimes wonder what Father would do in this situation," Fradel said.

I swallowed hard. It hurt. My throat was so parched, there was barely any saliva.

"He would tell us to have courage," I replied. "He would tell us to fight. He fought for us all up until the end. He would want us to do the same for each other. There is no choice."

Fradel rapped her knuckles on her wrist, bone cracking bone. It made me cringe.

"I've always admired you, Etcia. Even in the worst situation like this, you can find something good to talk about. But this is not good, Etcia. We have to face reality. We have been left here to die. They didn't throw us in the pit with the others. They didn't have to. We dug our own grave. They didn't have to tell us to lie in it. We did it ourselves."

I didn't want to hear anymore. "Shh, don't talk like that. Think about what we have already been through."

"I watched. Have you ever smelled people burning before, Etcia?"

I didn't respond. She already knew the answer.

"The smell never leaves you."

I waited for a minute, let the darkness soak up all the poison. "I'm sorry," I said.

"Don't be. You did not do this. We are still here because people are not all like that."

"True. And we are still here because God has not left us," I said.

Fradel whacked the side of the bed with her hand so hard, I could feel it in my legs. "You are crazy," she said, then laughed.

I took a deep breath. My body was so cold, I had no energy to move, to get under the blanket.

"Join me. Believe the men will find a way out. Belief. It's simply a choice," I said.

In some ways, it was almost a relief that it had finally happened. Living in the darkness deep under the ground, there was so much confusion. What we knew of life above ground was senseless. The people who had sealed up the cave at least were real. They gave me a place to focus my anger.

To talk myself down, I thought about sensible, organized things. In my mind, I walked through the rooms of our old house, of my parents' house, remembering dresses and furniture and paintings. I walked through the barn, naming the horses one by one: *In the first stall is a brown Russian don. She has a long, hairy mane and will snatch apples out of your hand. In the next stall is a white horse. She was four years old when we left. In the next is a black mare. My parents rescued her.*

I concentrated, catching the scent of the barn, musky with the bodies of horses and waste and hay. "Horse perfume," my father had called it.

There was a commotion on the other side of the cave. I dropped my legs onto the floor, pushed my body forward, and stood up. My hips creaked. The cold mud floor sent chill waves through my calves, and my knees felt as if they had turned to water. I had gotten up too quickly. I went over to Fradel's quarters for news.

"Fradel, it's Etcia. Are you there?"

"Behind you," she said.

I turned to face the place where she lay on the bed with the baby.

"Etcia, it's not good," my mother said from behind Fradel.

"Tell me."

"One of the men dug so high, the lamp gave out," Fradel said. "There was not enough oxygen for the kerosene. He left for a new lamp. When he went back, he found the tunnel had caved in."

"Is anyone hurt?" I asked.

"We don't know. Can you send Dunia to check?" Fradel asked.

I couldn't breathe right. It was as if someone had cored out my heart. "I will send him."

———◆·•••·◆———

I didn't pray so much anymore. I had a new relationship with God. It wasn't that I didn't believe. I probably believed more than I ever had before. It was just that praying required energy. And sometimes it felt like a futile exercise. We trusted in God but relied on ourselves.

When Dunia and my brothers were gone, I remembered to pray. I prayed hard, asking God to keep them safe, to make sure they weren't buried alive. I tried to remember the prayers. *Barukh ata Adonai Eloheinu, melekh ha`olam.*

I imagined the bats roosting in the spaces they'd dug, imagined their shrieking surrounding the men.

Barukh ata Adonai Eloheinu, melekh ha`olam.

The hole in my heart remained. It was as if I could feel the air leaking out.

Melekh ha`olam. Please, God, keep them safe.

Footsteps plodded on the earth. A man groaned. Then another. They were wheezing, coughing. Finally Dunia came back and collapsed on the bed next to me.

"Dunia, thank God you are okay," I said. I attempted to squeeze him, but he rolled to the other side of the bed. I grabbed his arm, touching his soft skin. I rubbed it. There was no dirt or mud on it.

"How are your uncles?" I asked.

"All the men are fine, Momma," he said.

The missing core of my heart returned. "What is it like?"

"Not good."

Behind me, a woman was singing a low dirge, a Hebrew song.

"Whatever they clear comes back down on them," Dunia said.

I leaned my head back on the pillow. The rhythm of praying continued. *Barukh ata Adonai Eloheinu, melekh ha`olam.*

Three days later, our prayers were almost answered—one of the men pushed his hand through an opening a few yards from the original entrance and felt warm wind and rain. Although it wasn't safe to be anywhere near the opening that had been discovered by the outside world, just knowing that it was possible to find another path out was a huge comfort.

The men sealed the entrance and covered it with a board.

Meanwhile, they continued looking for another exit, and we continued to wait.

<hr/>

The terrain of the cave was tough—blue clay thick as concrete in some spots. The men worked tirelessly to find places where it was penetrable, spearing their shovels into places that looked promising. They came back reeking of sweat and clay. Some of them were sweating so badly, they caught a chill, and we had to force them under a *varetta* so that they would warm up. A few times the overexertion caused them to vomit. There was not much food in their bodies, so only liquid bile came up.

When they finally broke through to the world above, the news traveled from the mouths of two young children, who ran clip-clopping into our sleeping area like an anxious herd of mountain goats. "They found it! They found it! There is a spot!" they screamed. Their voices were both sweet and bestial. They echoed through us. I touched Mania's hand, and we both started laughing.

Not too long afterwards, Yossel came back. He and Fradel came to our sleeping quarters. He knelt down beside me, talking softly, as if conserving energy, selecting only the most important details.

"There was earth that fell from two rocks above. It made a hill. It was enough for us to climb on. We built steps leading up. We are digging there now," he said.

"It looks promising, Yossel?" I asked.

"Yes," he said.

My brother had learned this manner of conserving speech from my father, who had been a man of action, not words. My father's direct manner of speaking had been a source of his pride. Yossel seemed to have taken it on in the cave during the most terrifying moments, when others' loudness belied a loosening grip on reality. I was again proud of the man my brother had become.

"When do you think you will know?"

"It is slow going. The earth is thick. We must be careful not to loosen the sand."

"I can send the children with water," I said.

"No need. We are taking shifts," he said.

Chapter Eighteen

September

THREE WEEKS LATER, most of the men had given up. They lay like rocks on their beds, waiting to die. A rage coursed inside me. I directed it towards the men because they could not find a way out, but it really stemmed deeper than that. I was finally enraged at the people who had done this to us, the ones who had blocked us in here, the ones who had taken over our village and forced us to run. I was mad at the police who had punched me in the nose and put me in jail, at the doctor who could not save my Chaim, at every person in the village who had turned my children away. I was angry at everyone, at myself. I was angry at God. I couldn't believe this was how we were going to die. It was just so unfair.

I walked over to Yossel's bed and touched him on the back. He jumped. "It's just me, Etcia," I said.

He moaned. On the other side of the bed, Pepcia was rocking the baby.

"You have not given up," I said.

"It's our own fault," he said.

My heart sank. I could deal with anything but my brother's disappointment. "Tell me," I said.

"We were distracted. Keeping busy. Making the best grinder. Building imaginary farms."

I laughed internally. The women had made jokes about the things the men did to entertain themselves, making contraptions on beds. When they ran out of things to do, they turned to their imagination. Mendel spent much of his days building an imaginary farm in another country. He had planned all the crops, the horses and donkeys. It was no different from what we women did. We wove rugs. We tilled old memories of places and people in our minds.

"That is not wrong. That is sanity. Keeping our minds sharp."

"Laziness. Complacency," Yossel hissed.

I touched his back. I said nothing. I waited.

"We should have looked for a second entrance sooner," he said.

"Maybe. But then, Yossel, maybe there wouldn't have been one."

———◆◆◆◆◆———

The cave was too quiet. There was no longer reason to speak. We no longer believed they'd murder us in our sleep. It was more likely they had simply left us here to die.

Nobody had been out of the cave in weeks. My children sinking deeper into blackness was an additional insult. My heart couldn't take it.

One morning, I started talking to them the only way I knew how. I lectured.

"Just believe, children. You cannot lose hope. We will be back home soon. One day, this cave, this life, will just be part of a dream."

"What for? Our friends are gone. They have already forgotten us," Mania said.

It surprised me that Mania was still thinking of girlish things like her school friends. It didn't matter to her that most of them were probably dead. Hope glinted occasionally like the metal bobby pins she kept in her hair.

"They have not forgotten you. Have you forgotten them?"

She paused, considering this for a moment.

"I don't know. Sometimes I can't remember their faces anymore. Barely their names."

"Try."

She didn't respond. I tried to remember Mania's friends. I remembered some Jewish girls—Sarah and Rebka—and I remembered a red-headed Polish girl. She wore pigtails and braids. She and Mania had played jacks in our yard. They must have been about ten.

"Do you remember your best friend when you were maybe ten? She had red hair, and she always wore it in braids. She had a green dress with pockets. Her last name was Yablonsky, I think."

"Oh yes, Vladka. Her name was Vladka. She was my best friend," Mania exclaimed. Her voice sounded childlike again.

I breathed deeply and exhaled, feeling my large breasts rise and fall, the light and air return to my chest. I knew what to do.

"Oh yes. Izidor Yablonsky was her father. He was the director of your school. Do you remember the school trip you took with your class to Zalishchyky?"

"I don't remember any trip."

"Yes you do, silly. Zalishchyky—that nice town in Poland, about fifteen miles from Korolówka. It is shaped like a horseshoe and is on the Dnister River. It is always warm there. The rich people from Poland often vacation there, but sometimes we did too. Your father and I went there a few times ourselves."

"You swam there," Marek said sleepily.

"Oh yes. And I remember there was one story about Zalishchyky I heard when you were just one month old, my Marek. You were so small you practically fit in the crook of my arm. This story takes place in July 1936.

"There was a teacher, Stephan Demkovich, and he and his assistant Galina Kubyak took some students from seventh and eighth grade there by horse carts one morning very early. Oh, they had such a good time. They visited all kinds of places, like a local museum and an agronomic station. They visited Poniatowski Palace, which has beautiful gardens and was built such a long time ago, in the eighteenth century."

"When was that?" Marek asked.

"A long time ago. I think I remember that place now. There was grass, and you could sit by the river, and we had ice cream and sweet water," Mania said.

I waited. The trill of her voice was delightful. She smacked her lips again and moved, just slightly, closer to me. Her rib cage didn't seem as high anymore, the way it was when she was constantly holding her breath.

"Yes. That is a nice treat.

"These students, after lunch they went to see St. Stanislaus, the Roman Catholic church. They also went to see the large synagogue in town. It was a beautiful synagogue, with one-meter-thick walls and copper plating and beautiful ornaments. It was so tall and glorious. Your father and I saw that one too.

"Later the teacher asked the students if they wanted to swim in the river near a nice sandy beach. Of course, they were delighted. The sun was still shining, and they went to the river and swam and played games. Their teacher was a good swimmer. He swam far. Everyone was in such a happy mood.

"After a while, the students were coming out of the river and drying themselves off with towels on the beach. The assistant, Galina Kubyak, was with them. She was a beautiful young unmarried woman, and the students all loved her.

"A few minutes later, everyone started laughing and pointing. The teacher, Stephan Demkovich, was walking out of the water. He couldn't figure out why everyone was laughing at him. It took him awhile until he was almost out of the water, and all the students were laughing so hard, they were practically crying at seeing what had happened. The teacher's bathing suit had somehow come off. He stood there for a second, trying to figure out what to do. He turned around and waded back to the water, showing his naked tushie, and he ran and swam until he was back under the water. Everyone was laughing so hard."

Dunia made his horse snort again, but underneath it there was laughter. Mania couldn't help herself. She started laughing too.

"So what happened, Momma? How did he get home?" Marek asked. He was laughing because his brother and sister were laughing, but he wasn't sure exactly why. His question made Mania and Dunia laugh again.

"Well, his assistant brought him a towel and handed it to him with her eyes closed. And the teacher laughed, and it became a great joke that he told every time somebody mentioned that school excursion to Zalishchyky. So you see, children, sometimes funny things can happen when you least expect them to. And a funny story can really stick in your memory," I said.

I combed Mania's hair with my hand, and she moved a little closer.

There were just six potatoes and a half-loaf of bread left, but at least we had a bit of light in our hearts.

Fradel, Meimel, Mania, and I stood by the buckets at the lake, washing clothes. Meimel agitated the clothes, stirring them with a stick in the bucket. Fradel wrung them out. I scrubbed and rinsed them and then handed them to Mania to hang while we worked. It was one small thing we did to return normalcy to our lives. It might have seemed important to wash the clothes to keep infections from us, to keep away bugs, to keep us more comfortable, but we performed this ritual more out of habit than anything else, for something constructive to do. We often wore the clothes so long, it almost felt as if they were growing out of our bodies. They itched. They always smelled a bit sour.

But we didn't really notice how fetid our garments had become until we took them off to clean.

Washing the clothes made them more threadbare. Pushing the brush over the clothes on the board tore them. We tried to scrub gently enough to keep them whole yet hard enough to actually clean them. We faced the same problem wringing them out. It took at least two days for them to dry, and even then, they were always still a little bit damp. Most of us had only one change of clothing. Some of us didn't even have that. And the longer we were down there, the more precious the water became. So even washing clothes left us vulnerable.

We mostly cleaned clothes for those of us who ventured above ground because the mud-caked clothes marked us as something other than ordinary Ukrainian peasants. We also wanted to be somewhat presentable to the families who helped us. But we didn't have this reason to motivate us on this particular day.

It had been nearly a month since we had been shut in. "The grain will not last. It's not enough," Meimel said.

"True," I responded.

"They have forgotten about us, the police and the Nazis. We would've been caught already. We would have at least heard someone at the boulder," Fradel said.

Meimel sighed heavily, then went back to sloshing the clothes in the water. The scent of the old clothes pervaded the part of the cave where we stood.

"The Ukrainians think we're armed down here. They think we travel the cave tunnels forever, that there are entrances for miles around," Meimel said.

"Where did they come up with that?" I asked.

Meimel laughed, a light, almost girlish laugh. The water sloshed. Fradel breathed heavily as she wrung out the clothes.

"Just a rumor. One of the men," Meimel said.

I laughed. Even in the cave, it was still fun to make fun of the men.

"It's amazing how even down here, where we are sealed off from the world, there is gossip," Mania exclaimed. The way she said it was womanly, as if she were trying to be part of our tribe. I had decided to treat her that way, to toughen her. Before we were trapped, I thought shielding her from the news was the best response to her frailty. But I had learned my girl was tougher than I had expected. She was wired like me—uncertainty and lack of definition bothered her. It was better for her to know what was real.

"It's possible they are just waiting for us to go outside," Fradel said.

The brush made a harsh scratching sound as it rubbed against the board. I cringed, imagining the clothes ripping. This was delicate work.

"It's possible," I agreed. "Still, we can't wait forever. My family can't last much longer. Everyone's supplies must be running out."

We worked in silence for a while. I handed a shirt to Mania, deliberately touching her hand, praying that the news didn't upset her. She touched my hand gently and took the shirt. She didn't seem fazed.

"True. We can't wait forever," Meimel said.

Chapter Nineteen

THE CHILDREN FOLLOWED me into a corner of the cave without knowing why I had called them there. They sat on a ledge. I took our precious candle, put it on the stand, and lit it. My head was covered with a kerchief.

"Children, it is September thirteenth. This is the day your father went to visit God. We light this candle to remember him."

I remembered the candle in the thick glass on my mother and father's windowsill when my grandmother passed. It burned for twenty-four hours. Chaim's candle would not burn as long. It was just as precious, though.

I went through the motions of prayer while the children sat open-mouthed around me. They didn't know what to do. I didn't really know either. Chaim's death had been only a few years before we went down to the cave. We were so young then, so foolish. We had no idea what human beings were capable of.

"Who would have believed back then how we'd be living now?" I said aloud without meaning to.

"How can there be a God when all this is happening?" Dunia said almost at the same time. "How can there be a God if he took my father?" he continued.

I stared at the flickering candle, alight despite the draft. I bowed my head slightly, then turned towards Marek and held his hands.

"Your father was ill. He had a disease. He died a natural death. He was buried in the cemetery. He had a headstone. He died because it was his time."

Mania whimpered softly behind me. She had been crying like that a lot. Often there didn't seem to be any reason.

"Children, come closer," I said.

Reluctantly, Marek and Mania moved closer. Dunia stood stock-still. I didn't let go of his hands.

"I do not always have all the answers. But whatever happens, I don't lose my belief. What I believe is that your father, my Chaim, is looking out for us, that he has always watched over us. I believe he is keeping us safe. Look at how hard we have been fighting, how we survive when so many have not. We are still all one family—you, me, and your father. I believe, children, that we will survive because your father is keeping us safe."

Dunia let me squeeze his hand, and then he ripped it away.

"Momma, you are keeping us safe," he said.

Tears sprung to my eyes, surprising me. I put my hand on my heart.

"Yes, Dunia. I will always protect you. But we are never alone. Your father watches over us. Your father also keeps us safe."

Chapter Twenty

October

I SAT IN BED daydreaming about my parents' house again: about my father's twinkling eyes when he sat at the end of the wooden table smiling and pulling his beard, about the nuts and dried plums and cheese and other sweet food we always seemed to have on hand. I remembered the way my father sounded when he laughed after making some kind of teasing joke that made my mother mad. It cleaned me out, that laughter, like the vibrating sound of the crystal glasses when my father rubbed his fingertip over the rim.

Then Marek came to me and clung to me, hugging my chest. His breath was sour. His hunger was aging him backwards, making him crazier than the older children. He had bouts of wild energy he didn't know what to do with. He held me, hoping I'd soothe him. But it was one of those moments when his need fastened down on my chest like a vise. It agitated me so badly that I could tolerate holding him for only a few seconds. I pulled him off me and practically wrestled him to his side of the bed.

"Be still," I scolded. The words left powder burn in my mouth.

Marek didn't move. It took every ounce of willpower I had not to hit him. "I'm sorry, Momma. What's wrong?" he whined.

I closed my eyes, counted slowly to five before I spoke.

"Nothing's wrong, baby. Momma just needs a little room. Why don't you go find your brother? See if he's done with the wood."

He stood, sulking and striking the mud with his feet.

I turned, composing myself. Marek wasn't good at navigating the cave, even when I hadn't distressed him

"Marek, baby. Where is Dunia?"

"With cousin Yohna. By the lake."

"You know where that is, don't you? Be a big help to Momma and go fetch him."

"Okay."

"Be careful," I said.

I put my feet on the floor and pinched my thighs hard until I felt the sting. I stood up and went to talk to my brother. My decision had already been made.

━━━━◆◆◆◆━━━━

Yossel and I met in his room. We rested our backs on the slippery gunk coating the walls. Pepcia was on the bed, coughing. She was trying to control her fits. They were getting worse. She coughed as if somebody had stitched her ribs tight. I thought she might have pneumonia, like my Chaim had.

"The moon, is it almost full now?" I asked.

Yossel cleared his throat. "Etcia, it's not safe yet to go out," he said.

It would never be safe to go out. We had to use the entrance dug right beside the one that had been blocked off.

"Did I calculate correctly?" I asked.

Yossel sighed. "The moon was fullest two nights ago," he said.

My brother was an outdoorsman. He missed breathing fresh air more than any of us. Even as a young child, hunting and fishing and farming had always brought him peace. He was the obvious choice to keep track of the light in the sky. Doing this kept him sane.

"They won't let you," he said.

I sat there for a while. The anger that I thought was gone rose from my stomach and settled on my ribs. I bit my lower lip, pressed my legs into the ground.

"It has to be done. The food is almost gone. Mania's stomach cramps are bad, and every time she goes to the bathroom, she has more and more blood. Pepcia, you need medicine too. Think about your baby, Nunia; he is only two. We must keep everyone healthy," I said.

My brother accidentally brushed my waist with his elbow as he brought his hand to his forehead, a habit he'd had since we were children when he felt confused.

"Listen to Pepcia, Yossel," I said. I was trying to manipulate him now, and it wasn't fair. But I knew his will was as soft as milk bread when it came to his wife.

"You could betray us. You could be followed," he said.

"If they haven't come back by now, they aren't coming. They've forgotten about us. There is too much land. They think we are armed. I will be careful," I said.

My brother and I sat shoulder to shoulder against the back wall. He was broader than I was and just a lot taller.

"We cannot make this place our grave," I said, the grit of my voice surprising me. "If we allow ourselves to be cowards, then they win," I continued.

Yossel moaned. He was the soldier among us. My technique was cruel but effective.

"Momma hallucinated," Pepcia said. "She thought they'd come down after us."

"It is a risk we have to take sooner or later. I'm going. And I will try to bring medicine."

Yossel sighed again. He knew better than to argue with me. It wasn't only that I was expected to be treated like the men. I was more sensible than my brothers. Common sense was of great value in the cave.

"I'm not asking permission," I said.

"I will go with you."

"It's better I go alone. I won't come back if there's any chance I was followed. It is easier for one woman to slip around unnoticed."

"One woman wearing suspenders and pants," he said.

I leaned my head back. In the bed, Nunia snored gently.

"I need you to get them to open the exit," I said.

"How?"

"Tell them you know what I'm capable of,"

"You are as stubborn as a donkey," he said and laughed. It was what Poppa used to say about me. He had said it up until my wedding day, when I refused to give up my determination to marry Chaim.

"And you are as wary as a bear."

Yossel elbowed me in the waist. I whacked him back. He laughed and tugged at my hair; then he let go.

Our heads were tilted back, our lips slightly open. Heavy air cocooned us. We drowsed, awake, in silence.

"When?" he finally asked.

"Tonight."

He sighed loudly. "The password has changed."

I squeezed his arm to let him know I understood. He would get me the new password. He'd get the men to let me out.

"The woods will be noisy. The wolves are restless, just like us. Some have been forced into hibernation. Even some of the animals who hunt during the day hunt at night now. They also adapt."

I let my head fall on my brother's shoulder.

"Pay attention. The animals have not lost their way," he continued.

Talking with my brother was such a relief. I felt the thick, dank silence of the cave give way.

"Just don't let them smell you," he said and laughed.

I elbowed him in the ribs.

"I will have a luxurious bath with bubbles before I go out," I said and laughed. Our detergent had long since run out. The sponge baths we gave ourselves didn't do so much good. Squeezing through the tunnel of the slippery cave made the yellow mud cling.

"Where will you go?" he asked.

"I don't know yet," I said.

There were still potatoes to steal in the fields, but the summer houses would be harder to access. How many people can you ask to risk execution for you in a lifetime? And how many were left who would offer? Every time we had gone outside, the village had looked less familiar. What had happened in the month since we'd last gone out?

There were once houses nearby where we could go to get food or to hide. Gradually, those places had disappeared. The families who would still help rarely spoke of other Jews. We didn't know if that was because there were more people dead, or if it had become more dangerous to admit knowing the ones who were left.

"You will be careful?" Yossel asked.

"Of course not," I responded

He elbowed me again.

"You don't have to worry," I said. "It works differently for me because I am doing it for the children."

A sigh escaped from my brother's lips. He knew what I meant. Something happened to me when I was out there alone. There was a strange, fierce determination that made me stronger than I was and that helped me do what I needed to keep my children alive. It was that force that had helped me break out of the jail, to survive all those nights alone on the cold mountain. There was no choice. I had to keep moving.

This is what gave my brother faith to invite me to provide for my family like the eleven men. I always kept this in mind.

"I'd never do anything to threaten our safety," I said.

He nodded. If I messed up and brought the police back, he'd most likely be responsible.

"You might try Kostaski again," Yossel suggested. "It's been awhile since anyone visited him."

I squinted my eyes, remembering what had transpired the last time I had visited Kostaski's house. It was impossible that Yossel knew my feelings for Joseph Kostaski.

"No. Not Kostaski. Not this time. We need medicine. Where do you suggest we find that?" I asked.

"Etcia, you don't have to..." Pepcia started to say.

"Yes, just get the food now, Etcia," Yossel followed.

"No." I shook my head, although Yossel couldn't see my face well in the dark. "I am worried for Mania. Right now we need the medicine as much as the food," I said.

"Stubborn as a donkey," Pepcia said and laughed out loud.

"Etcia, I learned a little trick when I was out there the last time," Yossel said. "If you are walking down the road and somebody sees you, maybe try whistling a little." He whistled then, a long, thin whistle, followed by a happy song.

"You are really a *meshugenah*," I said.

"Yes, but what the whistling does is to make it seem you belong there, that you are not worried about anything. It distracts them, like the animals, gives you a few seconds to run if you need it. They are not so bright, the ones who are left. Cruel, yes, but not so bright, especially not on their own. If you see one walking by himself, you are safe. They are like blind bats, Etcia. Believe me," he said.

I laughed, encouraged by my brother's wise sense of humor. I couldn't imagine having the courage to whistle if I were approached. I could imagine Yossel doing it, though. He always had a talent for trickery. My own wisdom was of a more practical nature.

"What about Doctor Tibels? Has anyone been to him yet?" I asked.

"Not a good idea," Yossel said.

I swallowed hard, disappointment shearing my belly. I'd been going to Doctor Tibels since I was a child. I had brought my children to him. He'd treated Chaim up until he died. He'd always been such a kind man. It felt as if he were part of the family.

"Why? Has he…? Does he…? How could he…have turned on us too?" I asked. The words were garbled in my mouth, reminding me of the dream I kept having that my teeth had all fallen out and I was trying to hold them in my mouth.

"It isn't that," Pepcia said gently. Some things only a woman understood.

"It is that the doctor is probably visited by the soldiers, by the Ukrainians who are our enemies," Yossel said. "Medicine is scarce. They have him under their thumb. Also, the road his house is on is a dangerous one."

"Yes, you are right. Of course," I said. "I don't know where my mind is sometimes."

Hunger made it harder to think. Like Marek, I had moments of behaving crazily, but I always tried to keep my emotions bottled up, contained in my mind. During these moments, brilliant things seemed to occur to me. After a few hours, I realized they weren't so brilliant after all.

"Your mind is still sharper than mine. Of course, that isn't such a great feat," Yossel joked.

I laughed. Nunia started crying gently. Pepcia rocked him, making soft hushing noises on the bed.

"Etcia, I heard a rumor," Yossel said. "I don't want to get too hopeful, but why don't you try Daria's house? Be smart, but I think it is a safe place. I think others have been there."

The nights were just starting to lengthen, so I left the cave a few hours after darkness to make sure I had enough time. Nobody was out. I darted between the trees. It felt too early to be so close to town. It had been so long since any of us were out, I didn't know what to expect.

The anger that had been nailed in my stomach the weeks we were sealed in was dissolving into my body. I held onto it when I could, using it as a compass that would keep me clear as I walked through the nearly unrecognizable streets of my childhood village. I stared down the empty road, examining the dark houses, and saw two Nazi vehicles parked by the side of the store. Even the rose bushes twining up the metal gate of a yard looked unfamiliar. This was no longer the place for which my children and I were homesick.

The night was windless. I curved through the streets, imagining a man walking behind me. He had no face or uniform. He was just heavy breath, a shape hovering in the background. The man might have been imaginary, but the danger was real. Walking the roads was suicidal. My mud-caked men's clothes couldn't protect me; neither could whistling.

It wasn't a decision but instinct that drew me towards Daria's house. It was the only house on that road still occupied by a person I knew, and Daria had always been kind.

Cautiously I walked towards the door in the yard, sheltered by a giant spruce tree. I knocked quietly, one time, two times. Then I waited. I knocked again as loudly as I could, praying I wouldn't awaken any neighborhood dogs. The house was silent. I wondered if Daria still lived there.

I put my hand on my heart. It wasn't so hard when I was walking, but when I stood still outside, terror gripped me. My breath was ragged. Going outside kept me in better shape than my children, who always stayed in the cave, but it was no longer possible to travel so far.

I counted slowly in my mind: ten, nine, eight, seven, six, five, four, three, two, one.

So far, I had been lucky. Some of the men told stories of people yelling out the windows at them to go away, threatening to call the authorities, even throwing balls and sticks at their head. I remembered the shots that rang out the last time I left.

I forced myself to stay put for my children. Besides, there was nowhere to go.

I told myself I'd stay five more seconds

Five, four, three, two, one.

The door opened. Daria stood there. As soon as she recognized me, she clenched my arm, her nails digging into me. She dragged me inside.

———◆◆◆———

I stood in Daria's house, waiting for her to tell me to sit. I could have collapsed from exhaustion. In fact, I often did on my trips above ground. Terror electrified my body when I walked through fields, but when I managed to make it to a house, I was drained. I longed for the cold, dark body of the cave, the heavy weight of my children surrounding me.

Daria's sister, Nusia, walked into the room. They had pulled the curtains. They exchanged glances. I knew how I looked. My clothes were disheveled. The mud and stench never really left us.

I had grown up with these women. Daria had always been kind. She'd given us food when the Germans first moved in.

"I'm sorry to bother you. I'll leave right away," I said.

"Wait here," Nusia said. She left the room.

Daria continued to keep her eyes angled away from me. She held her body stiff, as if she had to do so to maintain decorum. Did I imagine it, or was her expression unsympathetic? Of course, like everyone, she had less to spare. I tried to figure out if it was more than that, though. Had she started believing the ridiculous things that the Germans and her neighbors said about us to justify murder—that we were greedy and thieving, that we would take over all the shops in the village, that we would steal their livestock and murder their children? Even the strongest-willed people can start to believe lies if they hear them enough.

I reminded myself that she'd let me in. That's what mattered.

Daria had worked for many years for Mr. Shwartz, the village pharmacist and the husband of my old friend Fucia. I was hoping she'd have access to medicine that she'd gotten from the pharmacy before the Shwartzes disappeared.

For a second, I worried Nusia had left to report me, that in a few seconds, two soldiers would show up at the door with their rifles and take me away. It wasn't an outrageous idea. People like Kostaski and Grigori Ivasiuk had established reputations, not just among the Jews in the cave but among those the men occasionally bumped into on the road. There was no question we could trust them. Daria and Nusia had been good people, but good people often surprised us.

I was planning a ridiculous escape, running to the back door if they came to the front. Then Nusia came back in with a bag. She walked up to me and pushed it into my hands, meeting my eyes.

"There are potatoes, some eggs, some bread, beets, carrots, a little grain. I'm sorry it can't be more. We don't want to know where you are staying, and we ask that you don't come back."

"Nusia," Daria scolded.

"There is a reason. We have to be careful," Nusia continued.

She flicked her hand on the shoulder of her shirt. The bag of food was heavy. I squeezed it, relieved. There was enough in there. I wouldn't have to go anywhere else.

"Sit a minute, Panna Goldberg. Rest," Daria said.

The two sisters exchanged looks. I stood there, confused.

"Your children?" Daria asked carefully. I met her brown eyes. They were kind, filled with sorrow.

"There is a reason. We have to be careful," Nusia had said.

"There is a rumor. I don't want to get your hopes up," Yossel had said.

Her question helped me remember why I was there.

"They are alive, the children. All of them," I said, my voice filling with pride. "I came here because I am worried. I thought you might know where we might get some medicine. Mania, she is practically a young woman now, but her health is not good. She is constipated all the time. When she goes to the bathroom, she bleeds."

As I expected, the bluntness of my description of Mania's problem softened Nusia. She was a no-nonsense woman, a farmer.

"And my brother, Yossel, his wife, Pepcia, is sick. She is coughing all the time. Where we live, it is damp," I said.

Nusia's body moved a fraction of an inch away from me, like a door about to close.

"They have a two-year-old son, Nunia," I continued. "We're worried about Pepcia. A boy that age in these times needs his momma."

"I see," Nusia said.

The two sisters looked at each other seriously. The bag of food was heavy. It kept me grounded.

"Just your brother and your children?" she asked.

I nodded. Did she ask because no Jews had visited in a long time, or because she was going to turn us in? It was so hard to tell. I worried that I'd made a mistake. It would have been easier to visit Kostaski again, at least to ask him if Daria's was safe.

"Wait here for a second, please, Panna Goldberg," Daria said.

The sisters drifted into the other room. My back was to the wall, but the window left me vulnerable. I imagined somebody knocking on the door. In the next room, the sisters mumbled, arguing. Their voices were low but sharp.

"Etcia, please come in here," Nusia said when she came back. I hesitated. "It's okay. Bring the food. We have something to show you. It is safe here," she said.

I followed her blindly into a small, dark room beside the stairs.

"Please sit," she said, ushering me onto a straight chair. I sat, putting the supplies on the floor. Daria was gone. Silently, Nusia left the room.

•◆•×•×•◆•

I had nearly nodded off when footsteps came up the stairs. How dainty the sounds of the women's shoes were on the wood floor rather than the plodding of bare feet on mud or my own broken shoe soles flapping when I walked in the forest or on the roads outside. The sound soothed me until I remembered what I was doing, where I was. I looked up suddenly, ready to dart from the room, when I heard a voice so old yet so familiar to me, it was almost like hearing the voice of a ghost.

"Etcia Goldberg."

I looked up. A woman with a thin face, pale skin, close-cropped curly brown hair, and dark circles under her eyes was standing before me. She wore a housedress, the kind we once wore in the village. I recognized my old friend Fucia Shwartz and almost screamed. I jumped up then and hugged her so tightly, I might have broken her. Gently, she pushed me away.

"Oy. Thank God! I was worried about you," I said. "I kept asking. Nobody knew where you were."

"I didn't know if you were alive either," Fucia said. We both had tears in our eyes.

"Now you understand why we must be careful," Nusia said simply.

I was surprised again by Nusia's coldness but nodded at her to let her know that I understood.

I wanted to ask Fucia a thousand questions—how long she'd been hiding in Nusia and Daria's house, what she had been through, whom they had lost. Nusia was standing there, though, practically scowling.

"Your husband?"

"He is fine," she said.

"Thank God. I can't believe you are real," I said.

She laughed, then covered her mouth with her hand. Again I thought about my dream of the teeth falling out, how my great-grandmother always told me in Yiddish that dreams of teeth falling out signify grief.

"You don't have much time," Nusia scolded. "She has some medicines. Tell her what you need."

I'd lost track of the hours. I'd left early enough, and this was the only house I'd been to. I wouldn't need to go anywhere else. Still, I had no idea how long I'd been sitting in that chair waiting. There was nothing worse than walking back to the cave under a sky that had already started to drain.

"Daria says one of the children and your brother's wife are sick?"

"My Mania. She is constipated badly. She has blood when she goes to the bathroom. It is not menstruation. It is in her waste," I said.

"She has not been eating enough?" Fucia asked, but it was not really a question.

Fucia was a few years older than I. She had finished only the sixth grade but was always considered one of the most intelligent women in our village. She'd spent more time working at her husband's side at the pharmacy than I had at the leather store alongside Chaim. In the old days, she'd never sold medicine without her husband. Still, she was renowned among us women for offering medical advice. We often went to her when things were troubling us that we were too embarrassed to bring to a man.

"It is common these days. She probably just has hemorrhoids. But there is something we have, a type of oil that can ease her belly. We have some to spare. What is wrong with Yossel's wife?"

"We don't know. She is coughing all the time,"

"Is it a dry cough or a wet cough? Is it full of phlegm?"

I wanted to tell Fucia that we were living in a cave, that the temperature was a constant bone-chilling cold, that it was always damp, that even when we sweat we were in danger.

"It is a wet cough. Damp. She doesn't stay warm enough. We are always cold."

Fucia nodded, looking at me seriously, understanding. Relief flooded me, and I almost started to cry again. It had been so long since we had had any type of joy or good news. Here was my old friend standing before me. She and her husband had survived.

"I will go get you some things. Wait here," she said.

I nodded.

"Hurry," Nusia said, following her down.

"Relax," Daria countered.

Daria stared at me, almost apologetically, as her sister and Fucia made a racket downstairs. I picked up the bag. A scent I hadn't noticed before stunned me. It was heavenly—the scent of fresh, newly baked bread. I stood there inhaling, waiting for my friend. We had a lot to be thankful for, I thought. My friend was alive. The medicine might help us. The children would get to eat real fresh-baked bread. My eyes watered. I swallowed hard. The tears were almost insulting. I had lived all those months being a rock for the children. Even before the war, I had been a woman who rarely cried.

Then I heard the light yet purposeful footsteps beat up the stairs again. I looked up to see the sisters come in together but not Fucia. Nusia had a small bag in her hand. Did I imagine Daria was pinching her eyes?

"The syrup is for Pepcia," Nusia said. "Twice a day until it's gone. There are some pills too; that should help. She should take them the full course for seven days. You are very lucky, Panna Goldberg. These pills are precious."

I nodded as she put the other bag inside the one I hoisted.

"The crème is for Mania to rub on the inflamed parts. There is also some oil. Put a few drops in her food every day." She cleared her throat. "If there is no food, put it in water," she finished, almost as if she were embarrassed.

"Thank you," I said.

Daria kissed me on the cheek.

"Will you say goodbye to her for me? Tell her I miss her?"

"Of course," Nusia responded.

"She is being cared for," Daria said softly.

As if on cue, we all started walking towards the door.

"Avoid the bazaar road. There are soldiers always patrolling there. And don't go along Creek Road. Some Jews were shot there the other day," Nusia said in her matter-of-fact tone. What seemed like coldness was merely practicality.

"Etcia," she whispered as I got to the door. "This war will end eventually. Take care of your children. Stay alive."

⸻ ✦ ⸻

I wove through the quiet streets cautiously, relieved that the sky had barely lightened. My arm was strained holding the heavy bag, but my feet barely touched the ground. Emotions surged through me, awakening a part of my body that had gone numb. I was angry with myself for distrusting Nusia and Daria. A small dose of distrust was okay—as with the deer, our strength lay in our reaction. We have to be ready to flee before we are attacked. But Daria was once a friend. Just because we were living in crazy times didn't mean we had to lose our humanity too. It was the only thing we had left.

Joy also coursed through me, pure joy. My old friend was alive.

It was nearly dawn by the time I made it to the clearing. The moon had already dropped behind the mountains. The sky was just beginning to lighten into blue. It was a dangerous hour. I rushed, and my leg got caught in a prickly vine. Instead of yelling, I stomped the vine. A muscle in my thigh cramped. I waited, hollow inside as dry corn.

I'd been hoping to see another Jew in hiding. Sometimes, we saw someone others believed might be dead or might have been sent away to one of the camps. It was always joyous to bring that news back. Even if the person we saw was a stranger, the fact that there was more than one of us out there mattered.

I stood straight with my shoes planted on the ground, breathing downwards, waiting for the muscle to loosen.

New dawn sky exposed part of the village. Unlit houses sat on a hill. A white birch glowed in a yard.

It was beautiful.

It was also time to go.

I clenched my thigh muscle and released it, then wiggled my toes against the top of my shoes and hoisted the heavy bag.

A loud crack resounded in the distance behind me. It might have been a gunshot. I froze.

Then I forced myself to walk, one foot in front of the other.

That was one thing that always surprised me about killing. Afterwards, it was always so quiet.

<hr />

There seemed to be a threshold at the line separating the village from the woods. Every time we walked into the dense brush, everything changed. Few soldiers or police were ambitious enough to patrol all the way out there anymore unless they were deliberately chasing someone. I turned around. I wasn't being followed.

The woods weren't silent. They were filled with the sounds of animals—a high-pitched shriek, a chattering like teeth, a yowl beating deeply like somebody slapping a drum. Yossel had told me animal song was a sign of safety, that I had crossed the border.

I looked up. The moon was dim, but the Big Dipper was there. The sky clock was pointed almost all the way back towards the cave. It really was time to go.

I hoisted my bag up high and sprinted across the exposed field, my heart pounding into my throat. When I got to the entrance, I crouched down, waking the young guard.

"I'm here," I whispered.

The sleepy-eyed young man groaned.

"It's me, Etcia. The password is 'dark forest.'"

<hr />

When I was sure it was close to morning, I went to my brother's bed, tapped him on the shoulder, and waited. Yossel was not sleeping, but he groaned, then rolled out of bed. I saw only his shadow, the way he raised his hand to his forehead, maybe to gain equilibrium.

"Etcia," he said, and in his voice was a smile. "You are back."

I laughed inside because I thought he was still partially in a dream and because I was excited about what I had to give Pepcia. Something had shifted in me overnight or during the morning. It probably had to do with the deep, restful sleep that I always fell into after I went outside the cave. Nothing disturbed me, neither the children nor the dreams. When I woke up, I had forgotten the dead man in the woods. I was back in the cave, alive and well cared for, among my own family.

"I have something to show you. Come," I said.

Yossel followed me to a corner of the room, far away from his wife. We sat on a plank of wood above the mud and pressed our backs against the stone wall.

"I heard you come in. I was so pleased," he said.

I wondered if he knew what he was saying. We couldn't tell day from night. Sometimes we thought we were dreaming when we were awake.

"You were not followed, Etcia?" he asked.

"Don't be crazy. If I had been followed, I wouldn't be here."

"Right," he said, but I still wasn't sure I understood him.

"I brought you some medicine for Pepcia's cough. There are pills and some liquid. I got something for Mania too."

Yossel was silent for a long time. His breathing was labored, as if he were running back from that dream. The shadow of his chest moved up and down. The information I gave him came too fast. It was too much for him to take in. I sat with my eyes closed for a while, listening to Pepcia and Nunia breathe.

I touched my brother's hand. I spoke slowly, carefully. "I didn't see any soldiers. No police either."

My brother licked his lips.

"You visited Daria? Is this where you got the medicine?" he asked.

"You knew Fucia was there? How come you didn't tell me, Yossel? You knew how worried I was."

"There were rumors. I didn't want to get your hopes up," he said.

He spoke with a finality that left no room for argument. He was right, of course. False hope could be damaging. If you hoped someone you cared for was alive, if you kept that hope lit like a candle flame in your heart, and then you find out he or she had died, the flame snuffed out, you were left with a terrible darkness inside.

"You saw her, then, your friend?" he asked.

"Yes," I said

"It doesn't matter that there was medicine. Something didn't feel right about Nusia's. I don't think it's a good place to go."

"Why?" Yossel asked.

"I can't tell you exactly. It didn't feel right. Nusia treated me something like an inconvenience. She was acting strange. It's hard to explain."

We sat silently for a while. There was something else I wanted to tell him, but I couldn't remember what it was. Then the scent returned to me

"There were flowers, Yossel. At night. I could smell them." I could almost hear him smiling. "I believe they were Convallaria, Lily of the valley," I said.

"Whoa."

"What, Yossel? Tell me."

He paused so long, I thought he might have fallen asleep.

"White flowers shaped like little bells with a sweet scent?" he asked.

"Yes."

"You are right. They are Lily of the valley. They are my favorite flowers. Believe it or not, I often dream of them."

I sat there for a while, letting my head drop listening to my brother breathe. I thought that my heart couldn't hold many more memories, not anymore. Still, I had seen my friend. She was alive.

"About Nusia. Trust your instincts, Etcia. They are sharp. They've kept you alive."

Chapter Twenty-One

November

LAY QUIETLY IN that slow-motion place between sleeping and wakefulness. Remnants of a dream glowed. It was a pleasant dream that made me feel coddled, so I was trying to bring it back. I had dreamed about Mania—she had eyes as blue as they were when she was a baby, only in the dream she had grown into a woman. I grasped the *varetta*, smiling faintly. I scratched the dream like an itch, trying to recover the sensation, to remember how my Mania had looked and the fact that she had survived.

I finally sat up, moving carefully so as not to wake the children. Marek was on my left and Mania on the right. Above me was the sloping ceiling and below me the cold clay floor. There was something I was supposed to be waiting for. I tried to remember what it was.

I looked at the shapes on the bed and noticed people were missing. It came back to me then. It was probably dawn. Blue light might be filling the sky. It was the hour we dreaded most when we were outside. We'd all imagined ourselves shot in the back while we limped across the last one hundred yards of the wheat fields. My brother and nephew Mundek had gone out for grain promised by a merchant, a friend of one of the others. I stared into the dark hole of the sleeping room and prayed that it was still late at night. My children's heavy breath steamed.

I stood in case the men needed help. This was uncharacteristic of me. One of our unspoken laws was that people who went out took care of their own supplies. I was drawn through the corridors, though, step by step, ball of foot, then heel. I stayed close to the walls and counted aloud the five turns it took from Khatki to the end of the common area. It was easier to get lost just after waking, even in an area you know like the back of your hand.

I nearly knocked into someone on the way out.

"Etcia, is that you?" Meimel said, catching me in her big arms. "Thank God." Her voice was hysterical.

"What's wrong, Meimel?" I asked.

She put both her hands on my shoulders, pushed me down, steadying herself in the process.

"Mendel and my boy, Mundek, are still out there," she said.

I squeezed her arm, then walked over to the wall to steady myself.

"So, what's wrong with that?" I asked.

"Etcia, I keep checking with the boys standing guard. It's late afternoon now. They've been gone nearly two days."

I had been able to sleep a few hours here and there, but nightmares tore me apart. I always woke up in the middle and stared up at the ceiling, waiting for the rush of terror to pass through my body. I lay there, trying to remember the pictures. I thought if I could remember the dreams, I might be able to control them. Some were ordinary. Many times I was running, sometimes alone, sometimes alongside Mendel. I could not see the soldiers behind us, but I could feel them. They were barely human, just a terrible force pushing at us like a harsh wind that was impossible to outrun. In one, Mendel was lying near the tree with his tongue sticking out. In another, I was looking into the cave from outside and saw a bunch of skeletal children with yellow eyes and prominent cheekbones. They weren't crying. They weren't speaking at all. Yet their need was consuming.

I lay there quietly, taking in breath, trying to talk myself out of nonsense. If I didn't compose myself before I went to see Meimel, I wouldn't be any comfort to her at all.

"If you can see what you are afraid of, then you won't be afraid anymore," my mother used to tell me when I was a child afraid of imaginary monsters in my bedroom. The room was so bright. She would sit at my side, coaxing me out of my nightmare. It was strange advice coming from a woman who spent much of my early adulthood pretending anything she didn't like wasn't there. Still, it was good, solid advice. Some nightmares do go away when you name them.

The recurring dream that bothered me most was the one in which my teeth fell out. In the dream, I'd feel a loose tooth and then pull it right out of my mouth. I'd be left with a giant gap where the tooth was that made me look ugly and that I tried to hide. Sometimes I tried to put the tooth back in, attach it with glue. Other times it was more than one tooth. Sometimes all my teeth fell out of my gums at once, and I closed my mouth to catch them. It was a terrible sensation, holding all those teeth like stones in my mouth. Sometimes I swallowed one or two.

I lay there, everything railing inside me. This wasn't supposed to happen. Nobody down here was supposed to die. If my brother and my nephew didn't come back, seven people in the cave would be without providers.

We had never allowed ourselves to think about what we'd do if we lost people. We hadn't planned.

—◆◆◆◆—

My sister Meimel and I sat on stones by the water, where the air was more humid. Three terrible days and nights had passed, and Mendel and

Mundek still hadn't returned. The only thing we knew was that they were going to visit a local peasant, a friend named Kulchitsky, to buy grain. If they never came back, we might never know what happened to them. There would just be rumors.

"Etcia," Meimel said, squeezing my hand with her own.

"It's best to just stick to the now. We know nothing. They are alive. We must believe this," I said.

"That's what I thought in the ghetto," she said.

Meimel stirred the water with her hand, making a swishing sound. Under different circumstances, I would have corrected her. I prayed that she had washed her hands well.

"I'm a terrible person," she said.

"*Sha*," I said, using an old Yiddish expression. "That's crazy talk. Why would you say that?"

"Because my child and my brother are out there in danger, and all I can think about is myself. I worry how we will live. The children— Dorcia, Luzar, and Mania—are already so weak."

I took her hand and squeezed it. Mundek had been eighteen when we went down, old enough to take care of the family. Meimel wouldn't be capable of being head of household if he didn't return.

"They are smart. They will come home."

"But what if they don't, Etcia?"

"*Sha*, don't think that way."

"But what if they don't? We will die here."

I didn't have the patience for talk like that. If she had been one of the children, I'd have slapped her. If it had been anyone else, I might have walked away. But it was Meimel—kind, gentle Meimel. I'd often reflected on how remarkable it was that her sensitivity had remained intact in the cave. It reminded me that it was still possible to keep our personalities.

"Do you know how Fishel Dodyk brings food for Mayer and Hersch Kovalek besides his own family?" asked Meimel. "How brave and strong he is. I don't know why the Kovalek men don't go out."

I didn't respond.

"You are a woman, Etcia, and you go out. I cannot even imagine."

"I am terrified when I go out. But I have no choice."

She pursed her lips.

"If the worst happens and they do not come back, you won't starve," I said. "You are family. Yossel and I will provide for you and the children. Nobody is going to starve."

"No, that's no good either. Fishel has to go out more often. If you have to go out more often, you are risking your life. Etcia, you are strong, but you have only two arms. And you aren't a man."

"Why are you talking nonsense? It will do you no good. Calm down. Please, Meimel. Our dignity is all we have left."

This was a terrible thing to say. I was being cruel only because I knew it would work.

Meimel drummed her knuckles on the stone we were sitting on. It sent vibrations through our bodies.

"The thing that bothers me most is how brave my Mundek has to be. I am completely dependent on him, my own son. It makes me feel weak."

"*Sha*, Meimel. Don't you realize how brave Mundek is? It's true, but it's only because you raised him."

I ran my tongue along the ridges of my teeth. They were all there, intact. I couldn't whistle. Instead I pushed my palm into the stone and let my eyes close. I lightly hummed a song my mother had taught me when we were young.

————◆•◆•◆————

I was too exhausted to suffer another nightmare. My body had finally released me, and I drowsed on the pleasant breeze of a dream. I was at home with my parents. We were sitting at the dinner table. We had company. My mother made me wear a fancy dress that made me uncomfortable but brought out the green color of my eyes. People had traveled on horses and carts from other villages to be there. All the women there told my mother how pretty I was. The food was lavish: rich duck and beets and green beans my mother had ordered to be picked from the gardens. There was laughter, rejoicing.

The sound continued to trill, like the real ice cubes tinkling in the crystal glass, and I prayed for a few more hours of sleep to be able to stay in the dream.

It took me a few seconds to recognize that I wasn't dreaming, that I was awake in the underground cave, that the voice was not my father's but my brother's, Mendel's. The laughter was coming from Meimel and Mundek. I jumped up, mouthed a prayer as I plodded in my bare feet across the cave and joined the celebration. The men had come back. They'd returned.

"You two troublemakers must have just been playing a dirty trick on us, right?" I said as I reached them. My brother Mendel whaled me on the arm unexpectedly, the closest he ever came to giving a hug.

"Etcia, they are back!" Meimel squealed like a girl.

"Yes, I see that. Well, sort of," I said.

Everyone laughed. Mundek was holding a lantern. He squatted on the edge of one of the beds. The light it gave off was eerie, casting reddish shadows on a few men's faces.

"What happened?" I asked.

Mundek launched into a story, words spilling out of his mouth, along with some spittle. "So Kulchitsky didn't have the grain ready, and we were out in the woods. We heard noise. Bad noise, dogs barking. Then shots rang out. Boom! Boom! Boom! It was too far away. We didn't think it was because of us, but we couldn't tell. We didn't know who it was. Maybe it was Ukrainian police, maybe bandits, maybe the Nazis. We didn't know, so we didn't take any chances. We decided to hide. We hid in a storage unit in his neighbor's barn. That was the first night."

"The first?" Meimel exclaimed.

"Yes. So the next day we went to visit Kulchitsky again. He said the grain wasn't ready. He said to come back the next day. Of course, we worried maybe he was alerting the authorities, that we would show up the next day, and they would shoot us dead or follow us back here again. But Mendel says that was probably not right, that we should take the chance."

Mendel picked up the tail end of the story.

"I figured Kulchitsky was greedy. He wanted the money. And he wasn't smart enough to scheme against us. He's never showed a mean bone in his body. Besides, we had no choice. We hadn't been out for too long, and there's so little left out there. Also, we had already stayed out the one night; we figured we might as well wait another."

"So you hid again?" I asked.

"We hid again," Mundek said. "It was comedy. The next day we went back, and Kulchitsky told us to wait again. We stayed out of sight for three days before he finally coughed up the grain. He really came through. We circled back a few times just to make sure. But there's a lot here. It should last for a while."

"You were gone a long time," I said.

The men were silent for a minute.

"Yes," Mendel said. "You know what was really strange? Seeing Mundek's ugly face in the daylight. He needs a shave." He laughed.

"You don't look much better than that," Mundek joked back.

"Of course, I know this. I am grateful it was you I was looking at and not my own face in the mirror," Mendel said.

I laughed, but the comment startled me. Mendel had always been a strong man with wide shoulders and a cute smile. It was tough to imagine what my brother might have then looked like, what any of us really looked like. Mendel's face had probably turned sharp, his eyes shadowed. When I touched the skin on my own face, I felt it was softer. I wondered what the hunger had done to our skin.

"We were worried," Meimel said.

"I couldn't tell," Mundek said.

"Don't be fresh," Meimel said and then cuffed him on the ear.

"Well, you can't get rid of us that easily," Mendel said. He intended it as a joke, but there was something knotted in his throat. We tried to laugh.

"Let me get you both some water," Meimel said, then left.

The men shifted on the bed uncomfortably.

"What was it like being out there for so long? Did you get to feel the sun?" a small voice asked behind me. It was Dunia. He'd been there all along.

"Dunia, go bring your uncles some more blankets," I instructed.

"We saw the sun, Dunia. It's still there," Mendel joked.

It took a few seconds; then everyone laughed with him. The laughter died quickly. Awareness of what could have happened lingered like a strange presence.

Something had shifted. Something had changed.

Some said the fact that we were already living in hell protected us.

Every time we went out, we'd remember.

Chapter Twenty-Two

December

WHEN I STOOD in the forest looking at the empty fields in the moonlight, I was disappointed. The season had changed over so dramatically. I looked at the stalks of trampled wheat, remembering the way we used to collect the wheat in the summer and weave it into long strands that we fed to the animals. Life had a real rhythm back then. Now, the seasons passed, and my children missed them.

I waited, catching my breath, scanning the path I would take to the village for signs of disturbance. It was cold outside, nearly as cold as it was in the cave. Soon snows would come. Who knew how well we would adapt? Would we have to dig ourselves out? Would the trails be passable? How would we protect our feet from frostbite? How would we cover our tracks so nobody could find us?

An owl hooted, a long, low sound that comforted me. At least the air I was breathing was clean. Still, I was in the woods with my thick cotton *fufaika* buttoned up to my chin. The longer nights protected us, but the cold demanded I move faster. I was worried that my body and my mind would slow down as it sometimes did in the cave.

I started walking quickly, calmly, being careful not to make too much noise breaking sticks under my feet. The longer I walked, the more I noticed the quiet. Something had changed. Things felt darker, infected, as if killing and cruelty had finally seeped into the land.

⸻

My body still shivered even though I was nursing the thin soup Joseph had put in front of me on the table. I had to keep my mouth closed to ensure my teeth wouldn't clatter.

"I think it's colder outside than it is in the cave tonight," I said.

"Are there many stars out?" Joseph asked.

I nodded. I had learned that when it was very cold out, it was generally clearer, and there were more stars. These are things I would never have known in my old life. In my childhood, other people grew the vegetables, slaughtered the animals, turned them into rich roasts and stews and put them on our table. Chaim and I had some chickens, but the majority of our food had been traded or came from the store.

The way Joseph looked at me made me uncomfortable. I wondered if it was my less-than-perfect appearance, the strands of hair poking out of my cap, my cracked lips, my unbrushed teeth. I met his eyes, saw the tenderness in them, and knew that wasn't the case. I wondered how he could be attracted to me, being in the state I was in. Perhaps it was because he remembered me when I was a girl. Feelings didn't always have to do with appearance.

Worse than this, I was beginning to feel tender towards him too. It wasn't just because I had known him before the war or because of his kindness. It was something about the strength of his shoulders, the clumsy way he held his hands.

"I had a feeling you'd come visit. I was hoping. It has been such a long time," he said. He noticed my embarrassment and looked away. "You look well," he said.

I laughed.

"Different but well, considering the circumstances," he said.

I laughed again. He joined me. Humor was ordinary, part of our shared history.

"Well, do you want to know all the news?" he asked, mischievously.

"Of course not," I said.

He nodded seriously and adjusted his posture at the table.

"There are rumors the Nazis are building headquarters near Vinitsa, on the way to Kiev. Hitler himself visited. And worse, they are picking up more Ukrainians and shipping them out to work for Germany. It seems like they are making themselves comfortable here."

I rubbed my finger on the smooth wood of the table, then over its corner.

"They sealed us in. A few months ago," I said. The words barely made it past my throat. It was strange to speak them aloud.

He nodded. He already knew.

"Grigori Ivasiuk told me. That must have been terrifying," he said.

I took a spoonful of soup. It had already cooled. It was thin borscht, made from just a few beets. Still, its pungent sweetness reminded me of my parents' house, of the soup spoons made of real silver my mother polished herself.

"I make sure I get the news of you, of your brothers and sisters, and everyone in the cave. There are only a few of us left who still know where you are. It's our responsibility to make sure you are safe."

I was glad to hear he was not the only one left.

"Sometimes I can't sleep worrying for you," he said, a tenderness in his voice.

The heat rose to my cheeks, and I looked away.

"There is better news. The partisans in the Carpathian Mountains are active lately. The commander, Kovpak, is causing a lot of problems for the German army. Some sources told me the Russian army is beating the Nazis badly. They have already liberated the left bank of the Dnieper River in Ukraine, even Kiev. They could be here in five, maybe six months."

Joseph connected me to the world in the way that Chaim had. But it was different for me now because of my circumstances, of course. When I was with Chaim, I didn't really care to know much about politics. Now our survival depended upon knowing.

"The Nazis are getting nervous. Nobody has been here in weeks," Joseph said. He stared at me in that tender way again. "The children are well?" he asked.

"Mania is feeling better. I'm worried about Marek. He has lost so much weight, when I touch his face, I feel mostly bone. Food sometimes makes him vomit."

"Eat slowly," he said. "I have some things for you. It isn't much, but it was all we could spare. Some potatoes. Some oil. Kerosene. A duck."

His eyes sparked like a match flame, and he looked down. He grinned, embarrassed. A duck was a luxury item, even for him.

"I had a feeling you would come soon," he said simply.

"Thank you," I said.

We sat for a while. I sipped the soup slowly. Immediately my stomach started to churn. I gulped the water, trying to keep the cup away from my teeth.

"Your outfit still suits you," he joked.

I smiled. It was more out of habit that I continued to dress like a man. They weren't looking for Etcia Goldberg anymore. They weren't any less likely to kill a man.

"Etcia, I..." he started, then stopped when he saw my expression.

It was so quiet in the house. The curtains were drawn. I hadn't seen any soldiers on the street or heard any motorcycles.

"I have to start back soon," I said.

The light flickered in the kitchen. Despite the bright blue paint on the table, the room seemed gloomy, almost distorted. Joseph took my glass and brought it into the kitchen.

"There are not really patrols," he said from the sink. "Everyone is asleep or has passed out already. It is too cold for them to bother."

His steps were slow, lumbering. He came back and put the glass on the table. It was only halfway full.

"It is only one o'clock. There is enough food for all. It is heavy."

He sat down again, put his elbow on the table, and rested his chin in his palm. I drank the water slowly, savoring the coolness.

"Sit for a while, Etcia. Rest," he said.

He tapped my hand with his own, let it linger a second too long and then pulled away. Something in my belly dropped, reminding me I was still a woman. Joseph's cheeks reddened. I stood up to go.

As I walked, the weight of the bag tore at my muscles, sending a wave of pain through my veins into my wrists. By the time I put the bag down in the forest and kneeled beside it, I worried I'd ripped my wrists apart.

After seeing the dead man lying in the woods, I'd decided I would take only familiar routes back. I walked swiftly and was already at the edge of the tree line just before the clearing. I looked across the field. Nothing seemed disturbed. The night was quiet. I allowed myself to dip my hands into the bag, feel the waxy wrapped package stored between something round like turnips or beets or onions. I couldn't believe our good fortune.

I sat down, taking some pressure off my thighs. My calves were already starting to swell from the thrombosis. The cold night air pierced my cheeks. The clear sky was littered with stars. It was such a luxury to be able to see them, to breathe the cold air that rose from the ground. I examined constellations, the shapes that formed the basis of stories that ancient people all over the world told. My brother Yossel knew all those stories. I wished I knew some to take back to the children. I wished I could take a giant sack and collect all the stars and bring them back to the cave.

I looked up long enough to distract myself from the pain. Then I stood and hoisted the heavy bag up to my chest. Its weight made me hunch slightly. It was much heavier than it had been in previous trips to get supplies. This brought me joy. I reminded myself I didn't have to bring the children false stories about the sky or a bagful of stars. Those things didn't matter. You couldn't eat stars.

I hoisted the bag up higher to my breast, arched my shoulders back. It made me proud to know that in the bag I held something precious—a duck. A real duck. It would keep Mania healthy and make Marek strong, help him put on some weight. I was bringing real food to my children.

It would restore us, this treasure I held in my arms.

Knowing this, I decided right then that it didn't matter how or why it had been given to me. It was a gift. And I wasn't so proud or so stupid that I wouldn't accept a gift.

<hr />

I woke up later that night to Marek's shrill screaming. I sat up, and Marek clutched me so tightly, he nearly punctured my lungs. I pushed him off me without thinking about it, a long *shhhhh* sound escaping from my lips.

"What's the matter?" I asked.

"Momma, there were two big bright spots," he said and wailed.

"Marek, calm down. What are you talking about?"

"When I woke up, two bright spots were just so close to my face!" he shrieked.

I lunged to the rock shelf, quickly lit a candle, and held it up, just in time to see the red bushy tail end of a fox dashing away from Marek.

"Did he bite you?" I asked, practically shaking Marek. His face was tear-stained and red from screaming, but he shook his head no. I let out my breath. Then something terrible occurred to me. I reached back and felt for our food stash. The potatoes were still there, but the duck was gone.

I stood up, then dropped to the floor, reaching for the candle with one hand while searching for any remnants of the duck with the other.

Marek was crying.

"What's going on?" Dunia shouted.

My heart was in my knees, and I wanted to cry myself. This was unlike me. The food of course was precious to us; meat was a rarity, protein that would go a long way towards keeping us alive. It wasn't just that, though. It was partly sentimentality. The duck was a gift. Joseph had had to go to great lengths to get it for me. It was meant to be ours.

"Momma, what's wrong?" Mania screamed, alarmed.

"Nothing, babies. Don't worry. The fox is gone. Momma's just looking for something the fox might have taken," I said.

"A fox! It was a fox!" Marek shrieked as if giving his monster a name made it worse, not better.

"Just a little old fox," I said.

"Wait, what did he take? What are you looking for, Momma?" Dunia asked.

With that, they seemed to calm down. Marek still cried, but it was the hushed, sleepy sobs of a child.

I took a deep breath and slowed down, carefully feeling a square of dirt floor, then moving to the next. When my hand landed on the greasy duck, I almost cried myself.

"Etcia," I heard, the strong, firm voice of a grown man behind me. I turned the candle around and looked up. I followed the dirt-caked pant leg of my brother Yossel, then stood up until I met his blue-gray eyes with my own. I saw the fear draining out of him as I stood there, one hand clutching the candle, the other holding a fat, still-wrapped duck package by the leg. His face clouded in confusion, and I started to laugh. He touched my shoulders, shaking me slightly, as I had done to Marek.

"Children," Yossel said, "we heard screaming. What's wrong?"

I looked over to the bed where my three babies sat. Marek's body still heaved. I blew out the candle, guided my brother towards the bed, and sat down. I put the duck on the shelf behind us, grabbed Marek in my lap, and blew into the top of his hair.

"Marek just got a little bit scared because a fox came too close. But he wasn't looking to hurt us, baby. He just wanted to eat that old duck. It was a surprise. I got us a duck. Don't you worry," I said.

Marek started crying again, as if I'd reminded him of what he'd been scared of.

"A duck?" Mania exclaimed. She laughed lightly.

Yossel stood in front of the bed. I felt him watching us, rubbing his chin. "You sure he's gone, Etcia?" my brother asked.

"He's gone. I saw him run when Marek screamed," Dunia said and laughed.

My brother kneeled down in front of the bed. His breathing was deep, tired. The scent of smoke from the burnt-out candle lingered.

"I heard you come in. I was glad you were home," my brother said. My brother paid attention the best that he could.

"Is the duck okay, Momma? We can still have it tomorrow?" Marek asked.

"Shhh," Mania responded. "What do you have, wind in your head? Don't be annoying."

There was an awkward silence. The children knew their uncle was there, listening. It wasn't unusual for them to feel possessive of their own food.

"I just put it on the shelf. It's fine," I said softly.

"Marek, you know you don't have to be afraid of a little old fox," my brother said, changing the subject. "The fox doesn't want to bother with you. It's okay with him that you live here too." Yossel sat on the edge of the bed. It creaked. He felt my shoulder, then ruffled Marek's hair.

"How do you know?" Marek asked.

"Well, silly, the fox brought us here," my brother said. His voice was raspy. It was tough for him to start to find words.

"What do you mean, Uncle Yossel?" Marek asked.

The children relaxed into their regular spots. Marek put his head on my arm. I hugged him to me.

"We were looking for a safe secret place like this to live in for a while. A friend I had whose name was Munko was a forester, cutting trees so people could use the wood to heat their homes. My friend Nisel and I went to talk to Munko, to ask if he knew a good safe place we could live. He said we should check maybe by Priest's field, which was named after a nice priest whose property it had been. In the middle of the field, there was a ravine and a place where the foxes used to disappear when they were in danger. He told us where to go look.

"So that's what we did. Nisel Stermer and I, we went to the land, and we sat quietly, just like we do here, and we waited and watched. We were patient. Then one day, we saw a big, beautiful red fox with a fluffy tail like the one that you saw. The fox ran and ran, and then he disappeared. We went to the spot where the fox had been, and that's when we found the entrance to the cave. And when we went inside, we saw why the fox liked it so much."

Marek shifted in my lap. It was too many words.

"So you see, the fox knew a safe place. He wouldn't have shown it to us if it wasn't okay to share it. That fox was a gift from God. He was showing us the way. If you wait long enough and you pay attention, you will always find the answer you are looking for."

I scooped Marek up and cradled him, then laid him down on the bed. I kissed his forehead.

"You know, that fox and his babies live just like you," Yossel said. "They stay in a dark, warm place like this cave until they are big and strong enough and it is safe to come out."

Marek's eyelashes brushed my face. He closed his eyes and was getting ready to sleep.

"They are smart like you too, and your momma and your brother and sister. Their cleverness keeps them alive."

Marek's breath thickened. It traveled in and out his nostrils, the way it always had when he slept ever since he was a baby.

"Of course, Marek, this does not mean if you see a fox you should pet him or anything like that. He doesn't want to hurt you. But if you see him again, it's okay if you scare him the way that you did. The fox can be sneaky, and it's not good for him if he eats your food."

"I scared him?" Marek asked, sleepily.

"Yes. You were the big hero. We're lucky for you," my brother said. "Now, why don't you go try to go to sleep? It's been a long night for your momma."

My brother squeezed my shoulder and then stood up. I listened to his footsteps as he started to cross the room.

"Yossel, wait. I'll be right over," I told him

"Visit after you rest, Etcia. I want to hear you snoring," he said.

The children laughed. For once, I didn't have the energy to argue. My brother must have been tired too. I lay down. The *varetta* was pulled over all four of us. I had to breathe deeply only for a minute or two before my body crashed back into sleep.

— ◆◦◆ —

Yossel and I huddled on the edge of his sleeping quarters. His family was asleep. Momma was asleep too. Their breathing was labored yet peaceful. It relaxed me to listen to it.

I often felt this kind of serenity after I'd been outside. I'd noticed Yossel, and even Mendel, were animated the day after they'd been outside. Sometimes they chattered about how lucky we were. It wasn't surprising. The walk outside, the clean air, and the fact that we had cheated death under the moon restored us. The food I had brought back was as precious as breast milk for my babies. The few hours I spent walking on the topside always helped prove I belonged.

"I heard you come in. I was so pleased," he said.

I wondered if he remembered coming into my sleeping space the previous night, Marek screaming, the way that I had lost my composure looking for the duck.

"I'm going to cut you some of that duck," I said. "For your family. For Momma."

Yossel was silent for a long time. His breathing was labored, as if he were running back from that dream.

"Oh. That fox. We have to do something. We should try to catch it," he said.

"I guess he's not the only one who lives in Popowa Yoma," I said.

"No, probably not. Still, we must protect ourselves," he said.

I laughed. I refused to add the fox to the list of things I should worry about. But it was okay if it gave my brother something to do.

"I can't take the duck, Etcia."

"You can. You will. It was a gift."

"No, Etcia. We agreed when we first came down here to take care of our own families. Your children are lucky to have you, but you can't carry as much as we can. They need the nourishment. Make sure they get it," he said.

He coughed a few times. It sometimes happened when he spoke too many words at once. I leaned my head back, listened to the thick breath of Pepcia and Nunia and Momma, and to the silence of our neighbors on the other side of the rock. I wondered if I had let Yossel get enough sleep. It was our habit to check in with each other after we went out, to share news.

"It was such a clear night, Yossel. There were so many stars," I said.

"Did you see the Big Dipper? Cassiopeia? The ram?" he asked.

"I saw stars," I said and laughed. He laughed too. "It seemed to go on forever, the sky. It was so wide and clear and long, like a long black piece of fabric that we'd cut tiny holes in. So beautiful. Almost like the old world, like nothing had changed."

Yossel laughed. Then he coughed. Then he laughed again. "Etcia Goldberg, I've never known you to be so sentimental," he said.

"Hush," I responded.

He patted me on the shoulder.

"Birds were there. Many of them. You were right. They did make me feel less lonely," I said.

The dark air all around us was a blanket. It covered us.

"I know where you got the duck, Etcia," he said. "He's a good man."

"He's a friend. To all of us. He is loyal to Chaim," I said.

Yossel whistled a low, deep whistle. It didn't sound like any of the birds I had seen outside. It was soothing, though. Across the cave, someone whistled back. We laughed.

"I know, Etcia. Please do not take my words the wrong way. I'm not trying to pry."

There was nothing to say.

"Did he have any news?" Yossel asked.

"Good and bad. The Nazis are taking more Ukrainians to work in Germany. They are settling in. But the partisans in the Carpathian Mountains are causing a lot of problems for the German army. And the Russians are beating the Nazis bad. They have liberated the left bank of the Dnieper River all the way up to Kiev. They may be here soon."

Yossel rubbed his beard, considering all this. There was a faint smile on his face. "They give you a date?" he asked.

"Maybe five, six months."

He whistled again, a low, sweet sound that carried off the walls of the cave.

Chapter Twenty-Three

I T WAS EERIE being in the village so close to the holidays. It reminded me of how long we'd been in hiding. The wind had already picked up enough to erase my footprints from the few inches of snow on the ground. Cold seeped through the fabric I had wrapped my feet in to protect them from the giant holes in my shoes, searing my soles. The wind blew right through my threadbare clothes, practically knocking me off the ground.

I had stopped shivering. I walked blindly, as if in a dream. Several times I veered from the path. I found my way back, but it felt as if I were walking in circles. Every time I looked up, things seemed even less familiar. At moments it felt as if I had been walking for many kilometers, only to return to the exact spot where I'd started.

Panic beat in my chest. A jittery feeling coursed through my body. I had a bad stomach cramp. I was in a dangerously unbalanced place.

I considered going back to the cave empty-handed. I was too close to the village, though. A voice deep within me spoke reason. The snow would keep falling. There would be fewer opportunities to go out. Our food wouldn't last the week.

Stay focused, Etcia Goldberg, the voice said.

I arrived at the village. I traveled like a sleepwalker. My eyes barely registered the houses up and down the road. There were still Christmas wreaths on the doors. Through some windows, I noticed the trees and the boats and animals children had cut out of paper. It distracted me, these decorations, as if they too belonged to a world that was lost. At the moment, it was unfathomable to me how there could be a place where things were going on as they had been before, where people were celebrating holidays out in the open, perhaps even dressing in their best clothes, joining long processions and caroling around town.

Somebody watched me from behind. I kept moving by rote because that was the only way to keep him from shooting me. My thighs were heavy stones. I moved so slowly, I was practically moving backwards.

Wake up, Etcia. Pay attention. Your children need you. Do not let yourself die, the voice inside me said.

I turned the corner of a road and looked around. Nobody was there. Nobody was following me. I looked up, trying to get my bearings. I saw a sign marking the crossroads of Urampol and Zalishchyky. I had gone too far.

◆◆◆◆◆

It wasn't a decision that drew me towards the house of our old neighbor Nester Rosinski; it was instinct. I only knew only I had to make it somewhere inside. I reasoned with myself, remembering Rosinski had always been a kind, jovial man, that he was one of the customers who spent hours smoking pipes and laughing in the store with Chaim.

I walked towards the door in the yard, sheltered by the giant spruce tree that separated our houses. I knocked one, two times. Then I waited.

I turned to go, but panic slapped me awake. My cheeks were frozen. My mind was not working correctly. I needed to get inside.

I ran back to the door and knocked again, as loudly as I could, praying I wouldn't awaken any neighborhood dogs. The house was silent. A frozen clothesline shook in the wind.

Nester, the voice inside of me cried. *Nester, it's Etcia. Wake up!*

Please, God, I thought. *Help us. Please help.*

Did I imagine somebody standing in our old yard staring at me? *Rosinski*, I prayed.

A light turned on in the house. A stocky man hung out the window. Behind him was a woman.

"Rosinski," I called quietly. "It's me, Panna Goldberg."

The window slammed shut.

A chill passed through me. Everything inside me screamed, *Run! This was a mistake! You must go now!*

Instead, I stood still.

Nester came to the door. His face was unnatural, as if he were wearing a mask. His body was jammed against the side of the half-opened door. He stared at me and chewed the side of his mouth.

"I'm sorry to trouble you," I managed.

"Oh, Panna Goldberg. You have changed. You are wearing man's clothes. I did not recognize you."

He barely moved. His body was wedged like a boulder in the door.

"Just for a minute," I pleaded.

"Come," he said. There was something tinny in his voice, something untrue.

I followed Rosinski to the kitchen, where his wife, Anna, was standing by the stove in her nightgown. Her gray hair hung loose down her back. Her shoulders were slightly stooped. Even before she looked at me, I could see she was scared. She turned towards me. It took her a second for her to register who I was. Her mouth opened slightly; an "oh" sound escaped from her lips. She wasn't just surprised to see me; she was annoyed. She looked at me as if I were a ghost.

"You're shaking," she said. "Sit down."

She walked angrily around the room and came back to where I sat on a bench with a blanket. I wrapped it around me. The shivering racked my body. It was a good sign. Shivering meant that my blood was starting to warm again, that the feeling was returning to my body. It was one of the odd details I'd picked up from Chaim.

I was surprised to see Mrs. Rosinski come back to me with a mug of hot tea. She put it in front of me without a word. Her husband's eyes were on my back.

"You can't stay here," Rosinski said.

"I don't want that. I'm sorry. I will go," I said.

The room we were in was shabby. The light flickered, and the table was scarred. I didn't dare look at Nester too closely. I saw his wife's pale complexion, the uneven set of her jaw, the way her cheeks were drawn.

"You left the house a mess. It stunk," he said.

I looked at him uncomprehendingly. What did he mean? Rosinski was a carpenter. It was possible he was looking to the houses of the Jews who'd been killed for materials to use for his work. I imagined him in our house, dismembering the windows and staircase and fences, all of the things Chaim had so carefully built after we were married. Indignation cut me. The children and I were still alive. That was our house.

"What?" I asked.

"It was messy. The house," he said.

I realized I wasn't dealing with a sane man.

"I'm sorry, Nester. I didn't mean to," I said.

It seemed to pacify him. His expression changed. He resembled his old self.

"Why are you even here?" he asked.

"I don't know. I didn't mean to be. I got lost, I guess. I was walking, and then I looked up and saw I was on our old road. You were my friend here. Thanks. I will go now," I said.

I reasoned with myself that if they were both in the room, I would be safe. If they didn't leave the room, I wouldn't have to worry they would call somebody on me or go get a gun or a cleaver or a knife.

Anna walked over to me. Nester stared. I knew it was a rebellious act. She seemed so frail, so broken. Her heart was still intact, though. The fact that she was talking to me meant her courage might have been intact too.

She squeezed my arm. "What do you need?" she asked simply.

I sipped the tea, trying to think of something small that would allow her to continue to defend me because she believed she had helped, but would get me out the door quickly. I didn't want to ask for food and set Nester off. It was too dangerous.

"You know what would be nice? Some spoons. There aren't enough for me and the children," I said, taking a gamble. Bringing the children up would alert them they were still alive. Their children had gone to school with ours.

"And what else, Etcia? Please," Anna said.

"Maybe some clothing. My children are still growing. Their clothes are small and torn," I said.

"The children," she said, the faintest smile trailing out of her lips.

"Yes—Mania, Dunia, and Marek. They are all healthy," I said.

"We have some old clothes our children have outgrown," Nester's wife said.

"Anna," he scolded.

Nester's wife walked around him and went into the other room. She made a racket, slamming around. Nester leaned against the counter, his chest puffed out, deliberately not looking at me.

I sipped the tea, remembering the move Yossel showed me to use if I was ever in danger, to take my two fingers and jab them at the hollows of a man's throat, then kick him down below. The longer I stared at him with his smug expression, the angrier I got.

Stay quiet, Etcia. You don't know who his friends are now. It's not safe, the voice inside reminded me.

Anna came back into the room, carrying a bag in her hand. Nester wasn't looking at me. Anna met his eyes, longer than he was comfortable with.

"It's pointless," he said. "Can't you see? She will be killed. Her children will be killed."

I didn't move. Anna walked past her husband and slammed open a drawer, pulled out some silverware, and put it in the bag. She walked over and handed the bag to me.

"Thank you," I whispered, the words barely reaching the air. I put the bag to my chest the way that Anna carried it into the room. She nodded, then walked away.

I walked over to Rosinski. "Nester," I said. "Don't say these bad words."

I waited until he looked at me directly, so closely I could see threads of red veins in the white part of his eyes. I could see what was going on. He was not angry but scared.

"Tell me, what did we do to deserve this?"

I turned from him and walked down the long, dark hallway back to the door.

◆◈◆

I walked as quickly as I could through the streets and then into the trees behind the houses in our old neighborhood, cursing myself for being so stupid. Nobody in the cave had mentioned Rosinski's house. My actions were only a result of walking in the cold without enough calories.

I made a pledge to myself to be the old practical Etcia, to remember my old paths. The faster I walked, the more blurry my head felt. Something still wasn't right. Rosinski might have sent people out after me—soldiers, neighbors, people with dogs. I didn't dare stop walking, but I was still disoriented. I thought it might be wisest to make a run for the woods, to return to the cave empty-handed.

Two thoughts stopped me. The first was that if I were being followed, they would go back there with me, that I would be responsible for the deaths of the thirty-seven other people in the cave, including my children. The second reason was the weather. Soon it would be nearly impossible to get back out. I remembered peeling Marek's sweaty undershirt off his clammy skin, the sound his spoon made when it scraped the bottom of the bowl.

I started to run, holding the flimsy bag of clothes in my hand, darting through backyards, staying as close to the tree line as possible. My body was betraying me. Something was wrong. I stopped short near an old spruce tree and collapsed on my knees. I kneeled there, pressing my hands into the ground. A whistling sound pierced my ears. My stomach dropped. I felt that my bowels were about to fall out. I leaned over to steady myself, then vomited on the ground.

I kneeled there, swaying a little, until the world became solid again. Another wave of nausea rose up in me. I leaned over, vomited a little bit more, then wiped my face with one of the shirts Anna had given me. I waited. Slowly, my composure returned. I could breathe normally. My mind was clear. I pulled my hair back over my ears, wiped my hands on my trousers, then picked up the bag and stood. I started walking again.

———◆•❈•◆———

I stopped when I was on the outskirts of Joseph's neighborhood. It was miraculous that I hadn't been followed. My choice to visit Joseph then was more habitual than accidental, the flight path of a bird homing in on a familiar place without knowing why. I didn't want to intrude on his life, but I didn't have a choice.

When I got near his house, I cut through some yards. I put my empty bag on the ground near a tree trunk. The darkness protected me. I needed some time to think of a plan.

I leaned my back against the tree trunk. It felt so solid, so strong. Who knew something to lean on could become such a gift? The ridges of the bark felt good on my head. The cold air shocked me awake. I breathed deeply and rubbed my hands on the snow.

Snow had different meaning for me then. It was clean. It could be turned into water. I picked some up to rinse my mouth and shoved the blouse I used to wipe my face deeper into the bag. I felt the rest of the clothing Anna had given me. There was some cotton and something of a warmer material, like wool. I felt the stiff edge of a boy's pant leg. My knuckles banged on something hard, and I dug up Mania's spoon.

I sat there, imagining how the children would receive these luxury items. It didn't matter they were Rosinski's. Perhaps the spoons would charm Mania into believing life was still possible in the cave, that maybe there was a new dress in there that would make her feel pretty. I imagined her laughing as she did as a girl when I tied ribbons in her hair, made her pigtails and braids. I imagined her sitting on her knees on the tall stool in Chaim's store, watching her father ringing up a customer.

Stand up. Run. Get inside, the voice scolded.

I jumped up, straightened my clothes, and looked around. There were no trucks, no soldiers, no angry villagers standing by the woods with hatchets and knives.

There was nothing but a yard covered with unblemished snow.

The path to Joseph's house was clear.

———◆◆◆◆◆———

It was strange to be in Kostaski's kitchen again. I was intruding on his quiet family home and—if he ever got caught with me—on his life and freedom.

"You don't look well. Tell me what happened," he said.

"I went to see Nester Rosinski. It was a mistake, an accident. I wasn't thinking clearly. Maybe it was the cold."

Joseph nodded slowly.

"I thought he would follow, report me. But I circled around for a while. I don't think anyone was chasing me. I don't know, though," I said. My voice was shaky. It disgusted me. This was not Etcia Goldberg.

Joseph stood up. "I hear he's more a danger to his own family these days. He's a coward," he said. "There is soup on the stove. Please fix yourself a bowl. I will take a look around and make sure it is safe. Listen. If you hear me make a lot of noise before I come back, hide in the place where you hid with the children," he said.

"Joseph I can't ask you to—"

"*Sha*, Etcia. Don't be silly. We are friends. The war didn't change that. Eat some soup. Rest."

I sat there, my head shaking slightly, ready to nod off. I was in no position to argue. Maybe he would be gone long enough that I would regain my senses. Maybe I'd be able to plan.

When the door slammed, I looked towards the stove. I had no desire to walk over there. If I did, I thought I might fall over again. Besides, for the first time in months, the idea of food didn't appeal to me. I sat there quietly, praying to God to restore me.

I looked around the room. It was ordinary, solid, a room used as it was intended. There was a teapot on the stove, sturdy pans hanging on the wall, some sewing work with blue and pink threads that Marta must have made. On the shelf over the fireplace was a clock. Twelve-thirty. I nodded, thinking how remarkable the clock was, its round numbers measuring time. I didn't need a candle to read it.

Twelve-thirty was also a blessing. It was winter. Twelve-thirty meant I still had plenty of hours left, eight or nine, before dawn cracked the sky.

I looked towards the staircase, wondering about Marta. The cave had taught me that when some of your senses are taken away, others develop even more. When we couldn't see as well in the dark, we heard better, sensed the slightest motion of people moving around. Joseph's wife probably knew I was there.

I decided not to worry about it. I was there only to keep my children alive.

—◆·❖·◆—

When Joseph came back inside, his pale eyes looked happy, relieved. He'd always been restless, and in the winter, I guessed his urge to be outside was often quashed. I remembered in previous years when Chaim used to visit his workshop and come back happy. I imagined the workshop was both warm and cold, that the two men spoke about things happening in the village while Joseph mended shoes.

"There is no sign of anyone. The village is sleeping," he said. He came over to me, rubbed his chin. "You don't want some soup?"

"Thank you. My stomach is not right."

Joseph looked me up and down, stared at my boots, then sat down in the chair across from me.

"You look sad. Unlike you," he said. "We are the sane ones, remember? We do what is right. You are a mother trying to keep herself and her children alive. It is that simple," he continued.

"I am not bothered by Nester," I said.

"Then what, Etcia?"

"We are running out of time. Before the big snow. We will be trapped down there. We don't have enough."

Joseph stood up and walked across the room. He returned with a hot cup of tea and set it in front of me. The sight of the steam soothed me. I put my hands around the cup, warming them.

He stared at me the way he had the last time I was there. I'd never been a bashful woman. Still, the blood rushed to my cheeks.

"First thing, you probably got sick because you were chilled. Heat escapes through your head and your feet. You probably have no soles left in those boots. Am I right?"

I smiled. You couldn't argue that kind of thing with a shoemaker.

"So take them off and let me fix them. You have plenty of time. You don't want to go back and have the same thing happen. Maybe you will knock on the door of a Ukrainian police officer, ask them to arrest you."

I laughed despite myself. It was true. I had acted foolishly. The reason for my foolishness was a physical problem.

"So, the boots please, Panna Goldberg," he said.

"It's okay. I will be careful. I don't want you to wake the children," I said.

"The children sleep like rocks. Besides, this is no time for stubbornness. Some men from the cave let me fix their shoes for them. Did they not tell you? Your work is carrying food. Your shoes are your tools. You cannot get your work done with bad tools. Please, take them off."

Joseph deliberately turned his back and walked towards the stove, pretending to be warming himself while I took off my boots. I took the fabric I had wrapped around my feet off and shoved it in my pockets. My socks had patches all over them that I had sewed on, but they were still in one piece. I put the boots on the chair beside me.

Joseph came back and picked up the boots. He nodded at me seriously and then smiled. "Good. If you can't eat, you should try to drink some tea. It will improve your mood," he joked. "Relax. You don't have to rush out yet. It's winter. When I come back, I will have a solution. I get my best thinking done in the workshop," he said.

"Is that true?" I joked.

"Yes, of course it is true. You will see."

Joseph came back and handed me the boots. I examined them. The soles had been replaced. The holes on the sides were patched. They looked brand new. He was right. It would be an easier walk.

"They are wonderful, Joseph. Thank you," I said.

He stared deliberately. He wouldn't stop. Heat flooded my body.

"It's not proper for you to pay so much attention to me. I am a widow. You have a family. I care only that my children are safe." I half whispered these words even though I knew that his wife couldn't hear us.

"I'm sorry," Joseph said. "I didn't mean to offend you."

"You didn't," I said and stared at him. I know he saw the tenderness in my own eyes. He half smiled.

It was the truth. I didn't know what Joseph's intentions were, but I knew he felt the same way towards me as I did towards him. There was a small part of me that was happy. My love for Chaim was a strong, respectful thing, but I had been too immature in those years to know my true heart. I didn't know if what I felt for Joseph was love. I just knew that I kept circling back to him like a bird because he reminded me that there was a place that I belonged.

It was nonsense anyhow. I couldn't afford the luxury of worrying about anything other than the children. My love for them was the most important thing.

"You did not believe I would have smart thoughts while I worked. But you were mistaken. I had a good idea. Just listen, Panna Goldberg. It will help everyone."

I nodded.

"In three weeks, I will come with my horse and my sleigh and bring you some supplies, some grain and some pounds of potatoes. I will bring enough for many people—your brothers, sisters, whoever needs it the most."

I examined him, his eyes shining as if he had had a nip of vodka. I tried to believe that part of his offer was related to the fact that he was restless and needed something to do in the winter. He probably hadn't thought the plan through.

"On a Tuesday...three Tuesdays from now. After midnight. Have somebody stand guard at the boulder. Let them know. I will make our special knock. Is somebody there all the time?"

"Yes. But Joseph, it's dangerous. Absolutely not. I can't let you do that."

I'd always known Joseph was kind and did what he recognized to be right, but I never thought he was brave enough to risk his life outside too.

"You don't have a choice. Besides, don't insult me,"

"It's dangerous. What if you are followed?"

"If I am followed, I won't lead them to you. Trust me, Etcia. Let me do this."

I raised my fingers and started to protest. There were tears in my eyes, though. I clamped them back.

"Think of your children. And the others," he said.

I sighed. I could not refuse help for the others.

"They won't open with just a knock. You need a password."

"Give me one."

"'New day in Korolówka,'" I said.

"Now you describe to me how to get there," he responded.

Chapter Twenty-Four

MEIMEL STOOD BEHIND Mania, softly encouraging her as she pushed the stick over the rolled-out dough. The grain was running out. The way Mania was learning to bake made it even more precious.

"This way?" Mania asked.

Meimel stared down at the bread, squinting her eyes in the candlelight. Her face was more severely drawn than the last time I had seen her. A bit of extra skin hung down, making her look older. There were deep shadows under her eyes. Still, her eyes were so tender when she looked down at Mania. Her lips were arched in a smile. If it hadn't been for the candle, for the bunched-up rags we were wearing, we could have been standing in one of our kitchens at home.

"Good girl. That is just right," Meimel said. She moved closer next to Mania and stared at the dough. "Knead again like I showed you. Soon we will braid it like *challah.*"

Mania's body had not filled out yet, but she was taller. The quiet, concentrated way she kneaded the dough, pressing her palms up and down

233

like Meimel showed her, made me smile. *Mania isn't broken anymore*, I thought. *Even down here, she is becoming a woman.*

"Okay. Now, watch me first. Then we will knead it out, and you can braid it," Meimel said.

Mania stepped back, and we watched Meimel separate the dough into three sections attached at the top and braid it in a similar way that my mother had taught me to make *challah*.

"Isn't going to last so long," Mania said. She had started to imitate the clipped language so many others had started to develop in the cave. Sometimes the beginning of sentences were cut off, sometimes the ends. But the essential parts were always there.

"It's probably still snowing," Meimel said.

"Yes," Mania agreed.

It had been a long time since anyone had been able to go out, and it would probably be a long time before we could emerge again. I had dreams of the snow. Sometimes it was the snow outside the cave. It wasn't the real snow, though. It was imaginary. It was taller than the houses. It had fallen so deep, it obliterated the village, had covered horses and carriages and men. I always woke up feeling so cozy, an animal burrowing in a den. It was as if we were the only ones left in the world.

"I remember snow," Mania said simply, as if the word were a foreign language.

Meimel took the bread off the long slab we had built and walked over to the stove. I blew out the candle. Meimel slid the bread in. The scent of wood smoke filled my nostrils. It made our eyes burn.

"Do you know what I remember? How much we whined and complained when it snowed and we couldn't go outside right away? We were so spoiled then," Meimel said and laughed. We all laughed with her.

Meimel, like Mania, hadn't been out since we had gone down into the cave. She hadn't been stuck on the snowy hill with the animals all night after escaping from jail. The snow hadn't caused her to walk in circles, knock on the wrong doors, and throw up in the middle of the woods. It was still magical to her, part of a broken world she'd temporarily lost the right to visit. To me, it was poison. My last experience above ground had frightened me in a way nothing else had. It was as if my mind had been stolen.

"Hopefully, the snow will stop, and we will get outside soon," I said.

Nobody responded. Among the men, I was regarded as a hothead, demanding to go outside at times they believed were suicidal. But I demanded to go out only when it was the only thing we could do. It was neither bravery nor suicide. I did what needed to be done. The fact that they often couldn't see it themselves, or perhaps saw it but didn't want to act on it, made me angrier than anything else.

In the winter, I was torn. On the one hand, I was relieved for the snow. It gave me no choice. Even if I'd wanted to go out, it was impossible. The snow was too deep, and we were sealed in. On the other hand, winter could kill us. That loaf my daughter had just learned to make was our last.

"What if it never stops?" Mania asked.

I heard the bread being turned, logs moving around. When Meimel came back, she stood near Mania and sighed.

"I have a secret," she said. "The war will end. Life will return. When that happens, Grigori Ivasiuk will let us know. Because of course it could happen and we wouldn't know. We could be free for weeks and still keep living down here," Meimel continued. She stopped for a minute, catching her breath. She coughed a few times, then took a sip of water.

Something screeched. It was an animal, maybe a bat, roosting somewhere above us. It was a terrible sound, the way it bounced off the walls, and we could never tell exactly where it was.

"The way he will let us know is he will throw a bottle through the opening of the cave. He will put a note inside the bottle to tell us what happened. That is how we will know we are free. Mendel told me this," Meimel said.

I smiled. I'd already heard that rumor. I knew it was a premature gesture. Probably Munko had said that to give us some hope.

"That will be nice when that happens," Mania said.

"Yes. It will be nice," I agreed.

I sat on my bed daydreaming about life outside. It was nothing distinct, just Joseph and I walking on a trail beside a brook. I imagined us sitting down to a picnic and eating real food: fried chicken, corn, good cabbage salad. The sky was so clear and blue. Warm wind brushed my cheeks. Joseph was laughing. We weren't afraid to be there. The soldiers had all gone home.

The daydream was normal, and so it was unreal. The blue sky, the chicken, the safety were all as unfathomable as the ocean or outer space. It was okay to think about foolish things as long as they remained part of a dream.

The whole day had been nonsense. There was nothing to do. The laundry was clean. Our area was straightened. We had hours to go before food. It was no longer as tough for me to give in to nonsense, to linger in dream. It was practical. We conserved energy when we dreamed.

"Etcia. Me. Yossel." My brother's voice penetrated the dream. I sat up, embarrassed, as if he could have been viewing my dream.

"Down here," I yelled.

Yossel stumbled a little, stubbing the side of the bed with his toe. He kneeled down beside me, so close I smelled his beard. It had become our habit. If we were close enough, we anchored each other.

"I have bad news," he said.

"You are joking," I said. I laughed. He didn't.

"Your friend Fucia and her husband. They were turned in."

I rocked slightly on the bed, placed my hand on my chest bone. "Was she killed?"

He sighed deeply. I smelled the ripeness of him, his sour sweat. "They were arrested. Taken away. Nobody knows."

"Who turned them in?"

"Unclear."

I gripped the side of the bed, remembering the suspicious feeling I'd had in Daria's house.

"Daria, Nusia. Were they captured too?"

Yossel clicked his tongue no.

I sighed. Of course, we'd never know.

"I took a terrible risk being there," I said.

Yossel squeezed my shoulder. He left his hand there. He'd been the one who suggested that house.

I woke up to the sound of boys clamoring near my bed. I opened my eyes slowly, feeling as if I were underwater, as if the small hands reaching for me, poking me, were rescuers at a lake I had drowned in. It took me a second to touch the hands on my shoulders, to pry them off, to make out the words they were saying.

"Auntie Etcia, come on. He is here. There is food. He wants to see you. Kostaski," they said.

A heat flushed me. I put my hands on the side of the bed, held them for three seconds, and then pushed myself up.

"All right," I said. "Calm down. I'm coming. You should know better than to sneak up on an old woman when she is sleeping."

I got up too fast. The dizziness rushed me.

"Where?" I asked.

"At the entrance. He can't stay too long. You must hurry," Mundek said.

"Can we come, Momma?" Marek asked.

"I think it's better if you wait. I will be back soon."

"He came on horses!" the small boys said.

"Please, Momma!" Marek begged.

In the whole time we'd been down there, we'd never gotten a visitor. And on a horse and sled! These were creatures that barely existed in some of their imaginations.

"Okay, but you must promise to listen to everything Momma says. Do as I say. Exactly," I said.

"Yes, Momma," Marek said.

"Show me," I said.

Tiny hands grabbed my own, and we walked, as if in a parade, down the passageways. A younger one walked in front of us, apparently marking the route back. The entrance was new, but it was close to the old one, so the route was the same as it had always been. Normally, the children wouldn't be allowed anywhere near the entrance, but this time it was different. Although the children were all sleepy, they were running with excitement towards the entrance.

"He came on horses!" a child repeated.

Each step I took, I imagined Kostaski's horses plowing through the snow and was filled with equal measures of relief and dread. Was it a mistake that I had asked him to come? Kostaski had insisted that sled supplies would save us, but would they also bring the authorities? I imagined the clip-clopping of the horses over the fields, imagined them being followed. And where would he park them? What would people think if they saw a horse and cart parked in the snow? Did people suspect we were still down here? If they did, did they care? And was Kostaski savvy enough to outsmart them? Although he was respected for helping the Jews, I often wondered if the fact that he hadn't gotten caught was due to his wits or to dumb luck.

If it was Chaim who was protecting him, I prayed he would continue to do it.

When we arrived, people were bottlenecked at the entrance, and the atmosphere was one of reunion, laughter, and celebration. It seemed dangerous to me for everyone to be speaking so loudly so close to the world. I'd mentioned to my brothers that Joseph might come with some food, and I know they told all the other heads of household. Still, people were acting surprised. Anything that fell outside our daily routine, any change, took some getting accustomed to those days.

"Etcia, Kostaski has brought us grain and potatoes, enough to last the family for a while!" Yossel said. "He wanted to say hello to you. People are already out there. Join them."

"Are they sure it's safe?" I asked.

"Probably. If not, it's already too late," Yossel said and laughed.

He had a point. It would be rude of me not to go. Going back to my bed to sleep would draw more attention to myself, not less.

"Go quickly, though. Of course, he can't stay too long."

It was strange to go to the entrance with everyone watching. I was wearing the same clothes as always, but I hadn't even combed my hair. I didn't have all my layers on. It was only after I'd crawled through the opening, hoisted myself up in a familiar manner, and touched my bare hands on the snow that I realized I was also barefoot. I stood up.

"On the blanket, Etcia," a woman's voice said. It was Fradel. I walked towards her and stepped on a *varetta*. She laughed quietly, and I could feel her excitement. It was the first time she'd been allowed outside.

"Panna Goldberg," Joseph said. I looked up and saw him standing in the moonlight and wearing full winter gear—a wool cap, gloves, and a *koguch*. He looked so healthy and well-groomed compared to us. He looked handsome.

"I told you to tell them I was coming. Did I lie?" he asked.

"He brought supplies, Etcia. They will last for many weeks!" somebody in the crowd said.

"Thank you," I said.

I looked down the field towards the forest. It was windy enough. The faint footprints the horses had left had already been almost covered by the snow. I saw no evidence of human beings beyond it.

"There are so many stars, Etcia," Fradel whispered.

I smiled, put my hand on my heart. This moment would nourish my sister well.

"They gave me a fox," Joseph said and gestured towards his cart where a fox skin dangled. The men had been secretly trying to trap them. Laughter bubbled in my chest when I looked at Kostaski's cart. What if that was the fox his duck had attracted all those months back?

I looked at the horses, the solidity of their giant legs, the way their heads dipped as they waited. They looked magnificent to me, standing so still. One of the horses was white. His mane gleamed in the snow.

Joseph didn't dare look at me directly, but his attention shifted towards me. He was aware he might embarrass me.

"You ladies will catch cold with no shoes on," he said.

"You'd better get back before they catch you," I countered.

Everyone laughed. It was the truth. Still, we stood there in the snow under the moon for a moment longer. Then Joseph tipped his cap to everyone, mocking politeness. His eyes caught mine a second too long. We both turned away. A few men walked with him and hitched his wagon. I watched him walking, admired the sturdiness of his gait. It was like looking at the horses, who seemed so magnificent compared to us and who seemed to belong to a world we had lost.

"He is brave," Fradel whispered.

"Brave or a fool," I said and elbowed her lightly.

Fradel laughed. Her laughter sounded tinny.

I stood still, my body flooding with warmth, my head bent down to protect it from wind. I looked up only when I heard Joseph pull the reins. Then the heavy cart began to drag, and the horses started clopping through snow.

Chapter Twenty-Five

March

I WAS IN THE kitchen with Fradel and Mania. Mania and I were there only for company as Fradel cooked her thin, floury soup. Since Joseph had come, the kitchen wasn't such a depressing place for Mania to visit anymore. She saw the bags of grain and potatoes and was comforted by the illusion of food. She didn't know how long this food would be rationed, that we had only three more weeks at best before we ran out. I always hid our rations from the children. Though Mania was in some ways pretending to be a little woman by then, I still tried to shield her as best as I could.

In the darkness, I sucked on a raw potato, hoping she wouldn't notice. That night I would put the potato in their soup. I would eat only the liquid, giving the best parts to the children. This was a habit most of the women I'd spoken to in the cave had picked up.

"Hello, ladies," a male voice said.

"Fradel, Etcia, Mania," another man's voice said.

It took only a few seconds for Mendel and Ulo Barad to reach the part of the kitchen where I could make out their bodies in the dim candlelight.

Ulo stood next to Mania, and I noticed her move her hand to her hair, shifting her body nervously away from him. He was a few inches taller than she. It was still strange for me to see him standing upright.

"We have news," Mendel said.

"The Nazis have returned to Germany?" I joked.

"Somebody dropped some chickens down the entry?" Fradel continued. The men laughed half-heartedly.

I grabbed my shirt in my fist, as I had become accustomed to before receiving bad news.

"Tell us. It's better just to know," Mania said.

I had to remind myself that treating Mania like an adult made things easier on her, that it was better for her to know. She was trying her best to be independent, like me. She hadn't let me brush her hair in nearly a month.

"The water is running low," Mendel said.

"And the big pool? Has anyone measured it?" I asked.

Mendel ignored my question, cleared his throat, and walked over to Fradel, staring into the pot like a guard. There was a cruel tension between them.

"Stop hovering," Fradel said.

"Do not tell me what to do. You are using a lot of water in that pot," Mendel said.

Ulo mumbled something to Mania. She laughed. There was something girlish in that laughter that disturbed me. I brushed the feeling off like a leaf. She was only happy to have someone closer to her age to talk to.

"Please, Mendel. Fradel is doing nothing wrong. Just tell us. We have to know so we can all plan together," I said.

"It is low," Ulo said.

"How much longer?" Mania asked.

"Not long," Ulo said.

"There is hope because maybe not all the snow is melted yet. There could be new snow. It could run off, drip into the cave." Mendel said

"What if it doesn't?" Mania asked.

"It will last a month, maybe a little longer." Ulo said confidently.

"So we are careful. We make it last," I said.

Fradel took a sharp intake of breath. It probably had to do more with Mendel than the water.

"We don't panic," I instructed.

"Right," Mania said.

"When we go out, we must bring back water too," I said. "That is the only solution."

Mendel groaned. He knew as well as I did that that was impossible. Water weighed more than grain. We were getting weaker, not stronger. Each time we went out, we brought back less.

"And we pray," Fradel said.

Chapter Twenty-Six

SAT IN THE room with the men. They had long since lost their discomfort around me. I had gone out more than some of them, a fact that earned me respect. Winter was just starting to ease. We had been cooped up so long, we needed to remind each other it was almost time to travel.

The faintest scent of smoke lingered from a cigarette that was being passed around. When it came to me, I didn't take any but passed it to the next person, almost demurely—my concession to being a woman. They respected me for what I had accomplished, but some of the men were more conservative than my brothers.

I'd never smoked much until the war, when it became a small luxury, a substitute for food and comfort. I enjoyed the ritual of it, the sound the match made when struck, the satisfaction of taking a slow, long pull into my lungs. As the men passed it around, the cigarette tempted me. It evoked memories of better times, sitting on the porch with Chaim in the springtime, the birdsong rising in golden light. I made do with the memory.

"Did I ever tell you the story about the last time I was out?" my brother Mendel began. His voice boomed among the men. He was comfortable among them.

Yossel laughed. Mendel had told the same story a few times. It made him happy to tell it.

"I was coming back from town when I was approached by two peasants. Neither of them was very bright. I could just tell. They had nice clothes, but they weren't wearing them right. One's suspenders were falling over his shoulders. The kind of men who couldn't find wives," he said.

One of the other men chuckled.

"Well, they saw me, and I thought that was it. I knew the only reason I stood a chance was that they were dimwits. One stood at my front, one at my back. The tall one, the one with the suspenders, he took my bag. That was all the supplies. The other one took my cap. The one who took my cap pushed me lightly. The other laughed like a child. They stood there then, dimwitted, *behema*. They didn't know what to do."

Mendel's story trailed a little, and he beat his hand on his chest for emphasis. Someone laughed politely.

"If it had been three years ago, of course I would have beat them, no contest. I wouldn't have had to think twice. They might have been peasants, but they were Ukrainian," he said.

An uncomfortable silence passed. There were no class differences among us in the cave. But for a second, we remembered how much they had once mattered.

"I recognize that they are just two young guys out for a walk. They don't want to kill me, report me. Yet. But we know how fast that sentiment can change," Mendel said.

"So I think quick. I tell them, 'Okay, guys, you have my provisions. But just please give me back my cap. It's worthless. You see how old it is. It smells. But my wife would be mad if I lost my cap. You know how women are"

"They looked at each other. One tossed me the cap. It hit me square in the forehead, but I caught it. I put the cap on my head and bowed to them both at the same time, then walked away slowly, as if it were perfectly natural. I heard them prattling on, jostling each other, probably trying to figure out if they should go after me. Eventually, I got to the forest. I stopped near a tree. I looked back. The dopes, they were nowhere. Carefully, I took off my cap. I checked inside the hidden fold my wife had cut and stitched up for me. Do you know what I found there? Still stitched in the seam? My ten dollars! Our passage to Canada if we ever get out of here," he said.

Yossel whistled. There was low, polite laughter. I feared the men would be mad at him for mentioning money.

An older man cleared his throat. It was Nisel's father, Zeide Stermer. "Mendel was lucky. It will soon be time to go up again. We can't wait much longer."

"The ground is not yet thawed," somebody else said.

"Good. The earth is still frozen. We can move quickly in these conditions." Shimon said.

"That's good," Yossel agreed. "We will have to go soon. Aside from food, we need news. The Germans could have left already. We could be free now for all we know," he joked.

"Yes, they could be celebrating in the streets," I joked back. Yossel laughed. Nobody else did.

"We must plan better," Nisel said. "Every month brings more danger. Not just for us."

"What do you mean?" Mendel asked.

"Those who help us. The Olshansky brothers disappeared," Nisel said.

"We don't know what happened," Mendel said. "Maybe they were forced into labor for the Germans. Banderovtci could have taken them to fight for Ukrainian independence. Maybe they left and went to become partisans to fight the Germans. We just don't know," Mendel said.

"Maybe they were killed," Nisel said solemnly. There was definitiveness in his tone that quieted everyone.

"Is that the reason?" Mendel asked.

"What reason? No," Yossel said. "Who can tell? There is no reason anymore."

"This is true," Nisel conceded.

"Grigori Ivasiuk says they have taken Ukrainians and sent them to Germany to work," Shimon Kittner said. "Shot one who had a Jewish family living in their house. I have seen it."

Yossel whistled. Somebody lit a cigarette.

"Still, we must be more careful," Nisel said. "Protect those who have helped us, as they have protected us."

I swallowed hard.

"Etcia, when you go, do you think you can get over to Kostaski's, maybe have him fix our shoes?" Shimon asked.

I shuddered inside. "What do you mean?" I asked.

"The ground is cold. Our shoes no longer have any soles. It is more dangerous if we freeze out there. Get him to fix our shoes like he did yours."

I was glad for the darkness. "I am not the only person whose shoes Kostaski helped repair," I snapped.

An uncomfortable silence passed.

"Of course, Etcia, I mean no disrespect," Shimon said.

An anger rose in me I wasn't prepared for. Although we were all grateful for the food, I had been feeling wary since Joseph had left about how people regarded me. He didn't claim he had come to the cave specifically to help me, but everyone knew that he had. I didn't want them to judge me, to think I had done anything unscrupulous to deserve it.

"Kostaski is still good," Mendel said. "He knows how to keep safe. We can all visit him. We just have to take rotations again. Same with Grigori Ivasiuk. Who else has a place they know is safe, somewhere we could go?"

My awareness of the men's voices started to fade. I stood there stock-still, the way that I had that day in the snow. A whistling sound was trapped in my head. I couldn't tell if it was harmless, like one of my brother's birds, or the sound of something buried deep inside me, alerting me to danger.

Chapter Twenty-Seven

April

I SAT ON THE edge of my brother's bed watching Nunia, waiting for Pepcia to come back from the watch. Nunia wasn't asleep, but he wasn't quite awake either. He lay in that drowsy half state that had been so adorable in my other children when they had been toddlers. But in Nunia, it wasn't as much cute as it was cause for concern.

At two years and ten months old, Nunia seemed to be developing slowly. He laughed a lot but didn't speak much. He didn't stand or walk enough. He was malnourished, as we all were, but it took a harder toll on his body.

"Has he said any more words?" I asked Yossel.

"More sounds than words. He probably doesn't even remember the sun," Yossel said.

"When he is walking with two feet on the earth, he will remember. His body will heal," I said.

Yossel squatted on the floor, patching a rock that had fallen off his makeshift wall. He did things like that often. I often hoped the children would break something just so my little brother would have something to do.

Yossel dropped something metal on the floor, then clobbered the rock with what sounded like his hand. His breath strained with each motion.

"It's our turn to go out, Etcia. Tonight," he said.

"Yes."

"Will you go to Kostaski?" he asked.

I didn't respond right away. He pounded another rock into the wall, then picked up the metal again.

"Is there somewhere else I could go this time?" I asked.

I generally tried not to rely too much on the other men's routes; trusting my instincts would get me where I needed to go. But the experience with Nester startled me. The names of the Ukrainians who had been killed bothered me. Worse than that, my vanity was making me want to stay hidden.

"Etcia, nobody is judging," Yossel said. "Kostaski's is the best place for you tonight. Our options are getting slimmer."

"I will go. But Yossel, I want you to know—there is nothing going on between us," I said. "Nothing physical," I added.

He pummeled one rock into the wall and then another, his breath straining.

"Pepcia and me, nothing can break that. The more I grew to know her, the more I learned from her, the more I trusted her. It was like the way I trusted the men in the army, but even more. I trusted her with my life, all of it. She is my home."

He coughed, then punched his chest with his fist. It would have been impolite to interrupt. He had never spoken so many words in his life.

"Our parents loved us, Etcia, but they never taught us trust like that. We always had to prove our loyalty. We had to learn this from other people, Etcia. You, me, Fradel. Instinctively, we knew how."

"Yossel, I never knew you to be such an orator," I said.

"There are only two things we can be sure of anymore. The old rules don't apply. And we know who is decent and good," he said.

The metal reverberated as he pried out another rock.

"You have sacrificed so much for your children, your family. You must make your own choices. You know what is right. Don't deprive yourself of happiness, Etcia, wherever it comes."

Chapter Twenty-Eight

I WENT INTO KOSTASKI'S kitchen, bringing the warm, honeyed air with me. There was no longer any snow on the ground. Things were defrosting. The scent of crushed wheat and new grass and some other scent that was familiar, that came and went with the seasons, returned. It flooded my senses, made me almost light-headed.

"I can see in your eyes my appearance has changed," I said.

Joseph didn't flinch from the truth. He'd never been someone who lied.

"We have all changed, Etcia. I can't even imagine what you've been through. You do look a bit different. But you are still the same girl I knew," he said.

He stood up and I looked down at my arms, at the boniness of my hands, the extra flesh hanging off my forearms. I'd wrapped my pants with rope because they were at least three sizes too big now. My sweater had worn so thin under the arms, it was practically threadbare. My face was gaunt.

Joseph stood near the stove, ladling me a bowl of soup his wife had made, as had been our ritual. He put it and a spoon on the table. I nodded, thanking him. I dipped my spoon in the bowl, turned the soup both to cool it and to give me time to think of a response. I also didn't want to seem greedy.

The soup was mostly potatoes, corn, and carrots in a heavy cream, heavier than I was used to. I lifted the spoon and brought it to my lips, then swallowed. I took a sip of water to wash it down.

I always left Joseph's house without finishing all the soup in the bowl. I wasn't sure he understood why. How could you understand hunger if you had never sucked on a raw potato to keep it at bay?

"Your wife is a good cook. Please thank her for me," I said.

He nodded, looked at me sadly. "I'm tired," he said.

I stirred the soup in the bowl. My throat was parched. It was always dry. I looked up and met Joseph's eyes.

"I mean of the war," he said. "And it's a good thing. The German front is collapsing. The Russian troops are approaching. Sometimes at night, I go outside and can see the explosions, fire over the hills in the middle of the night. We are close, Etcia. Soon you will be free."

"I will believe it when it happens," I said.

He nodded sadly, rubbing his chin with his thumb and pointer finger.

"And if what you say does happen," I said, "then the Russians come? Even if they do, where does that leave us?"

"Didn't Mendel tell me Ivasiuk would throw the bottle to let you know?" he asked.

I laughed, a funny laugh that hooked in my throat. "I know we will find out," I said. "Eventually. That's not what I mean. We Jews are told it is safe to come out. And then what? Where does that leave us?"

"People will get used to normal life again. They will forget."

"That will not happen," I said.

"Etcia, I never knew you to be so fatalistic."

"You misunderstand. That is realistic. Even after all we have been through, I have no hatred in me. My conscience is clear. It will be harder for those whose conscience is not clear to forget. And so they will have trouble believing that we are here, even if they can see it with their own eyes. I know this is truth."

"Do you think you will stay here, Etcia?" Joseph asked. A sadness, barely discernible, tugged at his throat. It was the way a child sounds when he learns a favorite pet will soon die.

"I plan to live. That is all that I plan. I plan to walk with my two feet and my three children and all of their feet upright in the sunshine and pick flowers. I plan to watch Dunia play soccer and Marek go to the creek with his net and catch tadpoles and Mania play dress-up and fall in love. I plan to live. That is all that I plan," I said.

"That is good to hear," he said.

I ate in silence for a while. The rich cream made my stomach feel gassy.

"Do you think you will stay here in Korolówka, Etcia?" he asked. He made a motion to touch my hand, then pulled it away. A shiver passed through my body. I wanted him to touch me. I couldn't believe that part of me was still there.

"A lot of people are talking about where they will go if the war ends. Some to Canada. Others Israel, to follow the Zionists, like Chaim always said. I can't see myself having lived like a rat all this time, to have suffered and have foul-smelling clothes and cheeks like a skeleton, just to be forced away from my home. This is where we have always lived. This is where our ancestors lived. So it doesn't seem right to leave," I said.

Joseph fingered his chin again, deep in thought.

"But I can't say," I continued. "What kind of life will we have in the town, the *shtetel*, after losing so much? Will our lives still be miserable? What will be left of our neighbors?"

He smiled. I caught him staring at the hollow between my neck and my throat. I imagined him brushing his fingers there.

"I can't believe I just said all that," I said. "I haven't allowed myself to even think it."

"Then maybe you believe me. This land will again be free," Joseph said.

I shook my head definitively. The land would never be free. It had absorbed too much blood.

"Some things you can't erase from your memory," he said. Joseph was not usually that perceptive. "I'm sorry," he said quietly.

"There is nothing to be sorry for. You are a good man. You are brave," I said.

"I am not brave," he said.

"How can you say that? You are risking your life every day for us."

"I didn't know that I could. When I took you and the children in at the beginning, that was the first time. I didn't know that I could. Being around you made me strong."

I swallowed a piece of potato nearly whole and started to cough. I sipped water.

There was a long, awkward pause. I looked towards the clock. Three-fifteen.

"Etcia, there is something I want to tell you," Joseph said.

His eyes held mine. My stomach dropped. Joseph reached for my hand. First he brushed against it; then he put his hand on top of mine. I left it there a second, then pulled away. Heat rushed to my face.

"Don't Joseph. It's not right," I said.

"We can't stop our feelings," he responded.

I picked up my spoon, then dropped it back in the bowl.

"You don't have to say anything. But I need you to know," he said. "I care deeply for you. Every time I don't hear from you, I feel sad...worse than sad, like I have lost you. It's unbearable, the feeling. It agitates me. Every time I see you again, peace returns. I can't explain it. I've never felt this way before."

I stood up, pushed in the chair, and hoisted my bag. He stood up and met my eyes. We were exactly the same height, but at that moment, he felt so much larger than . I stared at his broad chest, keeping myself from letting my head fall on it. Joseph, more than anyone, knew my true heart. That whole year, he'd been my home. I was tired too.

I sat in the forest that night, languid, as if in a dream. I had made a conscious decision not to think about Joseph, though as I ran my fingers through my hair for a few seconds, I forgot that decision and imagined he was sitting there with me. I took a deep breath, remembering his scent: like musk and wood and shoe leather, the scent of a man who spent a lot of time outdoors. I imagined him wrapping his arms around me, hugging me, keeping me safe.

"Don't deprive yourself of happiness, whenever it comes," Yossel had said.

I craned my head towards the sky. The Big Dipper had shifted; the constellation almost pointed to the cave. It was time to go. I bent my knees to stand up but then stopped. A giddy panic struck me. I reminded myself my feelings for Joseph were almost irrelevant compared to what he had told me: "The German front is collapsing. The Russian troops are approaching."

Joseph's first thought came from a realistic place. It was true—we could be underground a long time before anyone got word to us. The problem wasn't that nobody knew where we were. People knew; we were sure of it. It's just that we no longer mattered. We were almost irrelevant. And so nobody bothered to remember us.

When we finally walked above ground in socks and shoes, would we continue to be invisible? Was it possible we had been gone for so long, we had really turned ourselves into ghosts?

———◆◆•◆◆———

Of course, I had not been the only one to get the news. The atmosphere in the cave had changed, but like the indefinable, senseless hours, our emotions were going haywire. Bouts of spontaneous laughter, joyfulness, and celebration were followed by anxiety, the sounds of people pacing and mothers scolding hysterical children.

When we lay down, we imagined the fronts moving back and forth, the explosions, a thunderstorm raining bullets.

Our lives had been suspended so long that the possibility that our imprisonment would finally end made us edgy. Some people didn't believe it could actually happen. Others were agitated that they had to wait. The last moments before release were the toughest.

One morning, Yossel came to talk to me. It seemed our worst fears had come true.

He sat on the edge of my bed, so close I could smell his sweat. "Are the children here?" he asked.

"Mania and Ulo are keeping company. Dunia and Marek are getting wood. What's wrong, Yossel?"

"Etcia, I tell you, we've come so close to our freedom. We've worked and slaved here underground so everyone can live, so we can keep our family together, so our two-year-old child can see the sunlight. We've come so close, and they want to take it away."

"Stop it, Yossel. Don't let the anger take over."

I waited, my brother sitting next to me on the bed.

"Okay, you are right," he said. He laughed. I laughed with him. "Oy," he said. "You are right. This is not me. I am a soldier." In the room next to us, a child cooed. "We were out there, me and Mendel and Mundek. We went out after you, just to be sure we had enough supplies in case we had to wait. It's wise to be prepared. Wars can linger."

"That is true. Smart," I said.

"On our way out, we stopped. There were two people dead—a man, Hersh Hollenberg, and his eleven-year-old boy, Chatzkel. They were good people," he said.

A groan escaped my lips. Yossel was close with this family.

"I'm sorry," I said.

"They tied them to the *schron* with barbed wire. Their faces were destroyed, off color, the tongue hanging out of the boy's mouth. Don't you see, Etcia? It was a warning. The Ukrainian bandits did it. They didn't like us so much before the Nazis came in. Remember?"

"I remember," I said grimly.

I wasn't the only one who was wondering what it would be like when we walked in the village again.

Dunia sat on the edge of the bed with his back to me. He was inconsolable. He hadn't been friends with Chatzkel, but we knew him. The boy was close to his age and had been killed close to our home.

My brothers shouldn't have told Dunia exactly how Chatzkel was killed. I didn't know if they did it to warn him, to toughen him up, or because they had long since stopped thinking of Dunia as a boy.

The longer we were in the cave, the less I tried to shield the children. They had seen dead bodies. They had seen a mass grave. Some of these things seemed to only graze their consciousness; others penetrated deeply. We could never gauge what their—or our—reaction would be.

"I can't tell you anything to make you feel better," I said. "What happened to that boy and his father is terrible. The Ukrainian bandits wanted to make a point. Now maybe you see how the darkness you always complain about has helped to save us."

"How can you even say that?" Dunia shouted.

Mania bounded into the room a few seconds before I heard the explosions of the other families around us. She ran like a small child, pounding the earth with her shoe soles.

"Momma! Momma! They found it! The bottle! We are free!" she screamed. She bounded down to the bed and tickled Marek. She squeezed me. I touched her face. Tears were streaming down her cheeks.

"We are free!" Marek screamed out.

"The boys found it," Mania said. "It was a glass bottle, old, blue. There was a note in it. The note was from Grigori Ivasiuk. It said, 'The Germans are already gone.' Isn't that amazing? Just those words. 'The Germans are already gone." Mania said.

"What does it mean, Momma?" Marek asked. "Are we free? Can we go outside and play with the ball? Can we go say hi to our old friends? Is it okay to go back to our old house? Can we go catch tadpoles in the stream? Will we see the sun? Let's go!" he shouted. "What are we waiting for? Let's pack our things, Momma! Let's go!"

It was too much at once. The words coming out of my children's mouths sounded like the screeching of the bats. They were talking a secret, angry, impenetrable language. I could make out only sounds.

"Children, hush," I scolded loudly. Mania and Dunia were hugging. Marek had smashed himself into my body.

"You are crying, Momma," Marek said, touching my tears with his fingers.

And so I was. All those years I had not cried, not once since Chaim's death. I didn't even recognize the wetness on my face as tears.

"Why are you crying, Momma?" Mania said sweetly.

"What's wrong?" Dunia asked.

"Nothing, children. I am crying because I am happy. This is beautiful news. But come, hug Momma, and let's have a chance to breathe a second. Let me think," I said.

The children stopped.

"All the things you said, we will do them in time. We will wear shoes and socks. We will walk in the sun. But slowly, my babies. We have been gone a long time. We must adjust. We will go up, but we have to plan first. We have to be patient."

We sat there, Marek pressed against my chest, Dunia rubbing my back, my fingers combing Mania's hair. I'd scared them a little. The fear would keep them in line. It was important to stay sensible.

All around us, people's emotions ran wild. I sat there, surrounded by my children, alive, unable to fathom the rest. I almost didn't believe what had happened.

———◆•◆•◆———

That night, the children's energy returned. Some of the girls deeper in the cave began singing, a light, airy melody I almost remembered. Mania had returned from a rendezvous with Ulo, flushed and embarrassed in the way she always was around him. Dunia had exhausted my brothers of tasks. It was a strange thing. We had been granted a reprieve. All figuring stopped.

"April 11, 1944—343 days. It will be 344 when we get up above," Dunia said.

I smiled and took a deep breath. We had made it. We had missed the one-year anniversary by just over two weeks. It would have been devastating to be down there a whole year.

"Three-hundred forty-four days," I said. "Just the blink of an eye. Like a dream. You have a long life ahead of you now, Dunia. Thank God," I said.

The girls' singing continued. Marek started acting like a three-year-old again. He took a running start and catapulted into my shoulder. I almost caught him, then heard him crash. He was making me dizzy. I'd forgotten how hyperactive children could be.

"Marek, you stop that right now. Act your age. The last thing we need is you breaking a leg," I said.

"Sorry, Momma," he said and giggled. "We are free, though, Momma, right? We are free?" he asked.

"We must be patient. We are going to go out in the daytime like real people," I said.

"Yes. And I will see my friends and go to the river and climb trees again."

"Why don't you children come and sit and rest with your Momma awhile? I would like to feel my precious children close to me this last night in the cave."

They gathered slowly. Dunia was on my left side. Marek sat on the edge of the bed near my right hip. Mania raked her hand through my hair and then drifted to the bottom of the bed.

"Are you scared, Momma?" she asked. Her voice trembled with its old fragility. Dunia cleared his throat.

"Of course not. We are strong," I said. "And you will be amazed at how good that sunshine feels on your head. And how good it feels to run and play and feel the wind and see the flowers again."

"Yes, that will be great," Mania said. "I would like to jump rope again."

I laughed. My Mania was too grown up for jump rope, but I was happy she still had the spunk of a girl.

"But it won't be perfect up there. He should be made aware," Dunia said, probably echoing my brother's words. The gravelly tone of his voice heartened me. We had made it. Dunia had practically grown into a man.

"It is true," I said. "It isn't perfect up there. We have been gone a long time. A lot of bad things have happened in the world. People are not all the way we remembered. When we go up there, we will conduct ourselves with dignity. We will move quickly and go to Granny's house first."

"Why not our house? Why can't we go to our own house?" Marek whined.

"Stop acting like a baby. You aren't a baby," Dunia scolded.

I wondered if my brothers had told Dunia that our house was no longer safe.

"We will go to Granny's house first to be with her," I said. "She doesn't want to be alone at first without Grandpa." I swallowed hard, something tugging my heart. It was strange to mention my father again.

"Okay. I'm sorry," Marek said.

"Hush. There is nothing to be sorry about. Do not ever apologize for who you are. Children, we have made it. We are strong and smart. Be proud of all the hard work we have done to survive down here."

"Some people up there, they won't like us?" Marek asked.

"Quit it," Dunia said.

"It is okay, Dunia. Your brother asks a good question. My children, there are some people up there who will be angry with us. We have done nothing wrong, but this war has changed them. They have been hurt too. Do not behave like everyone is your friend. Conduct yourself with dignity."

Dunia slammed his hand against the side of the bed. "They have no right to hate us."

"Some cannot help it. You know when you get a cut and it takes time to heal? The world is like that," I said.

"But they aren't all bad, right, Momma?" Mania coaxed.

"Oh no. There are good, brave, and strong people up there. There are people who risked their lives to help us. They gave us food and hid us, even though it could have cost them their lives. They are the people whom we have to thank God for. They are the people who remembered what is right."

"Like Kostaski?" Mania asked, Joseph's surname rolling off her tongue. She squeezed my calf.

It was a good thing we were still in the dark because I felt my face heating up.

It was that way all night. It was almost too much to fathom. All our senses were returning to us at once.

Chapter Twenty-Nine

April 12, 1944

THAT MORNING, WE lingered in bed a little longer, sipping the last intoxicating bits of drowsiness. Certainty that we would leave had settled overnight, yet fear still nuzzled against us. All those days in the cave, we had learned to strengthen ourselves by shutting down. There was a chance we would weaken once we were forced to stand up.

The others felt the same. Everyone had celebrated the previous night, singing and planning, but the next morning was solemn. Silence was broken by the occasional sound of pots banging, suitcases zippering, men dismantling walls.

It was our attempt at decorum to leave the place the way as we'd found it. Despite a few arguments, we'd managed to remain civilized. We hoped this would distinguish us from old neighbors we'd meet on the road who exploited the war to their advantage.

"What should we take with us, Momma?" Mania asked me that last day. Her voice was tenuous, strained from excitement and fear.

"Only the most precious things. What will remind us."

"I don't want a reminder of this place," Dunia said. It still surprised me.

"What will remind us of our strength, of the beautiful parts of ourselves," I said.

"But we don't have to live here anymore, right, Momma?" Marek asked.

"No, we don't have to live here," I said.

"Are you sure the bad men aren't out there anymore?" Marek asked.

"I am sure."

Dunia cleared his throat, possibly to let me know he understood there was still danger.

"You should each pick at least one thing," I said. "It is good to have a keepsake. I am going to take the most precious things I came down with, the photograph of your poppa and a bowl given to us from your great-grandma. You know it—the smooth one. I also have a hair clip for you, Mania, from your great-grandma. All this time, I was saving it for when we got out."

"Can I hold it?" Mania asked.

"Once we are bathed and your hair is washed and looks beautiful again," I said cautiously.

The children were silent. Perhaps they were stunned. The idea of a bath was incomprehensible.

"Where will we go, Momma?" Marek asked.

"Stop asking so many questions, little brother," Dunia said. "We have to take things slowly. The most important thing is to walk outside."

I wished Dunia was close enough that I could hug him.

"I will take the comb," Mania said.

"And you, Marek—what about your special rock? The sparkling one with all the creases you found by the lake with your cousin."

"Oh yes, can I pack it, Momma?"

"Put it in your pocket. There is no need for packing."

It wasn't humility. The things we had acquired weren't usable.

"I will keep my shovel," Dunia relented.

"Good," I said.

We waited for a while. I think we all felt a little nostalgic. No matter how bad things had been, this place had been home.

"Etcia, children, your turn," I heard Yossel's voice say.

"We are leaving. Get up, and let's clean first," Mendel said.

I sat up and saw Yossel and Mendel crouched down beside us, each of them holding candles. Behind them, the family waited, sitting on folded-up parcels on the floor.

<hr />

We stood in the tunnel of the cave, lined up like schoolchildren. Marek was in front of me, Dunia and Mania behind. Although I had been outside more times than any of the women and children and some of the men, it felt different this time. I was traveling through this passage for the last time, with the children. We were finally going to walk in the sunshine. The excitement was almost excruciating.

The passage that separated us from the entrance was pitch black. We sensed rather than spoke, as had become our habit. The line moved slowly, and each time it did, we were a step closer to freedom. It was unbelievable. Though we were less than seventy-five feet from our living quarters, in a few minutes that life would be memory.

"Momma, it's almost our turn," Marek said as he moved forward and loosened my hands on his shoulders. There were tears in his voice. I rubbed his shoulders, keeping myself from hugging him to me.

"Almost. Soon you will catch that sunshine, Marek," I said.

We took a step closer. There was slush and ice in the tunnel. The temperature was cooler. It must have snowed.

"I can see it, Momma. I think I see that sunshine," Marek said.

"Etcia, pass him up. Marek first," Yossel's voice echoed from the top of the shaft.

I stood at the bottom of the cave and lifted Marek.

"Now, pull yourself up, Marek," I said. "Crawl and you will find Uncle Yossel."

He squirmed out of my arms before I let go. My arms were empty.

"You go, Momma," Dunia said. "We will be right behind you."

"Go, Momma," Mania said.

We had agreed that I would go before them to help Marek.

My heart quickened as I made my way to the shaft. I had traveled that route many times, but still, as I jumped and hoisted myself up, it felt as if I'd never done it before. The intensity was again as if I were at the bottom of a river and pushing myself up to get air. The shaft was sloppy and frigid, and I squirmed up, the way I always had, up and up until I was finally at the top. On my knees, I breathed the air.

"Momma!" Marek shouted as he ran towards me. I hugged him tightly. The sound of light laughter from the others bubbled around me. I stood up and moved out of the way, joining the crowd to watch Mania's and Dunia's first breaths.

<hr />

When we were all outside, all thirty-eight of us, we stood there and bathed in the strong, even daylight. Some people were laughing. A few women cried. One child had fainted from shock when he first saw the sun. We looked at each other only long enough to recognize we no longer resembled the people we were. We were scrawny, with blue-veined, milky skin and thin, matted hair. Our mud-caked clothes barely covered our bodies. We nodded, acknowledging what we had been through, then averted our eyes, allowing each other the first few moments of privacy. Threaded through us was an indescribable awe. For me, it wasn't so much for the miracle of release as the fact that we had pulled ourselves through.

"It's real, Momma. The sun, the sky, the ground," Marek said and stomped his foot.

I laughed and tousled his hair. He cocked his head up. My breath hooked in my chest. There was something wrong with his eyes. The color was off; the white part was practically yellow.

Mania smiled shyly at me. Her cheekbones and hip bones protruded, and she still had the frame of a child. Her hair was so tangled, we'd probably have to cut most of it off. Still, there was a pride in her posture, in the way that she held her shoulders and head. *We made it*, her look said.

Yes, my darling, I thought, *we did.*

"Oy," I heard from behind me. I turned just in time to see my mother, Chancie, hit the ground in a faint. I rushed over. Mendel was already on the ground beside her, listening to her chest, slapping her lightly on her cheeks. She lay there, cold. Her skin was translucent in the sun, blue veins poking through. A sudden pain whacked me in the chest. *No*, I prayed inside my head. *No. After all this. Please don't let her be dead. No….*

"Wake up! Wake up, Momma!" Yossel was screeching like a child.

Just as I fell to my knees beside her, her eyes opened, her head still cradled in Mendel's hand. She breathed heavily. Collectively we did the same.

"Just rest, Momma. You've just had a fright. The sun. It was too much change for you at once," Mendel said.

"Oy, is she okay?" someone screamed.

"Yes, she's okay," Mendel hollered.

"Are you okay, Momma? Are you okay?" Yossel asked.

I looked at my mother, her head in Mendel's hand. Her face looked peaceful, shining. A slight smile formed on her lips. Her chin was cocked proudly towards the sky.

"Yes," she said weakly.

I laughed, then bent over and kissed her on the cheek. Her skin was thin, papery, like tissue. "We made it, Momma," I whispered, then stood up and walked back to the children.

I examined Dunia, wondering if it was dirt or beard scruff I was noticing on his face. He regarded me almost protectively, then scanned the field, waiting for a sign from his uncle.

We started off in a large group and headed towards the main road into Korolówka. We quickly began to see evidence of what we had been through—rusted and burned German tanks and cannons littered the gullies. The road I had traveled so many times in the dark looked foreign to me in the daylight, as if I had never walked it before. At first, we traveled in slow motion, unsure where we were headed. Then the first houses of the village began to appear, along with the birch trees we had known so well. We sped up. Although Korolówka was where we had been hunted, for most of us, it was also the only place we had ever called home.

When we reached the crossroads to the village, there were no people there to greet us. As if by some unspoken agreement, we hugged each other goodbye and split up, each headed down our own separate roads.

Our whole family turned together. We had made an agreement that we would go to Chancie's house first to get her settled in, but also because I knew our house was occupied. I didn't want to disappoint the children.

We passed the main street. There was a burned-out store on the main drag and a German motorcycle in the middle of the street. Beyond that, nothing seemed to have changed. Life occurred as it always had in the life that felt so distant now. A few people walked along the grassy road.

They were so clean and well dressed, it was almost as if they weren't real. I imagined what we must have looked like to them, a half-starved, disheveled group of Jews squinting in the sunlight in tattered, muddy clothes. Some of us were bareheaded. I imagined they would see us and scowl or start throwing rocks. Yet as we walked, nobody seemed to notice us at all. It was almost as if we didn't exist.

Chapter Thirty

M Y GRANDSON HAS stayed remarkably still through this story, as if a string had been pulled through his spine and knotted at the back of the chair. He's been staring at me, soaking it all in. I am surprised he is still paying attention.

"What happened then?" Valeriy asks.

I close my eyes. I am exhausted. The house smells of the chicken necks that are still warming in the oven. The table has to be set. I don't have the energy to move or provide my grandson direction. I have never before told this whole story in one sitting.

"Well, the war ended."

"There were only twelve Jewish people left in Borschow and none in Korolówka? After the war? From five hundred to zero?" he asks. Valeriy has always been good at math.

"Well, some escaped to other countries before the war, or even during the war."

"But there were more people than that in the cave with you. What happened to them?"

A bile taste rises in my throat. I swallow hard. "Many left—for Canada, America, or Israel too."

"But Granny, what I don't understand is why you stayed. You could have gone anywhere. Why do you stay here where they hate us?" he says.

"What, do you have rocks in your head? I told you. This is our home."

The way I snap surprises us both. The truth is I don't know exactly why I stayed. There was no plain reason for it. Joseph might have been partially to blame. I had imagined my feelings for him would last only as long as one of the candles we burned in the cave. I expected that when we returned to the ordinary world, the candle would burn down, the wick would be extinguished. The memory would be pleasant but dissolve, like the scent of smoke.

It would take many years before the world was ordinary again, though. And Joseph remained my touchstone. My feelings for him only deepened after I found my footing.

"It was all that I knew," I say to Valeriy.

Valeriy looks at his notebook and starts doodling songs he likes to play on his seven-string guitar. I watch him, remembering the long days Yossel sat with Marek teaching him to write. The children had some trouble catching up in school.

"What happened to your brother? The one who brought you down? The one whose grave we go visit with Mom on the holidays?" Valeriy asks.

The feeling that someone has taken an apple corer and pulled out a piece of my heart returns. The wind whistles through the hole.

"You are observant. Maybe you don't have rocks in your head after all," I say.

He smiles. I'm glad that I've flattered him. The knife has left a faint mark on his wound.

"Please, Granny, tell me. I'd like to know."

"Well, Valerchik, you are right that it was hard to get accustomed to our neighbors. The months after we came out of the cave, nothing seemed real. Our old house was occupied, so we lived instead in a two-story house on the opposite side of town."

"Were you scared of the neighbors?" Valeriy asks.

"I was living in an unreal world. Even though we were surrounded by neighbors who might have killed us months before, who might have actually killed some of our friends, I didn't feel anything bad could happen to us. It was as if we had passed a test surviving all those months underground. If we walked on solid ground, we couldn't be hurt."

Yet I had been mistaken.

Chapter Thirty-One

STOOD IN THE kitchen cooking my famous pierogies. I was making a special meal for Yossel. He was anxious because Pepcia had gone to the slaughterhouse two days before and had not come back.

It was summertime, and I had the windows wide open to freshen the house. It was still strange for me to see sunlight, to hear the birds, to stand upright and not clench my back against chill. Even though I knew we were back on earth and right side up, sometimes I couldn't tell if the cave was the dream or if this life was. I comforted myself by sticking to a routine, doing familiar things. I cooked as much as I could. I fed people. I encouraged people to talk. Often, I stood outside and just stared.

Nunia sat at the table with a pillow I'd turned into a car steering wheel, as my own parents had done for my brothers. He was anxious too, prone to screaming fits without his mother, Pepcia.

The boys were playing by the stream at my mother's house. Mania was with one of her old friends.

A knock at the door startled me. Yossel opened the door. There stood two Russian policemen. I turned back towards the pan and turned down the heat on the fried onions. They had just turned golden brown. They smelled sharp and tender. I pressed the edges of the pierogies into the perfectly even waves that everybody loved.

"Please sit down and eat before you go?" I asked the policemen.

"It smells good," one of the policemen said.

Yossel hesitated until I looked at him sternly. I fixed plates for each of them and set them on the table. Yossel kissed Nunia on the forehead. The boy wailed. I walked over, took his hand, and guided him away from the table. At the counter, I gave him a cookie. He calmed down.

"I can't take it anymore," Yossel said.

"Eat," I said to the policemen and Yossel.

They did as they were told.

"Tell me again why you are going to see Chechula," I said. Chechula was a bandit who hid on the outskirts of town.

"Mr. Rugitski told us that Chechula knows what happened to Pepcia," he said.

I paused, considering this. It didn't seem likely that Chechula would know.

"I tried everywhere else, Etcia. I even went back to the *schron*."

I watched the policemen's faces carefully for some trace of recognition after Yossel said this. One seemed to hunker down a little more, and something flashed in his eyes.

"It will be safe. We will surround the house and ambush him if he tries anything," one of the policemen said.

"You are kind," I responded. But in the back of my mind, I thought of the ways this ambush could go wrong. After all, Chechula was hiding from authorities and was probably armed. There was a strong possibility he would use weapons to avoid capture. In Yossel's quest to find Pepcia, he was risking his life.

I examined my brother, my big, strong brother, who was then wearing his clothes as neat and pressed as his old army uniform. My heart broke for him. He seemed so lost without Pepcia. He was imagining all the terrible things that could be happening to her. He had come above ground only to find himself powerless to protect her.

"I will hold on to Nunia as long as you need. Please be safe," I said.

<hr>

An hour later, I was scraping the dishes into the trash. I remember feeling pride that the men had finished every bite of their food, that I had fed them well and prepared them for their journey. I prayed Pepcia would be found. And I was looking forward to Yossel coming home.

I was still in this dream, believing we would be fine. I had tuned out my worry for Pepcia like a badly played song on the radio. It was always there in the background, but I didn't pay it any mind. It was partly that I was celebrating the new world we were living in. That was not entirely selfish. My body and mind were just starting to strengthen. I couldn't handle any more suffering.

Everyone has his or her breaking point. Sometimes you aren't even scratched by terrible things. Sometimes you are most vulnerable when you are the safest.

Yossel did not come back right away. After an hour, I heard the clip-clopping of horses and the heavy weight of a wagon stopping.

There was a knock at the door.

My thrombophlebitis was acting up a little, so I walked slowly. I noticed the solemnness on the policeman's face, his sad blue eyes.

I walked slowly outside the door. The air was warm. A faint scent lingered. It was so familiar, but I couldn't quite place it.

Convallaria. I remembered. Lily of valley…

Everything slowed down. I studied a horse the way I studied everything after we were free, as if it were a creature I'd never before seen. My eyes grazed its strong legs, its shoulders, the way the short hairs on its spine seemed to be brushed backwards, all the way back to its haunches.

I turned slightly then. I looked at the cart. Yossel was lying there, his limp body on top of a pile of straw. My first thought was that the man lying on the cart wasn't my brother. He looked like a doll, like a decoy.

"I'm sorry," the policeman said. He put his hand on my shoulder. It was too heavy, that hand.

It was as if everything had been frozen—the heat, the scent of flowers in the hot air, my heavy legs. A scream rose up in me. It was pulled from my gut to my heart to my throat and then poured out of me. "No!" I screamed. "No!"

I don't remember exactly what happened next. They tell me I ran to the cart and threw myself over my brother's body. I stayed there for a while weeping, clenching Yossel's cold hand. I cried hysterically, letting out all the grief I hadn't allowed myself since before the war. It just made no sense, how my strong brother, the one who had served in the Polish army and led our family to safety underground, the one who had protected us all of those nights, could have been murdered this soon after we were free. *It just makes no sense,* I cried to myself, *that I could be sitting here under the sunlit blue sky, free, holding my dead brother's hand. Why??* That one word screeched inside me.

I would not let go of that hand. I remember thinking that as long as I held onto it, I wouldn't have to let Yossel go. Eventually, one of the policemen had to pry my fingers from it. They stood beside me. They held me by the armpits and walked me through the doorway back into the house. Someone sat me down on the couch; someone else put a blanket over my legs. They narrated, as if in a dream, what had happened.

"Chechula was hiding on the upper level of the barn. The upper level was a loft style attic with a ladder leading up to it. Chechula put a German soldier's coat on the right side of the attic as a decoy to trick Yossel. As Yossel climbed up the ladder looking towards the right side of the attic, Chechula surprised him from the left side by shooting him from behind. We were waiting outside to ambush Chechula. We didn't know he was in the barn until he fired the shot. When we came into the barn, it was clear how the attack occurred. I'm sorry".

The policeman's words ran over me like the wind. I didn't move or breathe. I knew this could go terribly wrong, and it did.

"Yossel." The word found its way out of my mouth. My chest heaved. The tears didn't stop.

Eventually I heard the policeman's footsteps and the door close behind him.

Chapter Thirty-Two

"**G**RANNY, ARE YOU okay?" Valeriy asks.

I look up at him, see his soft cheeks, the bruise under his eye, the concerned way he is looking at me. I raise my shaking hands to my face, then pull a lock of hair behind my ear.

"I don't know much of what happened afterwards. They told me I was in shock for a month, that I was practically catatonic. A woman came and took care of me, feeding me soup. Joseph came too. He sat with me. He didn't speak much. Sometimes he sang. I wouldn't let them turn the lights on."

"Granny, it's okay. We're here now," my grandson says softly.

I look up at him, embarrassed by the tears that are flowing down my cheeks. He hands me a napkin from the table. I take it and smile at him.

"But you know what's good, Granny? You got to bury your brother. We can visit him now. You know where he is."

I look around my kitchen. Valeriy is still sitting at the table. His notebook is filled with songs. Joseph comes into the kitchen and stands in the corner, his eyes softening to my story. I think that Yossel had also brought me together with Joseph.

Just a few weeks after Yossel's death, I left Korolówka for Borschow with Joseph. Joseph left his house and all of his belongings to his wife, Marta, and his children. He never divorced Marta.

Pepcia was never found. Nunia lost both of his parents within days of each other. I wanted to keep Nunia and raise him as my own. But after discussions with my relatives, it was decided that Nunia would stay with grandma Chancie and aunt Fradel.

Joseph, the only one who will ever really know what this story truly means. It is instinct that always guides birds back to the place where they started. In those days after Yossel's death, the only thing I knew with certainty was that this man who is now still standing beside me was my home.

The tiny bell-shaped flowers are behind him. A woman at the bazaar once told me what Lily of the Valley really meant in the language of flowers—a return to happiness.

I walk to the stove and open it up. The scent of dill and onion floods me, and I remember my brother as he was when he was a child, sitting in my mother's kitchen eating the same dish. Yossel would be proud of me, I think, for continuing to live and raise my family. I remember the words my brother had spoken all those months before in the cave. "Don't deprive yourself of happiness, Etcia, wherever it comes."

Epilogue

AFTER THE WAR, Etcia Goldberg (and her three children, Mania, Marek, and Dunia) stayed in Ukraine with Joseph Kostaski. The other Priest's Grotto survivors immigrated to the United States or Canada. Etcia chose to stay with Joseph Kostaskis in Ukraine because Joseph wanted to help and support his children and Marta.

Etcia was grateful every minute of her life. She and Kostaski lived their lives as they both wanted to, taking care of Etcia's children. Kostaski continued to financially support his children and Marta in Korolówka after he moved to Borschow. His children, Victor and Lunducia, often visited them in Borschow.

Etcia was very proud of her children and the people they became. Etcia lived her life to the fullest, telling jokes even in the most difficult times. She always provided a hospitable and warm place for people to come and visit and to share their troubles with her. Her generosity was well known in Borschow.

She never forgot the family members she had lost. When I was a teenager, she took me to visit the grave of my great-grandfather, Chaim Goldberg, and the grave of her brother Yossel. She always remembered to pray for those who had died before and for those who immigrated to other countries after the war.

I was fortunate to live close to Etcia most of my life and to care for her in her final days. I gained invaluable perspective on life during my time with her.

Etcia Goldberg died on December 5, 1979, in her home, with my mother and me by her side.

Etcia's children and their families lived in Ukraine until 1992 and 1994. After "Perestroyka" started, they moved to the United States. Her four grandchildren—Valeriy, Boris, Malvina, and Tatyana—and seven great-grandchildren—Sergey, Elina, Michael, Konstantin, Victoria, Eduard, and Denis—live in the United States and Canada. Some of them have their own families.

Etcia Goldberg was one of a kind. Her bravery, selflessness, generosity, forgiveness, and love won over hatred, oppression, and cruelty. I am honored to share her story with the world and keep her memory alive for future generations.

You steal and kill and try to break my will,
But I keep pressing on.
My children cry themselves to sleep, their little bodies wilting.
I keep on pressing on.
No snow, no gun, no threat of death will stop me. I keep on pressing on.
One day this hunt will end, and I dare hope we will be the last ones standing.

By Elina Brim, Etcia Goldberg's great-granddaughter

Made in the USA
Lexington, KY
25 March 2017